NEW BEGINNINGS

Recent Titles by Pamela Oldfield from Severn House

The Heron Saga
BETROTHED
THE GILDED LAND
LOWERING SKIES
THE BRIGHT DAWNING

ALL OUR TOMORROWS
EARLY ONE MORNING
RIDING THE STORM

CHANGING FORTUNES

NEW BEGINNINGS

Pamela Oldfield

This first world edition published in Great Britain 2002 by
SEVERN HOUSE PUBLISHERS LTD of
9–15 High Street, Sutton, Surrey SM1 1DF.
This first world edition published in the USA 2003 by
SEVERN HOUSE PUBLISHERS INC of
595 Madison Avenue, New York, N.Y. 10022.

British Library Cataloguing in Publication Data

Oldfield, Pamela, 1934-
    New beginnings
    1.   Widows - Fiction
    2.   Great Britain - Social life and customs - 19th century - Fiction
    I.   Title
    823.9'14 [F]

    ISBN 0-7278-5865-3

Typeset by Palimpsest Book Production Ltd.,
Polmont, Stirlingshire, Scotland.
Printed and bound in Great Britain by
MPG Books Ltd., Bodmin, Cornwall.

For Sue and Richard
with love

One

C hloe climbed nimbly down from the pony cart and waved a 'Thank you' to her brother-in-law who had brought her to the gates of Fairfield House in Icklesham in Sussex. Beyond the elegant gates the warm browns of the rambling house were flanked by tall trees and crowned by a grey April sky. Three magpies strutted on the far from trim lawn and a squirrel took a few hesitant leaps in their direction. Chloe opened the wrought iron gates, trying to remember how she had felt almost five years ago when she had first come to Fairfield House for the interview. On that day she had been taken on as a companion to Jessica Maitland and her quiet life had changed forever. Since that time she had been married and widowed; had found happiness and lost it again . . .

Chloe swallowed hard. No more grieving, she reminded herself. 'Water under the bridge,' she murmured and, straightening her slim shoulders, hurried briskly up the drive towards the familiar house.

In 1890 she had been a young woman nearing twenty-one. Now she was twenty-five and liked to think of herself as a confident, much travelled woman.

As she tugged on the bell pull she waited in a state of excitement for the reunion with the family who had befriended her. The door opened and Fanny, the maid, stared at her blankly for a moment.

'Hullo, Fanny. Remember me?'

A broad smile lit the girl's face. 'Miss Blake! Oh lordy! Wait 'til I tell Mrs Letts. She was only saying the other day that it was a while since we'd heard from you and—'

'May I come in?' Chloe smiled. 'And it's Mrs Tyler now, Fanny. I was married, you know.'

'Oh yes!' Her expression changed. 'I'm so sorry, Miss Blake.' Fanny opened the door wider. 'I was forgetting . . .' Her voice trailed off as Chloe stepped past her into the familiar hallway.

Chloe looked around her with pleasure. The same elaborate hallstand with its oval mirror – and the umbrella stand beside it. Was it really only four years ago? Her time here seemed like another life.

Forgetting her duties in the excitement, Fanny scampered along the passage in the direction of the kitchen shouting for the housekeeper to 'Come and see!' Chloe slipped off her own coat and hung it up and then there were footsteps above and a portly man made his way downstairs towards her.

'Matty!' Chloe eyed him with a rush of affection. He hadn't changed much. A little fatter perhaps – and where was the cigar and the cloud of smoke that had always accompanied him? Seconds later Chloe felt a tightness in her throat as she saw the small figure coming down the stairs behind him. This must be Olivia who had been orphaned within days of her birth and was now being brought up by Jessica Maitland, her grandmother.

'By all that's wonderful!' Matty cried. 'Chloe Blake – or should I say Mrs Chloe Tyler. A married woman, no less!'

The little girl, overcome by a sudden shyness, peered out at Chloe who was holding out her hands to Matty. He was Jessica's stepbrother and one of Olivia's guardians.

Matty clasped Chloe's hands in his, beaming with pleasure. 'I never thought we'd see you again,' he admitted. 'Don't build up your hopes, I told Jessie. Especially when we heard that you were married. She may never return to England, I told her – but here you are and it's wonderful to see you again.' He regarded her with a critical eye. 'And look at you! Your hair's still brown. Jessica thought you'd be grey with all the worry. But you've lost a little weight. You need feeding up. Lots of dumpling stew and big helpings of Mrs Letts' date pudding and—'

'I feel well enough,' she told him.

'We were so terribly sorry to hear about Jeff.'

Chloe nodded, afraid to speak. Devastated by her husband's

death, she had waited to return from America until she felt more in control. Now, faced with such kindness, she felt vulnerable.

Instead of answering Matty, Chloe smiled at Olivia. 'Hullo, Olivia. It's very nice to meet you. Last time I saw you it was your birthday and you were one.'

The girl has her father's features, thought Chloe. Dark eyes and hair and a small neat chin.

Olivia offered a shy smile. 'Are you an aunt?' she asked.

Chloe hesitated but Matty said, 'Yes, she is. Aunt Chloe. Are you going to give her a kiss? Say "Welcome home, Aunt Chloe."'

Olivia obeyed and for a moment Chloe hugged the small figure to her. Oliver's child, she thought. She had missed the first four years of her life.

Olivia said, 'My nanny's gone to a wedding.'

Matty nodded. 'Alice's sister is getting married at Beckley. But come along into the drawing room and – oh! Here comes Mrs Letts now.'

Mrs Letts came puffing along the passage to welcome the new arrival.

Her face was woebegone and Chloe steeled herself for another difficult encounter.

The housekeeper took hold of one of Chloe's hands and rubbed it briskly. As though to rub away the sorrow, thought Chloe.

'We were so sorry,' Mrs Letts told her. 'Losing your poor husband like that. Terrible! Terrible! I cried for you. I really did. We were all so upset.'

This well-meant sympathy almost undermined Chloe but fortunately Matty sent the housekeeper away again to 'rustle up some tea and raspberry buns' for their visitor.

The drawing room hadn't changed at all and Chloe sank down into an armchair feeling very much at ease. Olivia settled herself on the floor with a doll and Matty looked round helplessly.

'No more cigars,' he confided with regret. 'Poor old Jessie can't abide the smell and the doctor says the wretched things make me chesty. I reckon it's a conspiracy.' He shrugged.

3

'Still, I'm not complaining. You're wondering where Jessie is, I expect.'

Chloe nodded.

He grinned slyly. 'She's with Bertha, *helping the midwife!*'

'The midwife?' Chloe stared at him. 'You don't mean . . . Bertha's baby?'

He nodded. 'A few days early, I'm told. They sent for Jessica first thing this morning. Something about complications, but don't ask me. I don't even want to think about such things. Thank God I was born a man!'

Olivia glanced up from her doll. 'Aunt Bertha is going to have a baby and the baby will be my cousin. And I can play with the baby and maybe if I'm good I can push the pram!'

How serious she is, thought Chloe. And so matter-of-fact for her age. Perhaps that was because she was with adults all the time. 'A cousin! How exciting,' she said.

Matty said, 'Which is why I'm left holding the fort. Jessie said I could look after Olivia –' he glanced at the little girl – 'but I said "Oh no! I'm just a poor old uncle. I can't look after people. Olivia will have to look after me!"'

At last the little girl laughed. 'I can't! You're too big.' She looked at Chloe. 'Uncle Matty is too big, isn't he?'

'Of course he is. He's just teasing you.'

At that moment Mrs Letts came in with a tray which she set down on the small table beside the fire. 'Binns says to say "How do" and he's looking forward to seeing you again.'

'How nice of him.'

'He's mucking out the stable or he'd say it personally.'

Without thinking, Chloe poured tea for two and handed Olivia the small glass of milk which Mrs Letts had sent for her. She sipped obediently and then began to lick the raspberry jam from the bun.

Matty opened his eyes in pretended horror and cried, 'Now what would your grandmama say about that?' and the child giggled.

After a moment or two Matty turned to Chloe and his expression had changed. He said, 'What exactly happened out there in America, Chloe? Your letter was so disjointed. Can you bear to talk about it?'

4

Chloe took a deep breath. She had dreaded the moment and yet had known it would come.

'Looking back, it seems like a whirlwind,' she confessed. 'I met Jeff soon after I arrived in Montana. He was working in a timber yard in Dubois – a small town near the Badlands. Jeff Tyler. Only son of a wealthy lawyer in Boston. Jeff was twenty two – the same age as me.' Her smile was a little shaky but she forced herself to go on. 'I had heard that there was an elderly Englishman on the payroll at the timber yard, so went along in case it was my father.'

'Ah, yes. The long-lost father. Jessica spoke of him. Left your mother with two little girls and didn't come back.' He shook his head. 'So you wanted to find him. Can't think why!'

Chloe smiled faintly. 'I don't really know why I did it, but I knew if I didn't try I would always regret it.'

'But all the way to America!'

'It was rash. I see that now but . . .' She shrugged.

Her trip to America had been planned years before with the sole purpose of tracking down her father who had left his wife and two daughters when Chloe was a child.

She said, 'The man on the payroll – it wasn't my father. It was the third or fourth disappointment but I always lived in hope. But Jeff had been told to take me to the man. When I met him he claimed his name was Blake Stanton. The men called him Blakey which was how the mix-up came about. Someone thought his surname was Blake, like mine.' Her face lightened. 'But I had met Jeff, you see, so the time wasn't wasted.'

'My mother would say that was "meant". She was a great believer in Fate.'

Chloe smiled at Matty. 'I don't suppose you believe in love at first sight.'

'Not my style,' he confessed.

She sighed. 'Well, that's exactly how we felt about each other from the start. Jeff was a bit wild . . . not in a bad way but . . . Maybe impetuous is a better word. I'd never met anyone like him. A bit of a rebel. He'd quarrelled with his father who lived in Boston and had gone out west when he was only seventeen, determined to show how independent he could be. The timber yard was his first job but he had great plans.' In her mind's eye she could see him, tall and bronzed, his unruly hair bleached by the sun to a pale straw colour, his eyes bluer than cornflowers, his head thrown back in a great roar of laughter. A sunny man – that was how she had always thought of him. Oh Jeff! *Jeff!* She blinked back tears.

'I'm sorry, Chloe. I shouldn't have asked.'

Matty was looking at her anxiously and Chloe realized she had been silent for some time.

'Don't apologize,' she told him. 'I need to talk about him. It's getting easier as the time passes and I know he'd want me to recover. He'd want me to be happy.' She swallowed hard and forced a reassuring smile. 'I wanted to meet his father and his brother.'

'Wasn't there a mother?'

'No. She'd died years earlier, so Jeff had been brought up by his father and elder brother. Jeff said it wasn't possible to meet his family but I tried to make him change his mind. Finally he agreed but it was such a very long journey and rough going. No decent roads and I was shaken to bits. Finally I . . . I was too ill to go on . . .' Chloe hesitated. Did she have to go into details? Unable to face it, she decided against it. 'We stopped travelling and I wrote to Mr Tyler, explaining the situation. He didn't answer the letter.'

Matty shook his head, dismayed.

'We had to turn round and go back to Dubois.'

'So Jeff's father wasn't up to much either – as a father, I mean.'

Chloe shrugged. 'I never knew what they had quarrelled about. Jeff wouldn't tell me.'

'I'm rather relieved *not* to be a father.' Matty grinned. 'And never to have married. I doubt I'd have been any good at it and I've obviously been spared all these worries.'

Chloe laughed. 'Jessica thinks you were too lazy to find yourself a wife although she hints that you had your chances . . .' She refilled their teacups and for a moment or two they watched Olivia playing with her doll. She had carefully removed the

6

doll's clothes and was now putting them on again. Her small face was creased with concentration.

Matty said, 'Some good can come from disasters. Olivia is a case in point – but do go on, Chloe.'

Wth an effort Chloe returned to the past. 'One day Jeff was sent along to the logging camp up river. He set off on horseback as usual . . . And he didn't come back. I began to worry. A couple of days later they found his horse wandering.' She sighed heavily. 'Then they saw Jeff's body among some logs that were floating in the river. A small log jam. Obviously he'd had an accident and fallen in.' She closed her eyes against the sight of her husband's body, cold and grey from the immersion. The blue eyes sightless, the limbs cold. 'He'd been crushed by the logs.'

'Awful!' said Matty. He patted her arm awkwardly.

'The coroner assumed something had startled the horse and he'd thrown Jeff into the river . . . I was in despair and almost decided to come home but I wouldn't allow myself the luxury. Then unexpectedly I found my father's grave, as I told you all in the letter. I wrote again to Jeff's father, telling him about the accident, telling him I was returning to England and asking to meet but he still didn't answer.'

'Jessie said you worked in an office.'

Chloe nodded. 'It was a land agency. I answered the telephone and typed a few letters with two fingers!' She smiled. 'People were very kind but I grew homesick and . . .'

'And here you are!' Matty beamed at her. 'A sight for sore eyes.'

Olivia glanced up at him. 'Have you got sore eyes, Uncle Matty?'

He laughed and ruffled her hair. 'No, little one. My eyes are fine. Now let me think . . . Have you shown Aunt Chloe your little cat?'

Olivia gave a shriek of excitement and scrambled to her feet. 'I'll go and find him,' she told Chloe and rushed from the room.

Chloe said, 'She's a sweet child. How sad that Oliver will never see her.'

Nor will her mother, she thought regretfully. Both parents

dead. Later on Olivia would realize what she had lost but in the meantime she had a secure and loving home in which she would hopefully flourish.

As if reading her thoughts, Matty said, 'She spends an afternoon with her other grandparents now and again. They adore her.'

Chloe glanced at the mantelpiece clock. 'I wonder how Bertha is getting on. I hope the complications are not too serious. A new baby in the family would be wonderful.'

'Jessie will also be exhausted,' said Matty. 'She's hardly slept these last few days. She wanted Bertha to stay at Fairfields for the confinement but George wanted the child to be born in its own home and I think he was right. They've got a very decent cottage and Bertha manages very well on their income – which is rising rapidly. Even Jessie admits that she was wrong about George. He is a good husband and his fame is growing. He has had several prestigious commissions from outside Sussex. People turn up from time to time to examine the wrought iron screen and gates.'

Chloe nodded. 'He had just started the work when I first came to Fairfields. It seems such a long time ago now.'

'It's not even five years but so much has changed.'

Olivia appeared at that moment, struggling to hold a large ginger cat in her arms. 'He's shy,' she told Chloe. 'He doesn't know you yet.'

The cat wriggled free and leaped to the floor and from there to the nearest windowsill.

'His name's Ginger.' Olivia watched Chloe for signs of approval. 'When it was his birthday Mrs Letts gave him a fish with a yellow ribbon tied round it.'

'Lucky old Ginger!'

Chloe could imagine how much happiness the child had brought to the family. Outside the sound of horses' hooves made them all turn expectantly to the window.

'It's grandmama!' Olivia ran from the room and Chloe heard her asking about the new cousin.

'It's a little boy named Robert,' Jessica told her as they came into the room. She looked much older than Chloe remembered and she smiled wearily at Matty before realizing that they had a

8

visitor. As she caught sight of Chloe, the old lady's eyes shone with delight.

'Chloe Blake! Is it really you after all this time!'

Chloe crossed to her and they embraced briefly. Chloe said, 'I've only been home for three days but I had to see you all. Matty will tell you all my news later but tell us first about Bertha.'

Within minutes they had settled Jessica in her favourite chair and Mrs Letts had brought a cup of hot milk with plenty of sugar. Willingly Jessica recounted the events of the past few hours, tailoring her words carefully for Olivia's ears. Reading between the lines, Chloe understood that it had been a very difficult birth. Bertha was very weak and the midwife had finally sent for the doctor. The boy was small and frail. Jessica sent Olivia on an errand so that she could elaborate in her absence.

'As soon as he arrived I asked George to run me home,' she told them between sips of comforting milk. 'The doctor will give Bertha a sedative and the midwife will stay the night to keep an eye on them both. Poor George is desperately worried but bearing up. I said I would call again tomorrow.' She smiled tiredly. 'Bertha will be so pleased you are back, Chloe. We've never stopped thinking about you but once you wrote to say you were married – Well, I confess we didn't expect to see you again.' She leaned forward and patted Chloe's knee. 'I want to hear all about America but it will have to wait. I am exhausted and can't think further than my bed!'

Chloe helped her upstairs and left her, then said farewell to Matty and Olivia. Binns, their groom-cum-gardener drove her back the few miles to the rectory at Icklesham.

There she was welcomed back by her sister, Dorothy, who was polishing the church plate. Her long-awaited child had been twins, who were now eight months old and thriving.

'It's really Mrs Evans' turn to do the polishing,' Dorothy told her, 'but she's got something wrong with her shoulder and it pains her to polish. Rather than search around for someone else, I said I'd do it myself. Bertie and Clara are out with Emily Franks. She's fourteen now and just left school and loves to push them out in their pram. It gives me a little time to myself. I shall miss her when she finds a job. Her mother wants her to go into service.'

Chloe picked up a pewter candlestick and a spare cloth and applied the paste and the two sisters worked steadily while Chloe passed on all the news she had gleaned from the Maitlands. She was halfway through the story of Ginger when Dorothy interrupted her.

'Good heavens! I nearly forgot. A man called in earlier looking for you. Said his name was Bourne. James, I think. No, Jack.'

Chloe stopped polishing. 'Jack Bourne. He's a farmer who's advertising for a housekeeper.'

Dorothy's face fell. 'Oh Chloe! Not so soon! You know we want you to stay with us for a while. You've only been back in England for a few days. We want you to rest and get your strength back.'

'There's nothing wrong with my strength!'

'You know what I mean. Recover from – from everything that happened in America. Albert says you seem brittle. That was his exact word. He thinks—'

'I'm fit and well, Dorothy, and I hate wasting time. Sitting about and brooding will do me no good at all.'

'But you've only been with us a few days!'

Chloe felt guilt creeping up on her. Her sister meant well but she was still trying to run Chloe's life for her. 'Look, Dorothy, I saw an advertisement on the noticeboard in Rye while I was waiting for the bus and realized how near his farm is to you and Albert. Jack Bourne farms sheep around Winchelsea. I must say he's been very prompt to follow up on my letter.' Chloe could see that the nearness of Jack Bourne's farm would influence her sister. 'I might have had to go much further to find a job.' Dorothy was still staring at her reproachfully, so Chloe rushed on. 'What was he like, this Jack Bourne? Old or young. Handsome or ugly?' She was trying to lighten the mood and eventually Dorothy relented.

'Tall and thin. Rather serious . . . He didn't have straw in his hair and mud on his boots but he looked like a farmer. Well-worn clothes but clean. It's market day in Rye and he'd been to sell a few lambs and thought he might as well drive on to Icklesham and speak with you.' She held up a silver salver and inspected it critically. 'He asked if you could visit the farm tomorrow morning. I said I thought so.'

'What did you think?' Chloe regarded her anxiously. She was determined to be independent but she had acted on the spur of the moment and was now having a few doubts. Housekeeper to a farmer? She should probably have waited for another genteel lady who needed a companion.

Her sister smoothed paste over the salver and gently worked it into the crevices of the design. 'What did I think? I wondered if he was married. You don't want to find yourself alone with a man in a remote farmhouse. Anything could happen.'

'I meant what impression did you form of him?'

'Not much. Quiet, polite, shy perhaps. I didn't ask him in because Albert was out. He didn't look very married.'

Chloe laughed. 'He could live with his mother or sister.'

'And he could live alone. You be careful, that's all I'm saying, Chloe. You've been married. You know what I mean.' She began to pile the church plate into a straw-filled basket and put a lid on the paste jar. 'Men get lonely,' she added and Chloe thought she was blushing.

'I'll be careful,' she promised, 'but I don't think there's anything to worry about.'

Friday April 5 – It was strange to be back at Fairfields. So much was different yet so much was the same. I felt almost like a family friend but also like an outsider. A visitor. Rather sad somehow. Tomorrow, after I have been to Monkswell Farm I shall call in on Bertha. I am seriously worried for her. Jessica's account of the birth did nothing to reassure me although I said nothing to alarm her. It is good to see Dorothy with her children at last. I began to think they would never have a child and now they have twins! Dorothy and Albert are upset because I am determined to find another position. No one understands this need I have to stand on my own two feet. Except my dear Jeff, and he is gone. I have to fill my days or the dark sorrow will return.

It is good to be back in England but I have one regret – that

11

I didn't meet Jeff's father before I left. It wasn't my choice but it feels like unfinished business.

I wonder what I will think of Jack Bourne and Monkswell Farm.

The following day Jack Bourne stared out of the kitchen window at the view across his fields. Taking Mrs Tyler round the farmhouse had brought home to him just how neglected it was and he tried not to dwell on her obvious dismay.

She said, 'It's a nice house,' but her tone lacked conviction.

'Four bedrooms! Are they ever used?'

'No. There's just me and I don't have time for visitors.'

She was going to turn down the job. He knew it. Without turning he said, 'It could be made very comfortable but I'm afraid I have little time for the niceties of life.'

It was hard for him to see the place from a stranger's viewpoint since he had been born at Monkswell Farm and had never left it. His mother had kept it as tidy as a farmhouse could be but the curtains had faded and dust lay on the shelves disregarded.

He said, 'A woman used to come in, mornings only, but the family moved to Hastings and I haven't got round to finding someone else.'

It sounded a flimsy excuse but it hardly mattered since this woman was never going to bury herself at Monkswell Farm.

She said, 'I love a big kitchen. I was a companion at Fairfield House a while back and their kitchen is vast.'

Jack glanced round. A large table minus tablecloth and the remains of his hasty breakfast. Shelves full of pots and pans, a very sickly pot plant, the name of which escaped him. Flagstone floor, old-fashioned cooking range, a large oak dresser and a walk-in larder that was half empty. Jude, the collie, kept a watchful eye on them and a chicken had wandered in from the yard and was pecking up the crumbs.

She asked the dog's name.

'Judy or Jude – but she doesn't like strangers.'

Undeterred, the woman held out a hand towards the dog and said, 'Hi there, Jude.'

The collie jumped to her feet and hurried over to her,

wagging her tail with every sign of friendship. Typical, he thought, half amused.

'Does she help you round up the sheep?'

'Yes, and she's good at it. But she's getting old and I'm looking for a pup to train to take her place.'

'I'm a cat person myself.' She laughed. 'I expect you have plenty of those to keep down the vermin.'

'Not at the moment,' he said defensively. 'The last one got caught in a snare. When I found him he'd strangled himself trying to get free.'

She made no answer and he thought perhaps his description of the cat's fate had deterred her. He said, 'I'm afraid I've wasted your time.' Even to his own ears it sounded brusque but this vivacious woman was hardly what he'd expected. Recently widowed, she had said in her letter, and he had imagined someone much older who would be grateful for a home. What his mother would have called a 'homebody'. This young woman would probably be married again within a year or so and he would be back to square one.

Glancing at her, he saw a pained expression in the hazel eyes.

She said, 'But I haven't seen the rest of the farm yet.'

'There's not much point. I think we both know that. I'm sorry but I don't think this job is right for you.'

'Why not?'

Argumentative, he decided. Jack hid his annoyance. 'I need someone more . . . mature. Stronger. It's not easy work.'

'I've just come back from Montana in America. Life is not exactly easy in a log cabin with no running water and logs to be chopped for the fire and—'

'I've got the picture,' he said brusquely.

For a moment they glared at one another and he was tempted to send her packing immediately but there was a steely look in her eye and if she argued further or refused to leave he would look a complete fool. He tried to imagine her in a log cabin and failed. Had she really been to America? Was she telling the truth? The silence continued as she stood her ground.

Then she asked, 'How many chickens have you got? How many sheep? How many acres?' She smiled. 'Do you grow any crops? Do you rear pigs? Or goats?' She was laughing at him but in a nice way.

In spite of his misgivings he found her interest inspiring and began to wonder if he had been too hasty. Perhaps she *might* consider the job. And if she wanted the position as house-keeper, did he want *her*? He knew suddenly that he did.

He decided to show her round. It was the least he could do. Then he would say he'd consider her for the job and let her know by letter. If he then thought better of it, he could write and say he'd chosen someone else. Someone older. He glanced at the clock. 'I've another woman coming later so I haven't got a lot of time.' It was a lie but he hoped it sounded convincing. 'There's not much to see but we'll have a look.'

They crossed the yard with Jude at his heels and passed the neglected vegetable patch and the small greenhouse which he rarely entered. It housed a few seedlings which had been given to him as well as wooden trays, trowels and a large watering can. He showed Mrs Tyler the large barn, the various smaller sheds and stores and she seemed to be interested. To his surprise, Mrs Tyler asked some intelligent questions. For a pretty woman she did seem to have a sensible head on her shoulders.

'I see you've got a pony trap. I can manage horses.' She smiled. 'America's a big country. If you can't ride over there life would be very limited.'

Jack noticed with surprise that a hinge was missing from the stable door and said quickly, 'I'll be getting that fixed.'

He watched her step carefully around a large muddy puddle and wondered if he should bag up some shingle from Winchelsea Beach to level the yard up a bit.

Suddenly Jude pricked up her ears and barked. She ran back towards the kitchen door, her tail waving a welcome.

It was Adam.

'My nephew, Adam,' Jack explained and it came to him in that moment that Adam would see Mrs Tyler as a possible conquest. He hid a smile as he introduced them. Adam, broad shouldered and with a cheerful open face, found women fascinating. He was twenty but Jack had lost count of the young women he had courted. Not that he had wanted to marry any of them. He would be single for years yet.

14

Adam raised his eyebrows as he looked at Mrs Tyler with undisguised admiration. He took off his cap. 'Glad to know you, Mrs Tyler.'

She smiled. 'Your uncle is showing me the farm.'

Adam looked at Jack. 'Where have you been hiding this pretty lady?'

'I haven't been hiding her. She's only been here for half an hour. Mrs Tyler was applying for the job.'

She corrected him. 'I *am* applying for a job.' She turned to Adam. 'Your uncle needs a housekeeper and—'

'Mrs Tyler may not be suitable,' Jack began.

Adam brightened. 'She's not at all suitable,' he agreed. To the woman he said, 'If you want a decent job you can come to us. Ma would be delighted to have some help.' He pointed. 'Our farm's next to this one but it's bigger. Bigger and better in every way.' He grinned. 'And I'd be delighted, too. We have a daily woman to do the washing and heavy cleaning. Come to us, Mrs Tyler. Uncle Jack doesn't deserve you!'

Jack glanced at Mrs Tyler who seemed to be both amused and flattered.

'But your father doesn't want a housekeeper. He's got Cathy.'

'Who is?'

'Adam's mother.'

Ignoring this remark, Mrs Tyler smiled at Adam. 'I'm open to offers,' she told him. 'If Mr Bourne considers me unsuitable I shall certainly be looking elsewhere.'

Jack felt his goodwill towards Adam cool. He was not about to let his nephew step in and steal his housekeeper and he shot him a warning glance.

Immediately aware of this slight tension Mrs Tyler stooped to pat the dog.

Adam crouched beside her and looked up into her face. He tickled the dog's ears. 'Her name's Jude. She's nine years old. She's one of the pups from our old bitch Susie, now sadly departed this world.'

Jack said, 'So what did you want, Adam? I've got rather a lot to do today.'

Mrs Tyler said, 'Your uncle has another applicant coming later for the job,' and gave Jack a coolly innocent look.

He knew at once that she hadn't been fooled by the lie and felt another wave of irritation. Perhaps he had underestimated the woman and she had recognized that fact. No doubt she would resent that. She might even go and work for his brother which meant that he, Jack, would lose out again. He closed his eyes briefly, beset by unhappy memories.

Adam said, 'Pa wants what's left of the drench.'

'Help yourself. It's in the barn.' To Mrs Tyler he said, 'We farm adjacent land but Patrick's mainly dairy. Some machinery we share. It's cheaper that way.'

Adam straighted up. 'Right, thanks. I'll fetch it and be off.' He winked at Mrs Tyler. 'You don't want to work for Uncle Jack. He doesn't appreciate women. Bourne Farm is a better bet! We'll look after you.'

She smiled. 'Thank you. I'll bear that in mind.'

As Adam wandered away in the direction of the large barn, Jude made to follow him but Jack whistled and the dog dashed back, head down, ears flattened, as though expecting a reprimand.

Jack took a deep breath. Time for explanations, he decided. As they walked through the farm gate and across the first field the blackfaced sheep kept a wary eye on them. 'Bourne Farm and Monkswell were one farm, but when Father died Patrick inherited because he was the firstborn. He's two years older than me and he was married by then with Adam on the way. Mother and I stayed on here and a new house was built for Patrick and his family. That became Bourne Farm. Mother insisted that I should inherit this house and some of the land, so two hundred and fifty acres were separated off for me to farm. I can run around six hundred sheep. Any more and I have to buy in feed.'

Chloe was watching the sheep, interminably munching as they moved slowly across the grass. The lambs were frisking in small groups ignored by the ewes who looked thin without their woolly coats. 'They were shorn a couple of weeks ago,' he told her, wondering how much she knew about sheep farming.

'Are they for wool or meat?' she asked.

16

He smiled. 'Both. We can use the wool. Mother used to spin and weave it. Now, of course, I sell the fleeces. We keep some of the lambs for meat for ourselves and sell the rest at market. The old ewes go for mutton.'

'And where does the name Monkswell come from?'

'That's the name of the lane at the rear of the house.' He suddenly grabbed one of the sheep, turned it over with a deft movement and examined its small hooves. With a satisfied nod he set it on its feet again. 'Have to keep an eye out for footrot since we had all that rain last week.'

'So Patrick got a new house. Did you mind?'

Jack hesitated. 'I like the old house and Mother didn't want to be uprooted.'

'But there were four bedrooms.'

'Patrick's wife wanted a new place.' He didn't say why she was so determined that they hadn't lived together as one large family. The Bournes' past history was none of her business.

'Did you ever wish you'd been born first?'

'No, I didn't. I didn't care one way or the other.'

He hoped this didn't sound as though he were bitter or that he was asking for sympathy.

After a moment she said, 'What did *your* wife want?'

'My wife? I don't have a wife.'

She stopped in the middle of the field and turned to him. 'So you really did want an older woman as housekeeper. Someone motherly.' Her smile was sympathetic.

He shrugged. 'I hadn't thought it through, to be honest. Just felt the need for some help in the house. I'm not much of a cook.' He shouted at Jude, who was sneaking around the bank at the edge of the field in search of rabbits. 'A bit of company, too, I suppose. Adam comes across most days but his father needs him most of the time. He's a good lad. His mother's seen to that.'

She pursed her lips briefly. 'So it's a live-in arrangement, this job?'

'I reckon so.' He glanced at her. 'Folk might talk.'

'Yes.'

They walked on and he pointed out the farm's boundaries and his brother's land and farmhouse. 'Black and white

Friesians mostly. Patrick's got ninety cows. He sells milk, butter and cream.'

'And your sheep – what are they? You'll have to teach me. I know nothing about sheep. In exchange I'll teach you about logging camps and timber mills!' She laughed at the expression on his face. 'My husband's work.'

'You're very young to be widowed. May I ask what happened?'

She explained briefly that he had been killed accidentally and for the first time the spark was gone from her eyes. 'I'll never be over it but I'm learning to live with it.'

He said, 'Loss is heartbreaking,' then wished the words unsaid. He hardly knew the woman and had never been a man for confidences.

She took a long slow look around then stared for a moment at his farmhouse.

She said, 'There is no other applicant, is there.' It wasn't a question.

'No. I'm sorry about that. Stupid of me.'

'I can put up with a bit of gossip if you can.' She looked at him expectantly.

'The terms – are they all right with you? I can't afford to pay you much.'

'It will do for the moment. If things improve I shall ask for a rise.'

'If things improve I'll give you a rise!' But they won't, he reflected.

She smiled slowly. 'Then I'll start Monday.'

Two

C hloe drove back to the rectory in Icklesham in a thought-ful frame of mind. Why had she been so hasty? she wondered. She had given the poor man no chance to decide whether or not she was suitable to be his housekeeper. Dorothy would be cross if she knew that Chloe had stam-peded Jack Bourne into giving her the job. And it was hardly promising – a small farm which was run single-handed and which had little obvious prospect for improvement. The money was only just reasonable – she should have asked for more. Plus there was the suggestion of friction between the two brothers.

Back at the rectory with Dorothy and her husband Albert, Chloe tried hard to make the best of her decision. Albert was polite but Dorothy was worried although she said nothing specific. As soon as the midday meal was over, Chloe offered to wash up while her sister fed the twins.

'There's no need,' Dorothy protested. 'You're a guest, remember.'

'I'd rather be family,' Chloe told her, filling the bowl from the large kettle and adding a few soap flakes. 'I need the practice if I'm going to be a housekeeper!'

Albert said, 'I'll leave you two ladies to argue it out. I'm wanted at Dove Cottage.'

Dorothy watched him go with her habitual expression of concern. 'It's Mrs Digby,' she explained. 'She only has a few days to live according to the doctor. Her daughter can't be with her all the time, so Albert sits with her for an hour or so. She likes him to read the Bible aloud.'

Chloe glanced at her affectionately. 'You made a good choice when you married Albert. He's a dear man.'

Dorothy nodded. 'I'm praying you will meet someone else eventually. I don't want you to be alone.'

Chloe let the comment pass.

'Poor Mr Lawrence lost his wife a few months ago and—'

'No!' Chloe laughed. 'No, no, no! I don't want to hear about poor, lonely Mr Lawrence. I don't want to hear about anyone. I want to start my new job and rethink my life.'

If she gave her sister any encouragement she would be lining up possible suitors and that would be impossible.

Ten minutes later she said goodbye to Dorothy and set off towards Bertha's cottage. At first glance it looked rather small and tucked away at the end of a narrow lane but as she reined in the horse outside the neat white gate, she saw that in fact it was larger than she had thought. Two large rooms downstairs and two under the eaves. She knocked on the front door but, receiving no answer, walked round to the rear of the cottage, where an extra room had been added at some stage. Pushing open the door, Chloe found herself in a pleasantly roomy kitchen. She was immediately struck by the comparison between this kitchen and the one at Monkswell Farm. Here there were blue checked curtains at the windows, tied back with broad red ribbons. A geranium bloomed on the window sill above the sink and there were rugs on the floor.

'Naturally,' she murmured, smiling. Jessica's daughter, Bertha, had been brought up in the comparative luxury of Fairfield House and she was going to make George's home as attractive as she could. But how was she managing without servants? Chloe wondered. No gardener and no cook. It must have been a struggle at first, being the wife of a blacksmith – even one as accomplished as George.

'Bertha? May I come in? It's Chloe!'

She heard footsteps on the stairs. Not Bertha, surely. A moment later George's mother, Ellen, appeared at the bottom of the stairs.

Chloe said, 'Do you remember me? I was Jessica Maitland's companion. I was visiting Fairfields and heard the wonderful news. I've popped in to see Bertha and the new baby.

Ellen's face broke into a smile of welcome. 'Of course I

remember you. You were very kind to George and Bertha. You're Miss Blake – or rather Mrs Someone. I forget—'

'Tyler.'

'Tyler. That's it. I know you married.' She put a finger to her lips. 'They're both sleeping, bless them, but you must take a peep at young Robert. He's the image of George.' She turned to lead the way up narrow wooden stairs.

Chloe followed, aware of a tight feeling in her chest. It would be hard to see Bertha's child but she would smile and say the right things. It was only a few years since she had lost her own child and she had told no one. Not even Dorothy. The loss was still so hard to bear that talking about it was an agony. Jeff had known, of course, and had shared the bitter disappointment but they had comforted each other and found a way to survive the grief.

Upstairs, the bedrooms were under the eaves, so Chloe ducked her head as she followed Ellen to the bed where Bertha lay asleep. There was perspiration on her face and Chloe could see a marked difference in her expression, even in sleep. A difficult labour left its mark on the mother, she thought, and prayed inwardly that Bertha would not develop childbed fever.

Beside the bed the small baby lay wrapped in a shawl, one tiny fist pressed against the rosebud mouth. There was a sprinkling of pale downy hair peeping from the white bonnet.

'Hullo, little Robert,' Chloe whispered and smiled at the child's grandmother who was bursting with pride. Leaning down, she dropped a light kiss on his head.

After a minute or so they went downstairs again and Ellen made them the inevitable pot of tea while she told Chloe the details of her grandson's difficult birth.

'I was so worried,' she said, 'that I sent for Bertha's mother. Just in case, you see. Because suppose Bertha had died? You know what I mean. You hear such dreadful things and it was so complicated. I had George with no trouble at all but Bertha is older, of course, and the baby was in the wrong position. The midwife did all she could to move it but little Robert was so stubborn!' She gave a small chuckle. 'His poor mother was so terribly tired. It seemed Robert never would be born.'

21

'Poor Bertha.'

'Well, of course, I say Robert but we didn't know then that he was a boy. If it was a girl they were going to call her Martha after Mrs Maitland's aunt and Ellen after me. But we didn't mind – boy or girl . . .' She sighed. 'Then the midwife sent for the doctor. We grandmothers were bundled downstairs. I think they didn't want us to know how worried they were. Touch and go! That's what the midwife whispered when she came downstairs and it was all over.' She stopped for breath, one hand to her heart.

'It must have been dreadful for all of you.'

'Oh, it was! Poor Mrs Maitland was very good, though. Never panicked. Not once. I never want to go through that again – nor Bertha either, poor soul. She was so brave. I was so proud of her. Men have no idea, do they.' She shook her head and added another spoonful of sugar to her tea. 'Not that you'd know, dear, but one day you'll have a child of your own. Leastways, I hope so.' She smiled at Chloe and patted her hand. 'You'll meet someone else, ducks, one day. Bonny girl like you.'

Chloe blinked hard, refusing the temptation to confide her own sad story. She would tell Dorothy one day perhaps. As for finding someone else to marry she had no illusions on that score. She would never find a man to move her the way Jeff had done. He had shown her all the beauty in life as well as the fun and the world had been a different place when they were together. The few years they had shared would have to last for the rest of her life but she was resigned to that.

She said, 'It's a very nice cottage.'

Ellen nodded. 'Bertha's done wonders, I'll admit that. A real hard worker. Of course she has a young girl who comes in Mondays to help with the washing and do a bit of scrubbing but Bertha does her bit. I did wonder when George first spoke about her. Thinking was she the right one for him. I should have trusted his judgement. She's the perfect wife – and now she's given me a grandson.'

'And little Olivia has a cousin,' said Chloe.

The Maitland family was alive again.

*   *   *

22

'So what was Mr Bourne really like?' Dorothy asked, the moment she and Chloe found time for confidences out of Albert's hearing. They were together in the nursery and Albert was in the shed in the garden patching one of his shoes. Dorothy had bathed Bertie and Clara and fed them and now she was settling them for the night.

Chloe had wondered on the way back just how much to tell her sister.

Now she said, 'Jack Bourne? He's a reasonable man. Doesn't look like a murderer, if that's what you mean. And yes, he's a bachelor and he's a few years older than me. Tall and thin. Rather sad, in a way.'

Dorothy tucked the babies into their respective cots and they tiptoed downstairs.

'I've made us each a sandwich to keep us from starvation,' Dorothy said. 'Albert won't be home until later – there's a Parish Meeting or some such – so I thought we'd wait for him and all eat together. I'll fry some liver and a bit of bacon.'

They seated themselves at the kitchen table.

Dorothy asked, 'A sad man? How, exactly?'

'He's sad in my eyes because he's never been married. You and I know how good it is to live with someone you love. He's sad because he's lonely and because his brother was born first and has a comfortable life while Jack Bourne is struggling.' She frowned. 'And he doesn't know he's sad. That's the saddest part.'

Dorothy wagged a warning finger. 'Leave well alone,' she advised. 'I know you and your good intentions. The road to hell is paved with them.' She glanced guiltily towards the door. Albert, the clergyman, didn't approve of such flippant talk. She said, 'He's probably never married because no one will have him. What's the farm like?'

Chloe finished the mouthful she was eating. 'Muddy. But he's got a nephew. Very attractive young man, I'd guess about twenty. Fair curly hair, well built. Plenty of charm. I think he took a shine to me and it made Mr Bourne jealous.'

At that moment there was a knock at the front door and Dorothy hurried to answer it. She returned with a plump woman in an elaborate hat whom she introduced as Mrs Markham.

'Mrs Markham is a wonderful needlewoman,' she told Chloe. 'She's been working on some hassocks that were on the point of falling apart. We couldn't afford new ones.'

From a large cloth bag, Mrs Markham produced three repaired hassocks and the two sisters marvelled at the work that had gone into them.

'No sign of the mending!' Dorothy sighed. 'I wish I was as nimble with my needle.'

When Mrs Markham had gone Dorothy continued her inquisition. Finally, guessing what was worrying her sister, Chloe said, 'It's a live-in job and he's there on his own but—'

'I wish you hadn't said you'll take it?'

'But I have.'

They stared at each other.

Dorothy said, 'Albert doesn't like it a bit.'

Chloe shrugged. 'Jeff and I travelled together before we were married. Nothing happened between us but no one knew that. No one pointed the finger.'

'But that was America and this is Sussex, England. And you don't know what was said behind your backs!'

'They didn't say anything.'

'You don't know that.'

She was right, of course, Chloe thought, but didn't put it into words. She had made up her mind that Jack needed her and being needed gave her a purpose in life. Right now, she had no sense of direction and a job that was a challenge would help her.

'He needs someone like me to cheer him up. Albert would approve, wouldn't he?'

'Not if people talk. Not if you get a bad reputation. You must insist on a key to the bedroom door. Does he drink, this Jack Bourne? You can never trust a man who drinks too much. Perhaps we should invite him here to tea—'

'But why?'

'To let him see that you come from a respectable family. To let him know that we'll be keeping an eye on you.'

'I don't think so, Dorothy.' Chloe gave her a reassuring

smile. 'I didn't have you with me in Montana to keep a watchful eye. I really can look after myself.'

Gossip or no gossip, Chloe had made up her mind and, if anything, her sister's arguments had reinforced her decision. She was a grown woman with a mind of her own. Come what may, she was going to Monkswell Farm to be Jack Bourne's housekeeper.

Cathy opened the door of the range, thrust a pie into the oven and slammed the door. Her husband looked up warily and said, 'What's up now?'

'Nothing.'

'That means "something".' Patrick laid down his newspaper. 'Out with it, Cath.'

She fiddled with her hair, which had once been auburn but was now dulled by the passage of years. She had been married to Patrick for twenty of these and believed she had been a good wife. Hard work had taken its toll and she had put on a little weight but at least she had given him the son he longed for. Adam was a credit to them both.

She straightened up from the oven and said, 'You've heard about your brother, I suppose. Taken in a young woman.'

Patrick tossed the paper aside. 'Hardly taken her in, as you call it. She's a housekeeper not a wanton woman!'

'She's young and pretty, so Adam says. A widow of twenty-five, to be exact. Been to America and back. I reckon there's more to it than—'

Her husband frowned. 'More to it? With Jack? Good God, woman! What interest has Jack ever shown in any woman – except you.'

Cathy swallowed. She must step warily, she told herself. She didn't want a row but she had to say something. She began to wipe down the table, sweeping crumbs of pastry into her hand and throwing them into the bucket for the chickens. Don't say too much, Cath. If you do, you'll regret it. 'That was years ago between me and Jack.'

Patrick snorted. 'Who are you kidding? Jack could have married but he didn't. That's his lookout. Don't blame me. If he wants to live alone, let him. I don't give a damn.'

'You never did!' She swallowed. There was so much unsaid between them; so much she longed but feared to say. 'He likes being alone.'

'Then why's he taking on a live-in housekeeper? Got tired of waiting, has he?'

'Waiting for what?' She feigned innocence.

'For you to get tired of me, that's what.'

Cathy felt her heart beginning to race. Last time she'd provoked him he had punched her in the arm and the bruise had only recently faded. Not that he was naturally violent but their rows tended to become physical and if she was honest it was frequently her own fault. She knew there was a point at which he would lose control, so why did she push him past that point? He wasn't a bad husband although he wasn't entirely faithful either.

Let it drop, Cathy, she warned herself but instead heard herself say, 'Her name's Chloe Tyler.'

Patrick studied his fingernails. 'That's it then, is it? Jack's got himself a young, pretty housekeeper. Good luck to him.'

'Aren't you jealous?'

'Are you?'

She should have expected that. Without replying, Cathy began to peel potatoes, wishing Adam would come in and put an end to this conversation. She had spent a restless night thinking about the new woman that had walked into Jack's life. 'There'll be talk,' she warned.

He shrugged and stood up, stretching his arms towards the ceiling. Patrick was the more handsome of the Bourne brothers and had worn well, Cathy reflected grudgingly. He was heavier than he had ever been but boasted that it was the fault of his wife's good cooking. He was not as tall as Jack but he walked well and could still catch the ladies' eyes.

Cathy said, 'Even Adam seems smitten with her.'

'Your son is easily smitten!' He laughed.

'Our son, I believe.' She cut the potatoes, put them in a pan and covered them with water. 'He's been over there several times in the past week on one excuse or the other. Let's hope Marion doesn't get to hear of it.'

She knew that would get her husband's attention. Marion

Lester was the eighteen-year-old daughter of one of Rye's councillors and was considered something of a catch. The Lester family had lived in Rye for generations and were, for the most part, well respected. Even elderly Eleanor Lester, who was rumoured to be 'strange', was liked by some and tolerated by most.

Halfway to the door Patrick turned. 'Adam's not that daft. He knows which side his bread's buttered. If he has to choose between a poor widow and the Lesters' daughter he'll do the right thing.'

'Let's hope so.' The thought of Adam leaving home touched a raw nerve but he would go one day and then she would be left with Patrick.

Now he said, 'Adam's too young to take any girl seriously but Marion's pleasant enough. I think she likes him.'

'I should think she would!' She glanced up. 'Any girl would!'

He tutted. 'You and your son!'

'Your mother was the same about you if I remember rightly!'

'I should think so too!' he mimicked. 'I'm off to deliver the piglets. See you later.'

And he was gone. Cathy glared at the door in lieu of her husband and sat down heavily. She would have to go over to Jack's place and see him. Ask a few questions. His answers would tell her if she had anything to fear. Jack would never lie to her. He never had. And if the woman had already started work she would see her for herself. Cathy brightened at the thought of doing something positive. It was always the unknown which made her anxious. What Patrick called 'her imaginings'. Once she knew the worst she could always do the sensible thing.

'Maybe tomorrow,' she muttered, eager for action. She would make Jack a pie . . . Or not. Maybe those days were over. The housekeeper would be cooking for him from now on. Mrs Tyler would see through the pie excuse at once. Women had a nose for these things. But she could take a couple of rabbits – Adam and his father had filled the pantry with their latest efforts. She would know at once if there was anything going on between Jack and the woman for she had known the brothers all her life.

'I'll go tomorrow,' she promised herself and began to wonder what she would wear. Perhaps she would iron her pleated silk blouse. Jack liked her in that. And she might even find time to put her hair in curling rags before she went to bed. If Patrick made one of his sarcastic comments she would say she was taking some eggs to old Mrs Parsons at The Manse. Everyone knew the old woman always managed to look bandbox fresh and nobody ventured near without making an effort to look good.

Feeling marginally happier, Cathy threw a handful of corn into the bucket with the potato peelings and went outside to feed the chickens.

Friday morning found Chloe hard at work. She had changed the bed linen, and the sheets and pillowslips were bubbling in the copper along with the towels. From time to time she took off the wooden lid, lifted the clothes with a stick and gave them another stir. Then she pushed a few more sticks into the fire beneath it. A copper seemed a luxury after the mounds of handwashing she had done in Dubois. Here there was even a mangle to ring out most of the water; there the clothes had hung on the line outside until the weather saw fit to dry them enough to be ironed with the old gas iron. Thinking of her home in Dubois brought a lump to her throat but she had resolved never to push that part of her life aside. Remembering her time with Jeff with sorrow was so much better than forgetting. Nothing that happened in the future could take away the magic of her few short years with Jeff.

Chloe had cleared the breakfast things away and washed up. Later she would make a start on what Jack Bourne called the 'best room'. It was in fact a sitting room which was never used and was therefore cold and smelled of mildew. She had found some beeswax polish at the back of a cupboard and would apply it to every wooden surface. And she had opened the windows to let fresh air in. At least it would smell better.

A knock at the back door alerted her to a visitor and her interest quickened. The neighbours so far were nothing more than names to her and she hurried to open the door. A large but handsome woman waited outside. She was neatly dressed in an expensive blouse and her hair curled round a plump face.

'I'm Cathy, Patrick's wife.'

The woman was eyeing her critically and Chloe saw suspicion in the pale blue eyes.

'I've brought you a couple of rabbits. Jack loves rabbit pie.' She pushed past Chloe as she spoke. 'I do them with bacon and add a few herbs. That's how Jack likes them.'

'How kind. Do sit—' Chloe stopped because her visitor had already seated herself. Making it plain that she had prior rights, thought Chloe. So this was Adam's mother. She thought she could see a likeness.

'Adam takes after you,' she said with a smile.

'So they tell me.' Cathy dropped the rabbits on the table. 'You do know how to skin a rabbit, I suppose?'

'Oh yes! And how to pluck sage hens and fillet fish.' Chloe was beginning to suspect that if Cathy had her way the two of them were never going to be friends. There was a spikiness about her manner that spoke volumes. 'I've even helped butcher a buffalo,' Chloe told her, 'but I confess I found that hard work.'

Cathy surveyed the kitchen in silence then said, 'My son has told me all about you, Mrs Tyler. You definitely have an admirer there but take no notice of him. He has a lot of charm but he also has a young lady.'

'I'd be disappointed if he hadn't!' Chloe told her and saw that the compliment pleased her visitor.

'Do you always do your washing at the end of the week?' Cathy nodded towards the copper.

'Only when there is too much for Monday's wash. Mr Bourne has been without help for some time. I'm trying to catch up.' She retrieved the jar of polish and found a cleaning rag. 'Mr Bourne has gone into Rye for—'

'For the market. Naturally. What a wonderful excuse it is for them. An hour's bargaining and two hours' drinking! You'll get used to it – if you stay.'

Chloe recognized the challenge and decided she could no longer allow the woman to walk all over her. She gave Cathy a very level stare. 'Aren't you expecting me to stay the course?'

Taken aback by this directness, Cathy stammered, 'I – Of course . . . I didn't mean . . .' To change the subject she added, 'I see Jack's given you plenty of kindling wood. That's so like him. Patrick never remembers it. I have to nag and nag him.'

'I chopped it myself yesterday. It's easier than nagging.'

There was a silence which became uncomfortable but Chloe was determined not to be the first to break it, but before either of them could speak, the door flew open and a man barged in.

'Patrick!' Cathy stared at him. 'I thought you were at the market.'

'I thought you were going to The Manse.'

Obviously surprised to find his wife at Monkswell Farm, Patrick Bourne blustered a little. He explained that he had changed his mind about the piglets and had decided to leave a message for his brother since they wouldn't be meeting.

Chloe recognized the lie and saw that Cathy did too. In a way she was amused. It was clear that all interested parties were going to call in to inspect Jack Bourne's new housekeeper. Better to be amused than annoyed, she told herself. It was probably natural in the circumstances.

Cathy began a lengthy but unnecessary explanation of why Chloe was still doing washing and Patrick seized on the topic gratefully.

'Not much of a housewife – our Jack,' he said and Chloe resisted the urge to defend her employer.

'So,' she said, facing Patrick cheerfully. 'What's the message?' She fetched paper and pencil from the dresser drawer and waited expectantly.

'What message?' he asked.

Chloe could see that he had expected a quiet chat with his brother's new housekeeper and was now confused by the discovery of his wife.

Chloe said, 'You said you had a message for your brother.'

Cathy laughed at his discomfiture and his face reddened as he turned to his wife.

'You can laugh!' he snapped. 'I'd like to know what you're doing here, all dolled up like a dog's dinner! You said you were going to The Manse.'

They glared at each other for a moment until Chloe took pity on them.

'I'm glad you're both here,' she said. 'Now we've met. I'm sure we'll get along.'

Cathy said, 'The important thing is that you do your job. It won't be easy. Farmwork never is.'

Patrick gave her a withering look. 'She's not being paid to do farmwork, Cath. She's a housekeeper.' He turned his attention to Chloe. 'So what's he paying you? Bit of a miser, Jack. You'll have to account for every penny—'

'I don't think that's anyone's business but ours,' Chloe said sharply. 'But you can always ask Mr Bourne. I'll tell him you enquired, shall I?'

Cathy glanced nervously at her husband and said, 'Take no notice of him, Mrs Tyler. You know what brothers are like. He didn't mean . . .' Her voice trailed off.

Chloe put pencil and paper on the table. 'I have some polishing to do but do leave your message, Mr Bourne, and I'll see that your brother gets it.'

It was as close as she dare get to a snub but as she left them to their own devices she caught the look that passed between them. She had no wish to make enemies but she was not going to allow them to dominate her and the sooner they realized it the better. From the sitting room she heard them talking in low tones and then the door closed behind them. When the polishing was at an end she returned to the kitchen. As she had expected, there was no message.

The following Monday Jack Bourne agreed that Chloe should have the afternoon off. There was no permanent arrangement but she would be given time off when it was suitable. She was also able to borrow the pony trap and and today she was off to have tea with the Maitlands.

'I see you drove yourself, Chloe,' Jessica said admiringly. 'You really are becoming very independent. Not that I altogether approve, mind you. I think men like a woman to be a little helpless. It makes them feel manly. I didn't bring Bertha up to be independent – although I realize that for you it might be desirable.'

31

'For me in America, it was necessary,' Chloe told her with good-humour. 'Women in America lead somewhat different lives.'

'I wouldn't want to live there, then. Not for all the tea in China!'

Chloe smiled. She had long since grown to like Jessica Maitland and understood that she was very much a product of her upbringing. They were standing in the sunshine beneath the big sycamore where Olivia was now swinging.

'Higher, Aunt Chloe!' she cried, her face alive with excitement. 'Uncle Matty pushes me higher than this.'

Jessica tutted. 'Your Uncle Matty is a law unto himself!' she grumbled. 'If I take my eyes off him for a minute he is up to something. Don't imagine, Chloe, that he is a reformed character. People like Matty are never reformed. I caught him smoking a cigar the other day. He was lurking in the shrubbery apparently unaware that the rising smoke was betraying him.'

Chloe smiled. 'It's one of his few remaining pleasures and it does him no harm.'

'It makes the furniture smell and dulls the curtains.'

'But he was in the garden.'

'You still like to argue, I see!'

Chloe laughed. 'I'm afraid I do.'

'Then you will never be fit for proper society. Men like women to be more agreeable – in every sense of the word.'

'I was lucky to find Jeff Tyler. He loved a good argument.'

'A good argument? There is no such thing between the sexes, Chloe – but you will never change your ways.' Smiling, she turned to Chloe. 'Fortunately we all like you in spite of your funny little ways.' She waited for Chloe to protest but, disappointed, decided to change the subject. 'So how are your sister's twins progressing? I'm afraid I never can remember their names.'

'Bertie and Clara.'

'Bertie? Another Robert?'

'No. Bertie's an Albert and they're doing well. They must be around nine months old now. There'll be a double birthday before long, I suppose. And how is *your* little grandson doing? And Bertha. I still haven't had a chance to speak with her. She was asleep when I called in and her mother-in-law didn't want to disturb her.'

Jessica looked troubled and chose her words carefully. 'They're both still very frail. I took Bertha some calves-foot jelly yesterday and I was made very welcome. George's mother is a very nice person and I'm sorry I didn't take to her earlier. I'm pleasantly surprised at the way she cares for Bertha. I couldn't do better myself.'

'She spoke very highly of Bertha when I was there.'

'Why shouldn't she? Bertha is a sweet girl and George is very lucky that I agreed to the match.'

Chloe, still pushing the swing, said nothing although her own understanding of those early days was rather different. Bertha had had to threaten an elopement before Jessica would accept the situation.

Jessica went on. 'Of course I would spend longer with Bertha if I could but I have Olivia to care for.' To Olivia she said, 'You must slow down now and stop or you will make yourself sick.'

Obligingly, Chloe allowed the swing to settle, ignoring Olivia's wails of complaint.

'Spoiled,' Jessica whispered. 'Matty just adores her and is putty in her hands! Let us go in now and see about some—' She broke off and frowned in the direction of the house. 'Now who is calling in the middle of the afternoon? We're not expecting anyone.'

Chloe saw a hansom cab draw up outside the front door and as they walked towards it a young man stepped from it. Catching sight of them, he removed his hat and hurried across the lawn to meet them. Jessica whispered something to Olivia and the little girl obediently skipped away towards the house.

'Little pitchers . . . !' Jessica murmured as she stared at the approaching visitor.

'Have I come to the right place?' he asked. 'I'm trying to find Matthew Orme.'

Jessica frowned. 'Do we know you?'

'This is Fairfield House, I take it? I was led to understand—'

'Matthew Orme does live here. Do you have business with him?' Jessica gave Chloe a look which signalled both suspicion and anxiety.

'I do, ma'am.' He smiled. 'I most certainly do.'

'And do you usually turn up unannounced at inconvenient moments?'

'Rarely, ma'am, and I think when—'

'And do you have a name?'

Sensing Jessica's hostility, he flashed a look at Chloe which was both charming and lazy and she felt an immediate interest. He was very good-looking, of average height with curly fair hair. Although he was smartly dressed with a gold-coloured waistcoat and matching handkerchief in his jacket pocket, his manner was unaffected with no hint of vanity. Chloe was surprised to see Jessica hesitate.

He said, 'My name is Terence Harkness. Terry to my friends.'

Jessica's smile was cool. 'Well, Mr Harkness, I'm afraid my brother is away at the moment – in London but he may well return tomorrow. Would you care to call again or better still, you could leave a message or your card and he will contact you if he wishes to make your acquaintance.'

Terence Harkness appeared to find her reluctance amusing but he fished in an inside pocket and produced a small business card. 'I'm afraid no one has left him any money,' he laughed, 'but I'm sure he'll be pleased to see me.'

Chloe, suddenly reluctant to see him go, said quickly, 'Are you staying nearby?'

'I have taken lodgings in Rye for a night or two. The Mermaid Inn. You might know of it. Very pleasant. I shall spend the afternoon exploring the town.'

For an exciting moment, Chloe toyed with the idea of offering herself as a guide but dismissed it immediately as quite out of the question. She had come to visit the Maitlands and it would be churlish to go off with a complete stranger. Madness, in fact. She was surprised and ashamed that the idea had even occurred to her. What on earth was she thinking of?

Instead she said, 'The Strand is interesting. Always boats unloading timber and the like. And the ships chandlers are fascinating.'

Jessica frowned at her before turning back to their visitor. 'There are several very rowdy public houses, so do be careful.

34

You might fall prey to the odd pickpocket and I'm told there are often fights around closing time.'

'Drink has never tempted me much,' Mr Harkness told her. 'I'm happy to say my vices are very few.'

His frankness was disarming, Chloe thought, and so was his smile. So why was Jessica so hostile?

He looked around him at the house and garden. 'A very handsome home,' he said. 'I particularly admired the gates.'

Chloe opened her mouth to tell him about George but Jessica gave her a discreet nudge.

'We won't detain you, Mr Harkness. I hope you enjoy Rye. We may see you tomorrow. Goodbye.'

She walked determinedly in the direction of the house and Chloe was forced to accompany her. She glanced quickly behind her when they reached the terrace and Terence Harkness raised a hand in a farewell salute.

Once inside the house Chloe said, 'But Matty isn't in London.'

Jessica tossed her head. 'A delaying tactic, that's all. Say nothing to Matty about this for a moment. I'll speak to him privately when I've had a chance to think.'

'But what was wrong with him? He seemed very polite. Quite charming, really.'

Jessica shook her head. 'I imagine most women find men like that quite charming but I've met his sort before. The sort of man Matty would be drawn to. If you must know, Chloe, I'm very much afraid Matty might owe him money. This sort of thing has happened before as you well know.'

Shocked, Chloe regarded her soberly. She well remembered Sid Jakes, sent to collect a debt. A vicious man who had come to their front door with a loaded shotgun.

'But that was different,' she protested. 'This man is nothing like Sid Jakes.'

'It's where it can lead,' Jessica insisted, looking uncharacteristically flustered. 'Someone from his past, maybe. I'll have a private word with Matty. You—'

A third voice said, 'A private word? That sounds ominous, Jessie!'

They both looked up to see Matty lolling against the door

jamb of the drawing room. A suspicious wisp of smoke floated behind him. He had obviously been smoking one of his forbidden cigars but to Chloe's surprise Jessica ignored it.

Matty continued: 'If it's about that young man I saw from the window, then I've no idea who he is. Use your thumb screws if you must, Jessie dear, but, hand on heart, I can tell you nothing.' Dramatically he placed a hand over his heart and looked at them earnestly.

Chloe grinned.

'Don't encourage him, child,' Jessica told her. To Matty she said, 'So you don't owe him money?'

'Certainly not. You know I've renounced gambling, more's the pity.' He winked at Chloe.

'I saw that, Matty!' Jessica glared at him. 'Then perhaps he owes you money. That would make a pleasant change.'

Matty thrust his hands into his pocket and sauntered towards them. 'He might be a solicitor. Maybe someone's died and left me a fat legacy—'

'He said not.' Jessica gave him a triumphant look.

'Well, you've obviously given him the brush-off. Presumably we shall never see him again.'

The word solicitor had made Jessica uneasy. She was frowning thoughtfully. 'He has left his card.' She handed it to Matty without reading it. A mark in her favour, thought Chloe. This was becoming intriguing.

'His name's Harkness,' she offered unnecessarily.

Matty peered at the card and shook his head. 'No mention here of a solicitor, more's the pity. Not for the first time in my life I'm at a loss. Don't know who he is but it will be fun finding out. I'll leave a message at his hotel to call tomorrow at eleven.' He smiled at Jessica. 'That OK with you?'

She rolled her eyes. 'OK?' she mocked. 'I do wish you'd stop talking like a young tearaway and be your age, Matty. Let's hope your visitor doesn't lead you into any mischief.'

Chloe said, 'You've condemned the poor man on very little evidence. He seemed quite harmless to me.'

'That's because the younger you are the more charitable you feel towards others. I've been around for many years and I know trouble when I see it.'

'Trouble? How can you say that when he has hardly opened his mouth. You sent him packing before he—'

'Thank you, Chloe!' Jessica snapped. 'This isn't any concern of yours. Matty and I will talk about it later when we are on our own.'

Curiouser and curiouser, thought Chloe, refusing to take offence. Come tomorrow, all might be revealed. She certainly hoped so.

I cannot get Terence Harkness out of my mind and this is oddly disturbing. I never expected to meet any other man who could intrigue me and I feel vaguely disloyal. He is so different from Jeff in everything except manner – the lazy, relaxed confidence that I find appealing and which poor Jeff had in abundance.

But who can TH be and what on earth does he want with Matty? Jessica has set her mind against him and was quite sharp with me because I defended him. Not that it matters for I shall most likely never see him again.

Bertha continues poorly and baby Robert is clinging to life, poor little scrap. Still, if he does survive he will have devoted parents and a comfortable life. Please God take care of mother and baby.

I am settling down at Monkswell Farm and learning so much. I only have to ask Mr Bourne a question and he gives me a lecture! We get plenty of eggs from the four hens and there are two beehives somewhere although I haven't found them yet. Apparently we sell most of the honey for income. Patrick is going to kill one of his pigs on Wednesday and I'm expected to go over to Bourne Farm and lend a hand. No doubt Cathy will be hoping I'm a complete duffer at it. Still, it does give me a chance to see their farm for the first time which will be interesting and to see if Cathy has softened towards me, which I doubt.

Three

Promptly at eleven o'clock the following day Terence Harkness arrived at Fairfield House and was shown into the drawing room. Matty, spruce in a maroon velvet jacket and dark trousers, went forward to meet him, his hand outstretched.

'My sister is busy elsewhere,' Matty explained. In fact she had chosen to begin a jigsaw with Olivia on the pretence of giving Alice a short break from her young charge. Mortified that Matty had ignored her advice and had invited 'this Harkness fellow' to the house, she had, somewhat illogically, been further insulted by his insistence that she should not be present at the meeting. If Terence Harkness was the bearer of bad news Matty preferred to deal with it on his own.

Matty said, 'Do sit down, old chum.'

'Thank you.' He remained standing, surveying the sitting room with obvious approval.

Matty eyed him nervously. 'I've ordered some tea. Would have liked something stronger but Fairfields is a female bastion. Jessica rules, if you get my meaning.'

He braced himself for an unpleasant reminder of past misdeeds but comforted himself that an early warning would give him time to plan his account, which Jessica would certainly insist upon later in the day. His schooldays had hardly been trouble free. He peered at the young man. There had been a dare, he recalled. He had dared another boy to climb out on to the roof in the middle of the night but he panicked. Clinging to the chimney, he had screamed blue murder and the teacher who discovered him gave them both a detention. Matty had received three strokes of the cane as well for his part in the ill-judged adventure. Could this be that boy?

Aware of the scrutiny, the young man smiled. He's as nervous as I am, thought Matty, but he is smiling. Not that that meant much. It might be a bluff. A way to soften up the 'target'. Is he going to blackmail me? He searched his memory for a worse sin that he may have committed during his misbegotten youth.

Terence Harkness said, 'This is a charming room. Very light.'

'It faces south.'

'Ah! That accounts for it.' His glance fell on the large grandfather clock. 'A handsome piece. My mother was very fond of clocks. Sadly she's dead now.'

'I'm so sorry.'

'I've recovered from the loss. It was several years ago.'

A short silence fell during which Matty prayed for the arrival of the tea tray. He sat down and the young man followed suit.

'So you're not a solicitor,' he said as soon as they were both comfortably seated. 'I was hoping a distant relative had seen fit to bless me with a legacy!' He chuckled to show that this was a joke.

'I'm afraid not. There's no money involved. It's more personal actually.' He drew a deep breath. 'I'm not here to ask for anything or to give you anything. The fact is . . .' He frowned. 'You won't recognize the name Harkness but you might recognize the name Downey.'

Fanny brought in the tea tray and set it down on the coffee table. She flashed Terence Harkness a pert smile and whisked out of the room in a flurry of petticoats. Matty stared at the tray but made no move to fill the cups.

'Downey?' Matty repeated. He shook his head. Perhaps this man had found the wrong Matthew Orme. 'Doesn't ring the proverbial bell.'

'Cicely Downey? I'm going back twenty-five years.' From his pocket he drew a crumpled photograph and handed it to Matty, who was already repeating the name with a shake of the head.

The photograph, however, jerked him back into the past. A younger Matty stared back at him. Laughing, carefree, this

39

other Matty was standing beside a young woman with blonde hair and beside her was an older woman in mourning black.

Matty whispered, 'By all that's holy! Old Ma Downey and Cis! Good Lord!' He studied himself with interest. He'd been a bit of a heart breaker in those days. His hair was darker and parted severely in the middle. His face was thinner and his smiling mouth appeared larger than he expected. Had he changed so much? he wondered.

Terence Harkness laughed. 'Ma Downey? She'd have been mortified to hear you call her Ma . . . So you do recognize Cicely. She later married Edgar Harkness. All a bit of a rush apparently. What they call a shotgun wedding.'

'Well I never!' Matty shook his head. 'I remember her as very prim. Very much on her best behaviour.' He'd finally 'had his way' with her but it hadn't been an easy conquest. She'd been very much on her guard until one day she simply surrendered to the moment. Much to his surprise. But it had never happened again. 'A shotgun wedding, eh! Edgar Harkness . . . I don't think I knew him.'

'Mr Orme . . . Cicely Harkness is my mother. Or was until she died. I was the reason for the shotgun wedding.'

But Matty was not paying proper attention. Fascinated by the unexpected glimpse of times past he was chuckling at his younger self. 'But I can't remember having this taken,' he mused. 'No recollection at all. But I remember her mother. Bit of a dragon, Ma Downey . . . What's that you say?'

'That picture was taken just before you disappeared from her life.'

It took Matty a moment or two to understand what was being said. 'I disappeared? Did I? That's rum.'

'Yes. And then Mother discovered she was expecting a child. You went off to enlist. In the Navy. That's what she claims.'

Matty swallowed but his mouth had gone dry. He felt a sudden chill of apprehension and looked anxiously at his visitor. It was becoming only too clear. This young man was a ghost from his past come to haunt him. He felt a fine sweat break out on his forehead, closed his eyes and tried to think. Dimly he heard Terence Harkness's words.

40

'I'm trying to break it gently to you. I'm your son.'

There was no rancour in the words and Matty risked a quick peep. Seeing nothing hostile in his expression, Matty scrutinized the young man for signs of a likeness. But Terence Harkness resembled his mother. He was a Downey. Matty covered his face with his hands and tried to think sensibly. Probably best to deny the whole thing. If Cis was dead she could hardly confront him . . . Unless she had left a letter revealing the truth. He tried to remember her. Surely she wouldn't intend him any harm. She hadn't seemed the vengeful type. God, this was awful. Whatever would Jessica say?

Terence smiled. 'How long were you in the Navy?'

'Never.'

'Ah! An escape route?'

'I suppose so . . . but I don't remember saying any such thing. If I didn't know she was with child why should I disappear?'

'Perhaps you suspected she might be?'

'I wasn't like that!'

But I was, he corrected himself, stricken. Love 'em and leave 'em. That had been his philosophy and it had served him well – until now. And now, all these years later he was being presented with a chip off the old block. Was that entirely bad? It was a shock, no denying that, but a son? A child after all these years? Was that good or bad?

'But Edgar Harkness?' he whispered. 'How did that come about?'

He listened carefully to the explanation. It seemed that Harkness had admired Cis from afar for years but knew that she was in love with Matthew Orme and wouldn't consider anyone else. When she fell from grace, Harkness found out and came to the rescue. Matty felt a pang of resentment. What a cheek!

'She should have told me.'

'You'd disappeared.'

'I would have done the decent thing.'

But that was another lie and Matty recognized it as such the moment the words left his lips. He would have run a mile! A wife had never been on his agenda.

41

'Well, Terence,' he said, still reeling from the shock. So he had a son called Terence. It didn't sound too bad. 'I suppose I have to . . . to apologize. What can I say except I'm sorry. It's a damned bad show.' A bit feeble, he thought, but what *did* one say in these circumstances? He stared at the pot of tea which had never been poured and the biscuits that had never been offered. 'Would you like a biscuit?'

'Thanks.' Smiling, Terence helped himself to an almond biscuit.

Matty watched him admiringly. Damned if he doesn't seem entirely at ease! Not at all embarrassed to meet his errant father – but what does he actually *think* of me? At least he hasn't pretended to see a likeness. But why would he want to? I'm hardly an encouraging sight although at least I'm tidily dressed and Jessica's idea of the red cravat works well. Oh God! I'm staring at him. *I'm staring at my son!* Say something, Matty.

'I'm afraid the tea will be cold. I'll get some more.' He stood up a trifle unsteadily. What on earth should he do next? He thought desperately. 'I'll fetch Jessica,' he said at last and rushed from the room in search of help.

Wednesday morning dawned bright and clear with a hint of a breeze and Chloe washed and dressed, pulling a wry face as she realized the pig-killing would go ahead as planned. It was nearly seven o'clock and downstairs Jack Bourne whistled to Jude and set off as usual to check his flock. From her bedroom window she watched them go with a small sense of loss. Jack Bourne was a quiet man but pleasant company and she liked to know he was near at hand. He was not a man of many words but maybe that was the result of living alone for so many years. Presumably, she thought, he had lost the art of conversation.

She was sorry she had come to the farm too late to be involved with the lambing. That must have been a busy time. She imagined her employer at all times of the day and night, struggling to save the lambs whose births were difficult. Maybe Adam, his nephew, had helped him. Or his brother . . . And then the shearing. A pity she had missed the most interesting months, she reflected as she tossed a few handfuls of corn to the chickens. She watched them for a few minutes, trying to raise some enthusiasm but they were of a uniform brown and to her eyes seemed entirely without personality. Nothing distinguished one from the other and she gave up on them and went to feed the remaining pig. She empied a pail of mash into the trough and admired the large pink animal with its sparse white bristles.

'Don't gobble your food,' she told it. 'You'll get indigestion!' The sow grunting ecstatically into the trough. A shame about pigs, she thought. This one was friendly and biddable and cleaner than she had expected. She had wanted to call it Amanda but Jack Bourne had forbidden it.

'You'll get fond of it,' he warned. 'My father never allowed it and with good reason. It's not easy to slit the throat of an animal that's been treated as a pet. That goes for the lambs, too. My mother had to hand-rear some of the weaker ones and there were always tears when they went to market.'

Chloe wondered how she would feel if it were this particular pig that was due for slaughter this morning. Bacon, she told herself sternly, and pork chops and sausages. The sow glanced up from the trough and grunted amiably and the small tail wiggled. Chloe resisted the urge to scratch the pink back. Use your head, Chloe, not your heart. Turning quickly away, she collected the four eggs and, carrying them in her apron, made her way quickly back into the kitchen. There she hesitated. There were vegetables to prepare for the midday meal before she set off for Bourne Farm but she had decided that today was the day she would cook a proper breakfast for Mr Bourne. He was up at six thirty every morning, ready to walk the fields with Jude to check on the sheep. When he came home hungry, he normally cut a slice of bread and smothered it in butter and jam. Not enough, Chloe, thought, to last him until twelve thirty when they sat down to the midday meal.

With a guilty glance at the clock, she put a frying pan on the stove and added three slices of bacon and thought guiltily of the friendly sow. Then for good measure she added a slice of bread. She laid a knife and fork for him and waited nervously for the sound of his boots on the cobbled yard.

Five minutes later he came into the kitchen frowning. 'Is that bacon I can smell?'

Chloe nodded and dropped an egg into the pan. 'You should have a decent breakfast,' she told him. 'No man should work on an empty stomach. By the time you've washed your hands it'll be ready.'

He hesitated but she was sure the tempting smells would disarm the protest which would inevitably spring to his lips. She glanced at him as he washed his hands in the sink. What was he thinking? That she was too forward? Or that she was taking an interest in his welfare.

They sat down in silence and she served the egg, bacon and bread.

He said, 'What about you?'

'I don't do the heavy work and I don't rise early. I toasted some bread. Who made the raspberry jam?'

'That's from Cathy. She keeps me supplied with chutney, too. She's a handy cook.'

Chloe was aware of a twinge of jealousy but brushed it aside. 'I'm not looking forward to the pig-killing,' she told him.

He grinned. 'The worst will be over by the time you get there but there'll be plenty to do. Once the blood has drained away there's singeing to remove the bristles as well as the innards to be dealt with. Don't worry.'

She smiled. Little did he know that her chief worry had been his own reaction to the breakfast but he seemed to be enjoying it and he hadn't been annoyed. Be thankful for small mercies, she told herself.

Footsteps outside heralded the postman and Chloe was surprised to receive a letter from Jessica.

She said, 'Oh no! I hope it's not bad news.' She explained briefly about Bertha and the baby and opened the envelope.

'I'll be off again,' Jack Bourne told her. 'Don't be too late at Patrick's place.'

Chloe nodded and began to read.

Tuesday, 16th April. Dear Chloe, You will be surprised and possibly dismayed to hear that Terence Harkness is Matty's illegitimate son . . .

'Matty's *son*!' Chloe blinked.

. . . The revelation has shocked us but we are coming to terms with it. Matty admits to a friendship with a woman named Cicely and I'm ashamed to say he abandoned her – although it is only fair to say that she had not told him of the consequences of the affair. Cicely then married an admirer (Harkness) with whom she subsequently lived for many years before her recent death. Naturally, because of your own search for your father in America, you will understand Terence Harkness's desire to find Matty. Matty, of course, has over-reacted. He has developed an excessive affection for Terence and wants him to stay with us but I have strongly resisted the notion and Terence Harkness continues to stay at The Mermaid. I write in haste to tell you this as the young man asked for your address and against my wishes Matty gave it to him. He may intend to contact you. Because we know so little about him, I do not think it wise for you to become too involved with him. Please don't think I am interfering – I have only your interests at heart. Yours, Jessica Maitland . . .

Chloe was astonished. She was also slightly irritated by Jessica's well-meant interference. 'I'm not your paid companion now, Jessica!' she muttered but there was no time to consider the full implications of the letter as she had to set off for Patrick Bourne's farm. She was pleased for Matty, she thought, as she made her way across the fields, her skirts held high above the dewy grass. But it was typical of Jessica to throw up objections. She was too cautious, by far. Chloe narrowed her eyes thoughtfully. Unless it went deeper than that. Five years earlier, Jessica had lost Oliver, her only son. It was possible she might subconsciously resent the fact that a sudden twist of fate had cast Matty as a father. Especially as Terence Harkness was a very attractive young man. Jessica might find it hard to bear if Terence Harkness replaced Oliver in everyone's affections.

Chloe thought again about Terence Harkness whose life story so closely resembled her own. They would have a lot to talk about if he ever did track her down.

* * *

45

The yard of Bourne Farm was the scene of great activity as the slaughtered hog was taken apart and prepared in various ways. The head was being boiled in a large iron pot over a makeshift fire and this meat would be chopped and turned into brawn. There was a large trestle table on which the dead hog lay in rapidly reducing splendour. Chloe forced herself to look nonchalant. Life in Montana had accustomed her to the casual barbarities of farmwork and she would not allow them to see her distaste. In time she knew she would find nothing offensive in the smell of blood or the sight of animal flesh.

Patrick was nowhere to be seen but two women were at work and a man with a narrow curved knife was butchering the carcase. For a few moments Cathy flitted to and fro, pretending not to notice Chloe's arrival, but at last she gave a cry of surprise.

'Oh! There you are, Mrs Tyler! I thought perhaps you had decided not to come. It is a rather messy business.'

Chloe smiled. 'I would have come earlier but Mr Bourne was late home for his breakfast.'

Cathy stiffened. 'Don't you worry about Jack. He can make toast with the best of them.'

'I wanted him to have cooked breakfast. After such an early start—'

'Oh, for heaven's sake! You'll kill the poor man with kindness!'

The other women were listening to the exchange and now laughed.

The younger one said, 'Cooked breakfast! D'you hear that, Cath? I doubt he knows a cooked breakfast from a hole in the road! Lonely old bachelor like that.' She winked at Chloe.

The older woman sniggered. 'Lucky old Jack! He must think it's his birthday.'

Cathy had failed to see the funny side of it and Chloe wished she had kept quiet.

Cathy gave Chloe a thin look. 'Well, now that you're here you can help me with the salting.'

This task, Chloe discovered, involved taking the pork portions handed to her by Cathy and rubbing salt into them.

46

She knew from her time in Montana that this way the meat could safely be preserved through the winter months. It was a messy job and Chloe's hands were soon sore but she made no complaint. She suspected that she had been given the most unpleasant job but would never give Cathy the satisfaction of describing her as helpless or mollycoddled.

After the best part of an hour they had finished.

Cathy pointed to a bucket of soapy water and said, 'Wash your hands in that,' and made her way into the farmhouse to make a large pot of tea tea for the workers. The large woman at once sidled over to Chloe and rinsed her own hands in the pail.

'Messy old job, that,' she said. 'I reckon she saved that one for you.' She accompanied the information with a sly look. 'I'm Meg. I got to clean the trotters. Sal there is making the tongue. Like tongue, do you? I put plenty of herbs in mine but Cath likes it plain.'

Chloe caught Sal's eye and gave her a friendly nod.

'Sal is Cathy's mother,' Meg confided. 'Comes from up yonder and doesn't spend a lot of time here. Can't abear poor old Patrick. Come to that, she don't get on too well with her daughter. Never has. But she's always willing to lend a hand, times like this. The chap carving is the local butcher. He's cutting chops and suchlike.'

Nearby on a trestle table, a pile of heart, liver and kidneys waited in the pan of a pair of large brass scales. Chloe had fixed an expression of interest on her face but tried not to look at a number of china bowls full of blood. But I must get used to it, she reminded herself. The time would come for Jack Bourne's pig to be slaughtered and at least she would be a little more experienced by then.

When the mugs of sweet tea arrived, Meg sat close to Chloe but kept a wary eye on Cathy.

Leaning towards Chloe, she murmured, 'I'd say she's taken against you. Cath Bourne I mean. Obvious, isn't it. You and Jack Bourne alone in that place. Stands to reason. She's not queen bee now, is she.'

'Queen bee?' Chloe pretended not to understand while she thought rapidly. It wasn't right to listen to Meg's insinuations but Chloe was curious. She had sensed Cathy's disapproval and wanted to know the reason for Cathy's ill-concealed dislike.

'You know,' Meg went on in a low voice. 'Her and the two brothers. The Bourne boys. Everybody knew. Years ago, I mean. Both boys were mad for her but she preferred Jack. Patrick was walking out with a girl called Lucy Aimes. Jack and Cath got engaged but then Patrick didn't like that. He dropped poor old Lucy like a hot potato and did his best to come between the lovebirds. And he did. In the end Cath changed her mind and said she'd wed him instead. Poor old Jack, he was broken up. Went off without a word and nobody saw him for three days. There was talk about calling in the police to find him but he turned up with a face like thunder.'

'Poor man.' It explained a lot, Chloe reflected. It was probably why Jack Bourne had never married. Maybe he had hoped against hope that somehow, at some time, Cathy would be free again.

Meg shrugged. 'Course then Cath was sorry but it was too late because Patrick had got her in the family way and she was expecting young Adam.'

Chloe saw that she was supposed to say something. 'How dreadfully complicated!'

'Tis that! Patrick and Cath got married but some say it's never been right between them. Might say it served them right . . .'

Chloe glanced at Cathy who was watching them suspiciously.

Cathy snapped, 'Aren't you two going to do any more work?'

Meg ignored the reproof and tossed her tea leaves on to the ground. Then she took Chloe's cup and peered into it. 'Ooh! I see a dark stranger . . . and the letter J . . . and a bell! Might be a wedding bell! Who can say?'

Chloe snatched it back from her as Cathy descended on them, whitefaced.

'Either get back to work or get off home!'

Chloe, taken aback, found herself scrambling to her feet.

Meg rose more slowly. 'Better get back to work, I suppose. Thank goodness I've finished with the trotters. Oh

Lor'! Black pudding time. I do hate the sight of all that blood.'

Chloe met Cathy's furious gaze as calmly as she could. 'What's next for me?' she asked.

Cathy glared at her. 'You can call it a day,' she told her. 'We can manage the rest. I'm sure you've plenty to do at Monkswell.'

Chloe left with a grateful feeling of relief and began her walk back to Monkswell. Her mind was busy with the information she had been given. She could now piece it all together and she found the finished puzzle depressing. Jack Bourne was still in love with Cathy and presumably she might well still have feelings for him. No wonder Patrick watched his wife so closely. Chloe frowned. Was it possible there *was* a reason for Patrick to be suspicious? She recalled the rabbit pies Cathy had made for Jack, the raspberry jam and the chutneys. Were they tokens of affection or guilt, or simply an excuse for her to call in at Monkswell Farm and spend time with Jack? And exactly how much time had they spent together before Chloe appeared on the scene?

No wonder Jack was so close to Adam. He was Patrick's child but he was also Cathy's son. The son *they* would have had if Patrick hadn't interfered.

She tried to imagine Jack and Cathy alone together in the big kitchen and saw that now they would find Chloe's presence a serious complication.

'Oh blow them all!' she muttered. What do I care? Jack Bourne advertised the job, so he must have wanted another woman in the kitchen. It just happens to be me.

To force the ill-starred lovers from her thoughts she searched for a more cheerful subject and began to think about Terence Harkness.

As soon as she reached Monkswell Chloe climbed the stairs to her bedroom. She was determined to give her hands another wash and to find a soothing cream for them. They looked rough and red and Chloe tried hard not to think too harshly of Cathy. In her place she would probably feel just as hostile.

As she prepared to go downstairs and do some belated

ironing, she caught sight of a man crossing the nearest field and coming from the direction of Bourne Farm.

'Oh no! Not Patrick!' she whispered.

A few more minutes and she could see him clearly. For a moment she stared and then she rushed to the mirror to study her hair and clothes. She quickly pulled off the coarse apron she had been wearing for the pig killing and tidied her hair. As Jessica had predicted, Terence Harkness was calling on her!

Downstairs she waited for his knock, counted to ten then tripped along the passage to open the door.

'Mr Harkness!' She gave a little surprised laugh. 'Mrs Maitland warned you might – not warned exactly!' This time her laugh was to cover her embarrassment. 'She said you might come to the farm. I was just about – oh!'

From behind his back Terence Harkness had produced a large bunch of carnations. He said, 'I think these must be for you.'

'For me? Oh thank you but I don't—'

'They're not from me,' he said hastily. 'I wish they were. They were here on the step.' He pointed. 'You have an admirer, it seems. And I'm not surprised. In fact I think I'm a little bit jealous. Flowers for a lady! Now why didn't I think of that?' He smiled again and Chloe wondered how Jessica could possibly suspect him of anything underhand. She looked from him to the flowers. 'Carnations at this time of year?'

'Probably brought across from the Scilly Isles. Flowers bloom early there because of the climate.'

'Do they? Oh dear! There's no message. I don't know who could have sent them.' She glanced around as though whoever it was might be lurking nearby.

'Maybe you should put them in water,' he suggested.

'Oh yes, of course I must.' Confused, Chloe turned to go in. Who on earth could have sent her flowers? she wondered. Not Jack Bourne or his brother . . . Not Matty or Albert, certainly. Could it be Adam? No, he had a young lady.

Terence Harkness said quickly, 'Is it too much to hope that you'll invite me in for a few minutes? I've been to Fairfield and then on my way here I met a man who said you had gone to Bourne Farm. So I went there but somehow missed you again. At last I was sent on down here.'

'Oh dear! You have had quite a runaround!'

'It was worth it to finally find you, Mrs Tyler. The truth is I was determined not to go back to London without seeing you again.'

Flattered but also flustered, Chloe opened the door for him and he followed her into the kitchen and stood at his ease while she found a jug and arranged the flowers in water. She stood the jug on the broad window sill and turned to face him. 'It's really very nice to see you again, Mr Harkness, but I do have work to do. I'm a housekeeper, you see, and not free to choose what I do.'

'And I'm keeping you from your work. I should feel guilty but I don't!' He grinned.

Disconcerted, Chloe smiled. 'I really shouldn't spend long talking with you. That's not be meant to be unkind . . .' Please don't let him take offence, she thought. Nothing would be nicer than the chance to talk with Terence Harkness but if Jack Bourne should return he would probably object. And with good reason.

Terence said, 'Could you spare five minutes without a crisis of conscience?'

'Of course. In fact I can talk while I work for this pile of ironing is my next task. Would you like to sit down?'

'I'm quite happy standing. My mother always said "Stand and grow good!"'

She laughed. 'And did you – grow good?'

'I like to think so.' He glanced round the kitchen briefly then returned to settle on Chloe. 'I suppose you know all about me by now.'

She nodded. 'Mrs Maitland wrote to me. I understand that Matty is delighted. Quite a shock, though.'

'It must have been, but my father's taken it awfully well. I'm so happy to have met him at last and found him so welcoming. After the initial shock, that is. He was telling me that you have just come back from the United States looking for your own father. That must have been quite a search. Puts my little adventure quite in the shade!'

Chloe stood the iron on top of the range to heat and folded an ancient sheet to lay across the table. 'I found my father at last but not in the way I had hoped,' she told him. 'He had died some time earlier and I was able to see his grave and put some flowers on it. Not that I felt he had earned them but since I didn't have the chance to ask him what happened, I didn't feel I could entirely condemn him. I met several people who *had* known him and were kind enough to talk to me about him.' She pulled clothes from the overhead airer and began to straighten them by hand.

'Did they speak well of him?'

Chloe hesitated. The mention of her father's name had met with a mixed reception. 'It seemed he had another family. Two sons. It was strange meeting them. He'd married bigamously, of course, and I found that rather worrying.' She looked at him earnestly.

'And hurtful.' His tone was gentle.

'Yes. I tried to be open-hearted but . . . it proved quite emphatically that he had given up the idea of ever coming back to us. I'm glad my mother didn't live long enough to know that. To be honest I wish *I* didn't know but Jeff, my husband, said it was not important. He tried to make me feel better about it.' She tested the iron and selected a pillowslip from the pile. Talking about her discovery still had the power to distress her and she hurriedly changed the subject. 'Was Mr Harkness a good father to you?'

'Fair to middlin', as they say.' Terence smiled. 'I only knew the truth when Mother was about to die. She told me as she lay on her death bed. She had had it on her conscience all that time. It was Christmas Eve, I shall never forget that day.'

'And Mr Harkness? Does he know that she told you the truth?'

'Yes, but he said the truth always comes out and he had done nothing wrong. In fact I think he had behaved very decently. Not many men would want to marry a woman who was carrying someone else's child.'

'Is he still alive? Does he know that you've found your real father?'

'No. He's dead, too. He only outlived my mother by nine

52

months. He was devoted to her and the doctor said he died of a broken heart. Poor Father. He seemed to dwindle away. Losing the will to live. So I found myself alone in the world – hence my search.'

Chloe glanced at him. 'I wish my father had been half as decent as yours! But as Jeff said, we shouldn't be too quick to judge.'

Footsteps sounded outside and they both turned as Jack Bourne appeared.

Terence said, 'Thank you for your directions, Mr Bourne. As you see, I caught up with Mrs Tyler at last.' To Chloe he said, 'I shall have to be on my way but would you allow me to write to you? I shall be down again but not this week. I'd very much like us to keep in touch.'

For some reason that she didn't understand, Chloe glanced at Jack as though seeking his permission.

He said, 'Why ever not, Mrs Tyler? You're a free spirit.'

He spoke in his usual gruff manner but Chloe was encouraged.

'Then do please write,' she told Terence Harkness.

After the 'Goodbyes' were said she watched him retreat across the yard. Saying nothing she began to iron one of the shirts.

For a moment Jack watched her in apparent indecision. Then he said, 'Carnations? From your friend?'

'No. Someone left them outside the back door but there was no note. I don't even know who they're for.'

'I don't suppose they were meant for me!'

Chloe didn't know how to respond. He seemed unexcited by the anonymous gift but vaguely disapproving. 'I don't have an admirer if that's what you think. Not that I know about. It must be a joke.'

'An expensive joke – carnations out of season.'

Chloe avoided his eyes. Finishing the shirt, she folded it over the clothes horse and reached for another pillowslip. 'They're lovely anyway,' she said defiantly.

'So . . . was that Matthew Orme's son? The one he didn't know about.'

'Yes. How did you know about him?'

53

'Word travels fast in these parts. He seems pleasant enough.' He waited for her comment but she remained silent. 'How did you enjoy the pig-killing?'

'I didn't – but I managed my share of the work.'

'I hear you did some salting.'

'It was no worse than any of the other jobs.' Chloe tossed her head. If he thought she was going to complain he was wrong. 'How was your morning?'

'So-so.' He shrugged. He sounded dispirited. 'I won't stay for lunch. Save you cooking. I have to get over to Guestling. I'll make myself a sandwich.'

Chloe put down the iron. 'I'll do it for you. I'll use some of the beef we were going to have for lunch.'

He protested but Chloe insisted. She cut and buttered four slices of bread, laid the cold beef across two of them and spread some of Cathy's chutney over the other two. She wrapped them in greaseproof paper, all the time aware that Jack was watching her. He seemed to have something on his mind but if he had, he decided to keep it to himself.

He thanked her and stuffed the package into the pocket of his old jacket then whistled for Jude, who was watching from her corner.

As he left, Chloe returned to her ironing. She had the distinct feeling that Terence Harkness's visit had not been well received. She wondered if anyone at Bourne Farm had spoken ill of her.

'Nothing you can do, Chloe, if they have,' she told herself. She was beginning to realize that life at Monkswell Farm was becoming complicated.

That night Chloe lay in bed wondering about the flowers. Assuming they hadn't been delivered to the wrong address, the puzzle over the identity of the sender still remained. It wasn't Terence Harkness because she was sure he had nothing in his hands as he approached across the fields. He only produced them when he arrived at the back door. Anyway, why should he lie? It would hardly make sense to bring them and then deny being the bearer of gifts. Chloe frowned into the darkness. It certainly wasn't Jack Bourne. He was not the type to give flowers – or if he *was*, there was no reason why he should give them to his housekeeper. Especially as Chloe now knew that he had been in love with Cathy for most of his adult life. That left Adam Bourne and she rather thought it might be him. He had that air about him – a certain confidence. Or perhaps 'cheek' was the correct word . . . But what Jack Bourne had said was true – the carnations must have been expensive and she understood that Adam had a young woman of his own. Surely he wasn't wasting money on a widowed housekeeper who was several years his senior. His flowers would go to Marion Lester.

'Time will tell!' she muttered, smiling into the darkness. At least someone admired her. 'More than one!' she reminded herself, for Terence Harkness was definitely interested in her. He was going to write and he would no doubt be in Sussex again to spend time with his new-found father. She smiled as she settled herself for sleep.

'Admit it, Chloe B. Tyler,' she whispered. 'You are rather taken with him!'

Not that anything would come of it, but the prospect of some pleasant male company was rather appealing.

She was up early next morning and began her round of early tasks – laying the fire in the big black range, collecting eggs, feeding the pigs and chickens and cooking a breakfast for Jack Bourne. He seemed strangely uncommunicative and she watched him for some time before plucking up the courage to speak.

'Are you feeling unwell, Mr Bourne?'

He glanced up. 'What's that? I was miles away.'

'I asked if you were unwell. You seem very quiet this morning.'

He tossed a crust to Jude who caught it in mid air and crept closer to the table. 'I've things on my mind, that's all.'

'Nothing I've done, I hope?'

'Good Lord no!' His surprise was genuine. 'Farmers always have problems. What's that phrase? . . . Ah! It goes with the territory.' His laugh was rueful. 'The banks are always breathing down our necks and the suppliers are never willing to wait for payment. Machinery breaks down, animals fall sick. Not that I'd want to be anything else but a farmer. I suppose it's in the blood.'

'Jeff felt like that about animals. It had to be stock with him. Cattle. He wanted some land and cattle to run on it. He did a number of different jobs, always trying to save enough to get started. He never forgave his father for not helping him – and neither did I!'

'What did his father want him to do?'

'Become a lawyer and go into the family firm.' She began to gather up some of the crockery and carry it to the sink. 'Well, I'm glad I haven't stepped out of line.' She wondered what he had heard about her small conflict with Cathy but was afraid to ask.

Jack said, 'No complaints, Mrs Tyler. You're doing well. Cathy was pleased with the work you put in up at her place. She's bringing round some brawn and a few chops by way of payment. It all helps.'

He wiped a slice of bread round the eggy plate and ate it with relish. 'I'll get fat if you keep feeding me like this.'

She smiled. 'You could do with a bit more flesh on your bones.'

'You make me feel like a Christmas goose!' He stood up and Jude sprang to her feet also. 'So do you think you'll stay on?' He tried to sound casual.

Chloe stared at him. 'Stay on? I certainly hope so.'

'Not going to run off with him, then?'

'Who?'

With a nod of his head, he indicated the carnations.

Chloe laughed. 'I'm not so easily bought!' she told him. 'Between you and me, I think it was Adam, so when I see him I shall thank him. Call his bluff!'

'He'll make a good husband for some lucky girl.'

'I'm sure he will. He's a nice lad.' She hesitated. 'Does everyone know about Matthew Orme's son?'

'I expect so. No good trying to keep something like that a secret. Only natural that tongues will wag but it was Patrick who told me. He heard it from someone who heard it from Binns up at Fairfield House. Straight from the horse's mouth, if you like!' He looked at her curiously. 'May I ask if it was welcome news?'

Chloe hesitated. 'The father is delighted but his sister, Mrs Maitland, is still rather dubious. A little cautious, perhaps, but I think she'll come round. At the moment she's more concerned with her daughter and the new grandson. They are both still under doctor's orders. Still, no one can say life at Fairfields is boring!'

'Were you happy when you worked there?'

'Most of the time. Oliver's death was a great tragedy, of course, but I've never regretted being with the Maitlands.'

'But you didn't want to go back when you came home from America?'

'They didn't need me and I think we all need change in our lives.'

'It was my good fortune, then.'

She glanced at him, surprised by what sounded like a compliment but he didn't meet her gaze. Instead, with a sigh, Jack stood up and ran his hand through his hair. 'I'm going to the far meadow to see how the wheat's coming on. We're going to need a decent crop this year. Pay some of the bills.'

Chloe took a deep breath. 'If we had some more hens could we sell the eggs? And there's the pond. Do you ever keep ducks? We could breed ducks and sell some for eating . . . And when you go rabiting I could come with you and learn. And did you know something has been at the flour in the larder? It might be mice and I notice we don't have a cat.'

He looked at her in surprise. 'You've been doing a lot of thinking, Mrs Tyler. Haven't you got enough work already?'

'I have and I haven't.' She laughed nervously. 'It's just I can see how much there is for you to do single-handed and I'm willing to make myself useful. Patrick's got Cathy and Adam . . .' She fell silent. She had probably been too presumptuous.

'Patrick's got more land,' he said shortly. 'Adam gives me a hand when he can. I manage. I've always managed on my own.'

'I'm sorry. I didn't mean to suggest . . .'

He slipped his jacket on and settled his cap. For a moment

57

he stared at her but all he said was, 'Back around noon, then.'

And he was gone. Chloe, hands on her hips, stared after him. 'But thank you for the offer, Mrs Tyler!' she muttered and went upstairs to make the beds feeling unappreciated and cross.

The next day Chloe visited her sister again and by three o'clock she and Dorothy were sitting in the rectory garden. In the large pram Bertie and Clara slept fitfully, one at either end. When one of them fidgeted Dorothy rocked them a little.

'I hope they're not too hot,' Dorothy murmured. 'It's unusually warm for April. Perhaps I should take off one of the blankets.'

'They seem quite comfortable as they are.' Chloe tried to keep her tone neutral but today she was finding her sister's motherly ways rather irritating. Dorothy's constant comments interrupted whatever news Chloe was passing on. Her constant references to the twins were also undermining her in ways she could not yet explain.

'You should remarry, Chloe,' Dorothy told her abruptly. 'You'd make a good mother. You need children of your own and a husband. You're twenty-five, Chloe, going on twenty-six. I'm sure Jeff wouldn't want you to remain alone all your life.'

'Of course he wouldn't.'

'You wouldn't want him to stay on his own if you had been the one to die.'

Chloe couldn't recall ever talking about death with Jeff. It would have seemed ridiculous to broach the subject with a man who was full of life and their plans for the future.

'I might get round to the idea later,' Chloe said. 'But for the moment I'm not interested in the idea.'

'But you must want to know who sent you the flowers.'

'Not particularly.'

'But you do like Terence Harkness. I can tell.'

'I hardly know him!' Her answers, she knew, were not satisfying Dorothy but she was trying to confide something which she had told no one; something which she needed to share with a sympathetic soul. Every time she steeled herself her courage failed at the last moment.

'Dorothy, I need to tell you something . . .' she began but as usual the tightness in her throat made it difficult to continue.

'Do look at Bertie, Chloe.' Dorothy laughed, peering into the pram. 'That little thumb almost lives in his mouth! But Clara rarely sucks her thumb. Funny, isn't it.'

'Very funny.'

Dorothy's expression changed abruptly as her earlier words finally registered. 'You need to tell me something? Something bad? Oh Chloe!' Her eyes widened. 'You're not ill? Please say you're not—'

'I'm not ill.' She clasped her sister's hand briefly.

'Then what? You look so – so terrible. Have you done something . . . ? Has someone hurt you? It it Mr Bourne? Chloe, please!'

'It's nothing like that. It's . . . something in the past.' Now committed, Chloe wished she had kept her secret but it was too late. She now had all her sister's attention. Haltingly, she began. 'When I was in America Jeff and I . . . we were lovers before we were married. It just happened. We were so much in love and – and at the time it didn't seem wrong.'

Slowly she looked at her Dorothy who was visibly shocked. Her mouth hung open as she stared at Chloe, her dismay unmistakable. How could it be otherwise? thought Chloe. Dorothy was a vicar's wife. Her life revolved around the Church and its teachings. As Albert's wife, Dorothy must be blameless. Having a sister who had committed a sin would not be easy.

Dorothy put two fingers to her lips, no doubt to hold back reproaches.

She said, 'If you truly repent . . .'

'That's not all.'

Once started on her story, Chloe had to tell it all. She may not have chosen the right moment but her need to talk about what had happened was overpowering.

Desperately she ploughed on. Her carefully rehearsed lines eluded her and the words simply tumbled out. 'We were both astonished by what had happened between us because, hand on heart Dorothy, we hadn't intended anything of the kind but—'

'I'm sure you didn't, Chloe. You're a God fearing—'

'We decided we'd get married. Jeff didn't propose or anything romantic but we just looked at each other and knew we had to be together . . . So we found the nearest preacher and tied the knot.'

'In a church?'

Dorothy looked anxious and Chloe guessed she was wondering exactly how much she would tell Albert.

'Yes. In a little white clapboard church.'

'What did you wear?'

'I didn't have a white dress but I had a posy of large white daisies.'

'Oh, you poor thing!' Dorothy was recovering from the shock and leaned into the pram to adjust Clara's bonnet which had slipped round her head.

Chloe drew in her breath. 'But then I found out I – we were going to have a child.'

The censure in Dorothy's eyes changed at once to an expression of delight which immediately gave way to confusion. 'But where is it – the child? What happened?'

'I had . . . an accident. I was watching Jeff school a difficult horse. He was so wonderful with animals especially horses . . . He warned me to keep well away because I was at four months by then and I did stay back but suddenly it broke free and galloped towards me and I had nowhere to go. I just froze and Jeff was shouting and I couldn't understand what he was saying and . . .' Her voice broke but she forced herself on. 'It bowled me over and I was knocked unconscious.'

'Chloe! Oh my dear!'

As Chloe's tears began in earnest Dorothy's arms went round her and they clung together as they had done so many times before.

Dorothy said, 'You lost the baby? Is that it? Is that what you wanted to tell me?'

'Poor Jeff blamed himself although it was nobody's fault. Just one of those unkind tricks of fate.'

'You poor darling!'

Dorothy's arms tightened around her as Chloe gave way to her pent up grief. The sense of loss filled her again with unbelievable force and she could no longer speak. Dorothy comforted her with kisses and kind words and although Chloe could not see them, Dorothy's own eyes were full of tears.

As the minutes passed, however, Chloe began to feel the relief that speaking of her loss had brought her and the flow of tears gradually eased.

'I'm sorry,' Chloe muttered.

'I'm glad you told me. Now you wait here.'

Dorothy brought them both a small glass of sherry.

'So I should be a mother by now,' Chloe said sadly. 'We were both devastated and we had already written to Jeff's father with the good news so we then had to write and explain.'

'And he never answered any of your letters? What a cold, unfeeling wretch!'

From Dorothy they were very harsh words and Chloe smiled faintly.

'He had his reasons,' she said. 'He and Jeff had always been at loggerheads, apparently. He was jealous of Jeff because his mother made such a fuss of him. His father occasionally drank too much and would sometimes hit his wife. When Jeff grew up he tried to intervene and they had colossal rows. The father said he would never let his son inherit either the business or the small ranch they owned. One day it became too much for Jeff and he left home and never went back.'

Dorothy frowned. 'But he wrote to his mother, surely?'

'Of course but that probably made things worse between his parents.' She sighed. 'It was all very sad. But don't let it upset, you, Dorothy. It's all in the past. Jeff's mother died and Jeff died, so the story's over.'

Dorothy looked at Chloe with undisguised compassion. 'You'll marry again,' she promised. 'You're very attractive. You always were prettier than me.'

Chloe shrugged. 'I've had a husband and a child and I've lost them both. So much loss. It's such heartache, Dorothy.

When it happened it turned the whole world grey. I sometimes wonder whether I will ever have the courage to try again.'

They sat in mournful silence for a while and then, greatly daring, Dorothy said, 'Finish that sherry, Chloe. I think we need another one!'

Four

Winchelsea Church had once been a much larger edifice but marauding French many years earlier had attacked and set fire to it, so that part of it was now a ruin. Chloe listened to the service with interest but decided that although Albert's church was smaller and less imposing, Albert's sermons were infinitely more bearable and not only because they were shorter. The Winchelsea hassocks were far superior, though, in her estimation and a great deal of time and possibly money had been spent on the flower arrangements – which reminded her of the mysterious arrival of the carnations. The congregation was larger than at Icklesham but that was to be expected. Wealthy people had chosen to live in Winchelsea and apart from the church, there was a thriving school and a jail.

Chloe sat alone halfway back on the left side of the church. It seemed that Jack Bourne was not a regular churchgoer and had refused Chloe's suggestion that they should both attend. Chloe watched with amusement as the young choirboys passed sweets to one another or whispered discreetly when they thought no one was listening. Ouside, a light rain fell, so that the cloudy sky made the interior of the church a gloomy place, cheered only by the enthusiastic singing of the hymns. Ahead of her she saw Cathy Bourne with Patrick – but they could afford extra help with the farm and could both be spared for an hour or so. Jack Bourne enjoyed no such luxuries and she had left him setting a trap for the mice which were still helping themselves to the chickens' corn at the back of the larder.

When the collection had been taken and the final prayers uttered for the sick, Queen and country, the congregation stood. People stretched their limbs and made their chattering way out into the soft rain. Along the length of the perimeter of the churchyard, various traps and dog carts waited for their owners. Restless horses shook their wet heads and scuffed their hooves impatiently while small boys waited for the pennies they had earned by holding the horses' reins.

Chloe had no wish to meet up with Patrick and Cathy and slipped quickly from the church without waiting in line to shake the vicar's hand. She drove herself back to the farm in a happier frame of mind. As always the church service had cheered her. The familiar words of the prayers and the music of the hymns had dispelled the lingering sadness that had followed her talk with Dorothy and she felt soothed and renewed. Humming to herself, Chloe unharnessed the horse, rubbed him down and coaxed him back to his stable with a few handfuls of oats. Then, opening the door of the large barn, she manoeuvred the trap inside and wiped the upholstered seat with a cloth. Above her, huddled in a corner of the rafters, a small owl watched her. From time to time it shuffled nervously but didn't fly. Jack had told her it was there and it pleased her to know that the bird felt safe enough to stay.

Chloe hung up the harness and reflected how quickly this routine had become familiar. Before she had finished, Jude came hurrying into the barn to greet her. The dog presented herself to be patted, then scurried around the barn, sniffing in the corners and behind the straw in the hope of finding a rat to chase.

'Come on, Jude!' called Chloe and with a last glance into the rafters, she left the barn. Closing the heavy door once more, she left the owl to its seclusion in the darkness.

Jack Bourne was in the kitchen adding up some figures in a ledger with what looked like a pile of bills spread around him on the table. There were two empty mugs on the draining board and Chloe wondered who had called. Had Terence Harkness descended unannounced? If so she had missed him.

'You had a visitor,' she remarked lightly, removing her damp coat.

'Cathy called in. Look in the corner there.'

Chloe followed his pointing finger and found a small tabby kitten asleep on an old cloth.

'Oh, what a sweet thing!' she cried, resisting the urge to waken it.

'Is that me or the kitten?'

Chloe looked at him in surprise. His eyebrows were raised and he was smiling. It made him look very different. Jack Bourne rarely joked and Chloe grinned at him. 'Both of you!' She laughed. 'Is it a he or a she?'

'A she – so you'd best think of a name for her. Consider her yours. A present.'

'From Cathy?'

'From me. I knew they had a litter, so I chose this one this morning. I hope you like tabbies. Mind you, she's a bit small to face a rat but I've set the mousetrap in the larder, so don't touch it. She's a bit young to actually catch one but her catty smell might deter them.'

'She's sweet. Thank you.'

He bent his head again to the work in hand; then, without looking up, said, 'There's a letter come for you on the dresser.'

'Oh!' The exclamation rang with expectation and excitement and Chloe wanted to kick herself. It was probably from Terence and she had no wish to remind Jack that she had an admirer. 'I'll read it later.' Deliberately she ignored the letter. Instead she said, 'No more mysterious gifts, I hope!'

'Not that I know of.' He picked up one of the bills, studied it and frowned. 'I'm beginning to be a bit wary of Mellows & Co. Every bill's just a little more than I expect. He delivers some of the feedstuffs but he's only the delivery man. I reckon he's creaming off a bit for himself. Adding a bit of commission, you might say, and hoping I won't notice. Well, I have and I won't be paying that one just yet.' He put the offending bill aside and picked up another.

Chloe sat down opposite him and swallowed nervously. 'I was wondering . . . Please don't think it an awful sauce but do you ever invite anyone to supper? Or to Sunday lunch? I don't at all mind the extra work and it would be nice and sociable.' She had his attention and rushed on. 'I was thinking maybe your brother and Cathy and Adam . . . but maybe not.'

He said, 'They've never come for a meal. They don't expect it.'

Chloe was silent. If she said that Jack seemed lonely he would be annoyed. Had he made a conscious decision not to entertain them or had it simply not happened because he lived alone? Now that Chloe had broached the subject she would have to go through with it but she was already regretting the impulse.

'I thought maybe on your birthday . . . Adam let slip that it's your birthday shortly and that you are usually invited to them for Sunday lunch.'

'I go because I don't like to refuse,' he told her, 'but I've always thought birthdays a little overrated – except for children.'

Overrated? Chloe was appalled. 'They could come here for a change. Now you have somebody to cook for you . . . Oh, never mind!' Seeing his expression, she stood up, regretting the suggestion. 'I'm sorry. I can see you don't care for the idea and it's really not my place to—'

He looked up at her. 'Have I disappointed you?' He smiled. 'Forgive me. I suppose there's no reason why they shouldn't come. Would you like to invite them?'

'That's up to you. I don't know who your other friends are.'

He smiled. 'They're probably rather thin on the ground! I'm not very sociable. Let's keep it simple. We'll ask Patrick, Cathy and Adam for lunch next Sunday. How's that?'

Chloe was positively beaming. 'I'm sure you'll—'

He held up a forefinger. 'On one condition. That you join us at the table. I won't have you waiting on us like a servant.'

Her delight cooled instantly. 'But that won't . . . Surely it will look all wrong. I mean—'

'You'll cook and serve the meal – Cathy might offer a helping hand – but then you'll sit down and eat with us. As a friend of the family. Agreed.'

She said slowly, 'It wasn't what I had in mind.' Cathy would hate it, she was certain but she could hardly say that.

He grinned suddenly. 'Bit of a dilemma, isn't it?'

Chloe's doubts remained but she nodded.

'Is that a deal, then, Chloe?'

'It's a deal.'

Too late now to back out, she thought. It served her right for meddling. And what should she wear in her dual role as cook and family friend? As Jack reached for another bill she took her letter from the dresser and hurried upstairs to the privacy of her own room.

For a moment Chloe was almost afraid to open it. With hindsight it had been a rather rash thing to agree to correspond with a man who was almost a stranger and she wondered what Jack Bourne had thought of her.

> *Friday 19th April. Dear Mrs Tyler, I was delighted when you said I might write to you. Meeting my father after all these years was a thrilling event and meeting you was what my mother calls 'the icing on the cake!'*
>
> *We have so much in common that I'm sure we will become great friends. I have been invited back to Fairfields the weekend after next and I am hoping you might be there although I know you have to work but I shall keep my fingers crossed. If not, I shall call in on my way back to Rye Station just for a few words. I wish you lived nearer London so that we could meet more often but I must be grateful – and am grateful – for small mercies!*
>
> *I look forward to our next meeting. Your hopeful friend, Terence Harkness.*

Chloe reread it with relief. There was really nothing to which she could object. If they met again she would be at Fairfields among mutual friends – and he was, after all, a member of their family. She certainly hoped to be invited to Fairfields as she was not happy about Terence Harkness making too many visits to Monkswell Farm. Folding the letter, she slipped it back into the envelope and stared out of the window across a landscape that was already becoming familiar. Broad fields dotted with sheep, well kept hedges and the occasional small copse.

She found herself wondering just how severe the financial problems were and how Jack Bourne would solve them. Then she remembered the birthday lunch and felt guilty. More expense. But he had agreed to it without protest, so maybe it didn't matter. She would think of a reasonable menu . . . Maybe a piece of baked ham – there were two hanging in the larder – with carrots and roast potatoes and early spring greens. Or would they like a pie – pastry was cheap and filling and she made a good, crumbly pie crust . . . Or a stew with dumplings – no. Not grand enough for a special lunch.

And she would try to think of a birthday present for him. Something simple. A book marker would be appropriate, for he sometimes read in the evenings for half an hour or so before he went up to bed.

She was still day-dreaming when she saw Adam coming up the lane. She hurried down.

As she reached the bottom of the stairs she heard Jack say, 'So you're sending my housekeeper flowers, are you?'

He was standing at the dresser riffling through one of the drawers.

'Me? no – but I might have done if I'd thought of it.'

Chloe went into the room, smiling. 'It must be you, Adam. Why not confess then I can thank you.'

'Because I haven't sent you any flowers. Sorry but I haven't. You must have an unknown admirer. I'll have to challenge him to a duel!' He turned to Jack. 'Before I forget, Ma says to come over for your birthday as usual. Just the four of us as ever, I'm afraid. Not very thrilling but . . .' He made a dismissive gesture with his hands.

He looked slightly embarrassed and Chloe realized at once that she had not been invited. Not that she would have expected it but Jack had insisted on her inclusion at his own lunch. Maybe he would now have second thoughts.

Jack closed the drawer and opened the next one. 'You're too late this year, Adam. I'm inviting the three of you to have lunch here. Nice change for Cathy. She won't have to cook.'

Chloe saw the surprise in Adam's eyes, followed by delight. So at least *he* was pleased by the invitation. Maybe Cathy had been hoping to let Chloe know exactly where she stood in *her* book – most definitely a servant.

She said quickly, 'You can't say no. I've already worked out a menu.'

'A *menu*, eh!' He rolled his eyes. 'What is it – champagne and truffles?'

Jack grinned. 'Hardly, but you certainly won't go home hungry.'

'We-ell! Ma will be surprised.' He seemed to relish the idea. 'Thanks. Nice surprise.' He regarded Chloe with amusement. 'So you can cook, can you?'

'Of course I can. I'm a housekeeper, aren't I?'

'The housekeeper. Yes, that's exactly what Ma said!' He gave her a look that wasn't too hard to read.

Chloe felt as though he had slapped her. Jack's eyes darkened. 'It'll be just the five of us.'

He looked steadily at his nephew, who said, 'Ah! . . . Good. That should be interesting.'

For a moment or two it appeared that he had something else to say but he simply shrugged. 'Well, I mustn't keep my young lady waiting. She can't go in to The Fox on her own and hates to hang around outside.'

Jack winked at Chloe. 'He has a new young lady every week. I can't keep up with him.' To Adam he said, 'Who is it this week? Not still the schoolteacher's lass?'

'You know darned well it isn't! That was Daisy Lynn. Not exactly a beauty but she's got very nice ankles!'

Jack raised his eyebrows. 'Ankles?'

'Yes. She rides a bicycle and has to hitch up her skirt for fear it tangles in the wheels. But now it's Marion Lester, as you well know.'

Jack turned to Chloe. 'I can't see what they see in him, can you?'

Adam said, 'Of course she can. It's my fatal charm. Ladies can't resist me.'

Chloe laughed. 'So why do you keep losing your young ladies?'

'I can't help it if they don't last the course. All women are fickle.' He looked pointedly at Jack. 'You of all people should know that.'

Chloe caught the implication and hastily intervened. 'You should treat them better, Adam. Send them some flowers!'

Adam grinned. 'I *didn't* send them! Why don't you believe

69

me? Maybe it was the new chap at Fairfields. I heard all about that.'

Jack said, 'Word gets around. Anyway, you get along to your young lady before she too rides off into the sunset!'

Adam looked at Chloe, doffed an imaginary hat and swept her a low bow.

She said, 'Goodbye, Adam.'

When he had gone Jack said, 'I'm sorry about that. About Cathy I mean. She can be a bit . . . Well, she has her funny ways like the rest of us. None of us are perfect and she can be a bit sharp.'

Chloe hesitated then decided to speak out. There was no point in pretending ignorance.

'Meg told me – about you and Patrick and Cathy. I understand how it is – for all of you. Not easy at all.'

'Meg's a blabbermouth!' His face flushed. 'I don't know why Cathy employs her. Meg is the local busybody.'

'It doesn't matter, Mr Bourne. Truly. It helps me, to know what happened. I needn't take everything personally now because I understand everyone's point of view.'

Closing the second drawer but still empty handed, Jack sat down. 'There was a lot of trouble at the beginning of their marriage. The truth is that Patrick told Cathy he thought the boy was mine. Cathy and I knew, of course, that that was impossible – there'd been nothing improper between us – but Patrick wouldn't listen. He'd got it into his head and nothing would shift it. He led Cathy a hell of a life.'

'Poor Adam.'

'Yes. Even as young child he must have felt something was wrong. He's never been as close to Patrick as he should be. They've both missed out over the years – but I've had to be careful. Adam turned to me for affection and I loved him because he was part Cathy's. Should have been hers and mine but it wasn't to be.'

'But Cathy . . . I know it was her own fault but . . .' She stopped, wary of speaking ill of Cathy Bourne. Presumably Jack still loved her. The eternal triangle was hardly new but surely two of the three people involved should have been happy. In this case it seemed that none of them were. Stealing a glance at Jack's face, she saw only resignation.

He rubbed a hand over his face and sighed. 'You know what they say? That we all get what we deserve from life. A frightening thought, that!'

'Very frightening!' Chloe agreed. 'But I don't believe a word of it!'

Next morning at Bourne Farm, Cathy awoke and immediately her mind was filled with the problem that still rankled. Jack was expecting them to share his birthday with his new housekeeper. How on earth had that come about? Unless the housekeeper had somehow wheedled an invitation for herself. Jack was always weak where women were concerned. She stared at the ceiling. Watching the daylight creep in over the top of the curtains, she sighed deeply. If it hadn't been the housekeeper's insistence then Jack was doing it to aggravate Patrick – or maybe to punish *her*, for all his years of loneliness. Am I never going to be free, she wondered miserably, of this terrible sense of failure; of the knowledge that I have made a mistake that can never be righted; of the sense that I do not deserve happiness?

Outside, she heard the cuckoo but it was the third time this year and nothing to get excited about. Turning her head slightly, she regarded her husband's sleeping form with distaste. His mouth hung open and his florid complexion appeared darker against the white sheet. She had loved him, all those years ago but she had loved Jack, too. Jack, so quiet and sensitive and Patrick so bold. Why hadn't she seen Patrick for what he then was – a shallow young man behind the teasing and laughter? The older cocksure brother that always had to win. That boldness, the *arrogance*, had been what excited her. In Patrick's company she had been sure of the limelight because that was the sort of man Patrick was. If he couldn't be the centre of attention he wanted to be somewhere else.

Jack was so different. So shy, always hanging back, admiring his older brother and desperately wanting to be like him. Jack hated centre stage. He was always trying to blend in with the crowd, enjoying life in his own quiet way. How could she have

71

chosen the wrong man? If she had married Jack she could have given him the self-confidence he lacked. She could have made up for all the years he had spent in his brother's shadow. And dear Adam would have been *their* son.

'Leave me, Patrick,' she whispered. Run away with another woman and let me have Jack. Give me a few years to enjoy his company before it's too late. She could bear the scandal and the pity and even the disapproving looks if only she and Jack could be together at last.

She slipped from the bed, reached for her wrap and made her way quietly down the stairs. On the few mornings when she awoke before her husband, she treasured the solitude. The kitchen clock ticked stolidly while, outside, the birdsong had begun. Hastily feeding twigs into the range, she waited for the kettle to boil. She spooned tea into the pot and fetched a mug from the shelf and found milk and sugar.

'And now there's you!' she said to the absent Chloe. This wretched Mrs Tyler who was about to take away the only pleasures she had. She could no longer look forward to those visits to Monkswell Farm with the rabbit pie or the bread-and-butter pudding. Cold of course but they warmed through nicely enough. Not that anything was ever said between them and she had never miscalled Patrick. How could she? He never did anything wrong. Well, he did, of course, but it was nothing she could talk about with Jack. Patrick didn't beat her or keep her short of money but he did let his fancies stray and there was more than one young woman in the village who had spent stolen hours with Patrick Bourne. That said, his only real crime was that he wasn't Jack.

Sipping her tea, she heard her husband rouse up and the creak of bedsprings told her he was getting up. He came downstairs in the ghastly green pyjamas he had chosen in the shop in Rye. He was bleary eyed and with yesterday's bristles on his chin he looked a sorry sight. Cathy wondered what Jack looked like first thing in the morning – and whether or not Mrs Tyler knew. Handing Patrick a mug of tea without speaking, she watched him add sugar. Then he stirred his tea until she wanted to scream. Round and round went the spoon, scraping the china, grating on her nerves. He knew how she hated the sound but he always claimed that he didn't know he did it.

She snapped, 'So we have to put up with Mrs Tyler! Some birthday party!'

'It's hardly a party. It's—'

'You know what I mean. Makes you wonder what's going on there.'

'Why should we care?'

'Well, you should care. She might be after him for all we know. A widow like that.'

He blew on his tea. 'So what? She's welcome to him. He's got nothing. A farm that's on its last legs. Debts.'

'Debts? How do you know?'

''Cos I keep my eyes and ears open, that's how. Cut me some bread.'

She rose automatically and cut two slices. She watched him butter one slice and stick the other on top. Choke on it, why don't you? she thought angrily.

He went on. 'He's not buying at the market. He's never in the corn chandlers. Never in the pub.'

'Then how come he's inviting us round to lunch?'

'That's nothing, is it. He grows most of it. Be interesting to see what she does for us. I doubt she cooks as well as you.'

Cathy glanced up, surprised and pleased by the unexpected compliment. 'Oh? Don't you think so?'

'Well, she's a lot younger than you. Stands to reason. You've been cooking for years longer than her.'

'Not that many!' Trust Patrick to ruin even the smallest compliment. She said, 'Anyway, I'd rather not go.'

'So you keep saying but we're going. He's my brother and it's his birthday and we're—'

'You and Adam go without me.'

'We're *all* going!'

'I just don't like the woman.'

'I know that! And don't think I don't know why. You're jealous of Chloe Tyler. It's written all over your—'

'Jealous?' Cathy gave him an indignant glare. 'Are you mad? Jealous of a little housekeeper?'

'She's sharing his house, though, isn't she?' Patrick looked at her with the beginnings of malice.

Cathy instantly regretted the conversation and where it was heading. Why hadn't she kept her mouth shut? She stammered, 'You're being ridiculous. What's Jack got to offer? Why should I be jealous? You said it yourself – he's got nothing to offer.'

'Then why take against her for no reason? You've had your knife in her ever since she set foot in the place. Before you even met her.' He leaned closer. 'And I'll tell you why. Because she's younger than you and prettier and you know he must fancy her or he wouldn't have taken her on. You've got a rival at last, Cathy. You've had Jack all to yourself all these years – oh, don't think I haven't noticed all your little errands.'

'Little errands? I don't know—' She felt the colour rush into her face and wanted to slap the triumphant look from his silly face.

'Errands. Whatever you call them. Pies and stuff.' He adopted a high-pitched voice that was supposed to resemble hers. 'I think I'll pop a jar of this chutney over to Jack.'

She said, 'Sometimes I make too much. Sometimes . . .' Her throat dried.

Patrick watched her humiliation. 'It's been going on for years. If I haven't said anything before it's because I don't ruddy well care!'

For a moment Cathy felt breathless with fright. These things shouldn't be said. She knew they shouldn't, but she heard herself say, 'Well, you should care!'

'Why? Because you say so? I don't lose any sleep over it because you're not worth it!'

His cruel words robbed her of speech. He had never spoken to her like this in all the years of their marriage and she had only herself to blame. Tears threatened but she would *not* cry. Instead she went on the attack. 'If you ask me, you're a bit keen on her herself. Younger . . . prettier. Perhaps it's you that's jealous! Perhaps you wish we had a pretty housekeeper. You wonder what they get up to at night, don't you?'

74

Instinctively she knew that there was no going back. Grievances that had gone unexpressed were being aired but it was dangerous.

Patrick's hands were clenched. 'What if I do wonder? I'm only human. First time Jack's taken an interest in anyone but you. So of course I wonder.' He was glaring at her, breathing quickly. 'But there's not a ruddy thing we can do about it so let it lie. And not a word to Adam.' He stood up abruptly. 'Whether you like it or not, we're going to lunch on Sunday.' Stabbing the air with his finger, he added, 'You're going to sit with Mrs Tyler and you're going to keep your mouth shut. One wrong word and . . .'

She gasped. 'Are you threatening me?'

'Too right I am!'

And before she could answer he stormed out of the room.

Unaware that he was the source of such anger, Jack sat in the bank manager's office. He wore his decent suit and fiddled with the cap which rested on his knees. On his way to the bank he had stopped in Rye High Street to look at the clothes in the menswear shop, wishing he could afford a better suit for high days and holidays – but knowing that in his present financial state he could not. He wasn't quite sure why he felt the need to improve his image and he kept the idea of Chloe Tyler firmly out of his mind. Of course. It would make a better impression on the bank manager if he looked like a man who was comfortably off and could afford to dress well.

Now, ensconced in the bank's cramped office, he regarded the manager with misgivings. Some men were wined and dined by their bank manager but Jack had never been one of the fortunate few. His account was rarely out of the red and probably never would be. Once, Jack knew, Patrick had been taken out to lunch but it had never happened again.

Running a finger around the inside of his collar, Jack said, 'It's very warm in here, isn't it.'

Edmund Salter gave him a thin smile. 'Our clients appreciate it.'

Thus quickly put in his place for his impertinence, Jack fell silent. He stared past the manager's head at a calendar on the wall. Realizing that it was a month out of date he felt that he had scored a small victory.

The manager buried his face in a spotless handkerchief and gave a discreet cough. Edmund Salter was a small, plump man with a deceptively genial face which reminded Jack of a benevolent grandfather. In matters of business, however, he had a reputation for ruthlessness and these meetings always made Jack nervous.

Now, Salter tapped a pencil on the desk as he turned the pages of Jack's file.

'It's now seven weeks,' he murmured. 'I confess, Mr Bourne, I am a trifle worried . . .' He glanced up, smiling gently. 'But I expect you are, too, Mr Bourne.'

'Of course I am!' Jack hadn't intended to snap but the words were sharpened by fear. 'I've had a few purchases, some unexpected.'

'Which were?'

'Wood to repair the barn. It was rotting under the eaves and the wheat was—'

'Wood.' He made a note on his pad. 'And this wheat? I thought you were a sheep farmer.'

'I grow a little wheat for our own consumption.'

He made another note. 'And . . . ?'

'And the shearing costs went up.'

'Don't you do your own shearing?'

Jack regarded him with something akin to loathing. The same futile questions year after year. Shouldn't a bank manager understand something of his client's problems? 'I have around six hundred sheep. I have to employ help with the shearing.'

'Hmm . . . And any other purchases?'

Jack swallowed. 'I have been forced to take on a house-keeper who also helps around the farm. That frees me up to get on with the real work.'

'A housekeeper? Oh dear! Yes, I can see that would be an added expense. What a pity you haven't married, Mr Bourne. But you mentioned purchases.'

Jack racked his brains. 'I had to get a new gate for the far meadow. The sheep got out and—'

'Ah! New gate.' He nodded, wrote again, turned back a page

76

and studied its contents. Then he looked up. 'I see you intended to buy a cow to replace the one that died.'

It was news to Jack but he assumed he had said so at their previous meeting. Now he thought quickly. 'I couldn't because the prices were too high. I was hoping they would drop but they didn't. I still hope to get one.'

Jack groaned inwardly. How pathetic he sounded – all these excuses. Yet none of them were false. Farming was a constant battle against the unexpected but how would a bank manager be expected to comprehend the subtle shifts of farming? There were so many imponderables. The weather, the current prices, fluctuating as they did from month to month, the price of fodder, of labour . . . He despised the plump manager, sitting in his leather chair in his cosy office, making life and death decisions for those who were scraping a living from the land while he was being paid a steady income come what may. Jack said, 'I might buy a calf from my brother and rear it.'

Salter's interest quickened. 'For slaughter, you mean?'

'For milk.'

'Ah yes! Your brother. I seem to remember that I suggested you shared some equipment with him. I thought that made a great deal of sense.'

Jack wanted to strangle him. Was he being deliberately dense? He said stiffly, 'We don't necessarily need the same stuff. He has a dairy herd and I run sheep.'

'But he has a few sheep.'

'He also grows some oats and has a field full of geese but he has a bigger acreage than I do. He can do more. If I had more land . . .'

'I hope this isn't leading up to that perennial request for a loan, Mr Bourne. Buying more land doesn't necessarily mean a better financial position. I thought I made that quite clear last year when you raised the subject.'

Jack sighed. He knew it was pointless. It was a vicious circle. To have more land to run more sheep he would have to borrow more money and already he was finding it difficult, if not impossible, to pay back the previous loan. He said, 'If you can give me a bit longer, I'm sure things will look up. I'll be selling on the lambs in the autumn.' This was true but he dared not admit that there would be fewer lambs than usual to sell on. It had been a cold, wet spring and in spite of all his devoted care he had lost eleven to the inclement weather.

'I'm really not happy about the situation, Mr Bourne.' Salter shook his head with a show of regret. 'My superiors aren't going to like this at all and I do have to be aware of the guidelines. Is there the smallest gleam at the end of the tunnel that I could mention to Head Office?'

'I can't think of anything.'

'Wouldn't your brother help you out?'

'No!'

The manager leaned forward, a kindly smile on his face. 'Your brother is comfortably placed, Mr Bourne. I know you have your pride but a small loan from a family member is nothing to be ashamed of. I can assure you—'

'I said, "No"!' Jack glared at him, struggling with his temper which was beginning to fray. The wretched man was patronising him. 'I'll never ask my brother for a penny! I've told you before.'

Salter sat back, shook his head and sighed. He fiddled with the pencil and stared at the open file. 'You do realize that we may have to call in the loan?'

Jack felt a coldness seep into his bones at the fateful words. He had survived bad times before now but had never heard those particular words uttered.

He tried to speak but his throat was tight and unresponsive. At last he stammered, 'I hope it won't come to that.'

'Oh, so do I, Mr Bourne. So do I.' Salter smiled. 'Provisionally I will give you another three months but I shall have to notify my superiors and they may not agree. At that stage it will be out of my hands. Do you see, Mr Bourne? I've done my best for you but I won't be able to help you after that.'

Jack stood up, feeling unsteady. Shock and shame seemed to weigh him down. Somehow he shook the plump pink hand that was offered and stumbled to the door. He had failed. Outside, in the soft rain, he put his cap on and stared round the familiar High Street. He dared not tell anyone or the final demands would flood in. He thought briefly of Patrick but his pride would never allow him to confide this disaster and Cathy must never know.

'Oh God!' he muttered. 'What's to be done?' He shivered although it wasn't cold.

He needed a drink. Thrusting his hands into his pockets he made his way unhappily in the direction of The George Hotel.

Chloe straightened her back and surveyed her handiwork with pride. She had found six young tomato plants in the old greenhouse and had planted them in a sunny spot not too far from the kitchen. Later they would need stakes, she knew, but at present they were no more than ten inches tall and looked sturdy enough to survive the spring weather. She glanced down at Jude, who was mournfully following her about.

'What do you think, Jude? Have I done a good job?' She patted the dog's head. 'Don't look so sad. Your master will be back soon. He could hardly take you to the bank with him.'

She would mention the plants casually to Jack Bourne and hoped he would be pleased with her initiative. There were other plants but none as healthy looking and some she did not recognize. Anything that saved money must be a good idea, she told herself and, gathering up the fork and watering can, she set off towards the kitchen.

'Hey! Missus!'

Surprised, she turned to see a scruffy boy on a rusty bicycle weaving an erratic course across the yard as he dodged the hens who had set up a loud squawking as they fled from the wheels of his bicycle. The boy looked about ten, she thought, with a large mouth, untidy hair and a coat two sizes too big for him.

'What is it?' She looked at him curiously and Jude growled a warning deep in her throat. 'If you want Mr Bourne he's—'

'I want Mrs Tyler. I got summat for her.' He stopped and pulled a small paper packet from somewhere inside his coat.

'I'm Mrs Tyler. Who are you?'

'Tom Finch. I was told to give you this. I was given a sixpence to bring it and hand it over personal.' He held out the packet.

She didn't immediately take it and he said, 'Go on! If you're Mrs Tyler it's yourn!'

Before she could argue, he tossed it towards her and she instinctively reached out to catch it.

'Who sent you?' she asked, already convinced that this was another mystery present.

He grinned. 'Can't tell you 'cos I don't know. That's how it works, see. This geezer gives it to this other kid and he passes it on to me.'

'So it's a man.' She thought quickly. 'Old or young? Fat or—'

''Ow do I know? I just said – I never got to see him.'

'And this other boy? Do you know his name?'

Laughing, the boy swung his leg over the cycle bar and prepared to ride off but Chloe caught hold of the handlebars. 'There's threepence for you if you tell me.'

'Threepence? No fear! A shilling more like!'

Chloe released her hold. 'A *shilling!* Why, you cheeky monkey!'

She watched him go, then turned her attention to the package. It was about ten inches long, slim and weighed little. Hurrying indoors, she removed the string and tore open the wrapping. Inside, she found a pair of white lace gloves and as she stared at them she felt her pulse quicken. They were beautiful. Someone admired her enough to send her such a gift and the thought lifted her spirits immediately.

'A someone who goes to a lot of trouble to remain anonymous!' she said. 'Who are you?'

She wondered whether she should tell Jack Bourne and hesitated. If she did he might not be too pleased but if she didn't, and he found out later, he would think her deceitful and it would somehow make her look guilty. If it turned out to be Adam she doubted if anyone would mind – but it was an extravagant gift for such a young man to give. She put them on the dresser, where Jack would be bound to see them. Then he would ask and she would answer. That way she wouldn't appear to be flaunting the gift.

When he returned, however, he seemed rather subdued. Jude rushed to him and he fondled her ears absentmindedly, then sat in silence sipping a mug of tea. Chloe wondered whether she should ask how the meeting went. That was what a wife would do, she reflected, but she was only a housekeeper and he might consider it presumptuous. She busied herself making an apple pie, snatching the occasional glance in his direction. At last she was driven by his gloomy silence to say something.

'I bedded out the tomato plants,' she told him.

He said, 'Did you? Let's hope we don't get a late frost.'

'Oh!' Her face fell. 'I hadn't thought of that.'

'It doesn't matter. They never do that well. Cathy usually nags me about them. She brings the plants across. It's never my idea – but thanks, anyway.'

After a moment she said, 'Mr Bourne, is something wrong?'

'Nothing that concerns you.' He gave her a weary smile. 'With a farm there's always something going wrong. It's just the way it is.'

'Is there any way I could help?'

'No, my dear.' The endearment slipped out and they were both surprised by it. Chloe thought at once that perhaps it was a phrase he used when he spoke to Cathy. Confused, he added, 'But thank you for offering.' Disconcerted, his gaze lingered on her face for a moment and then shifted slightly. Chloe saw his eyes widen. 'Lace gloves? Not another present, surely!'

'Yes. I hope it's not Adam. I don't think his father would approve of him wasting his money on me. I can't think of anyone else it could be.'

'Will you wear them?'

She laughed. 'I don't know. Perhaps not. When I discover the sender I may feel I should return them. Meanwhile I'll put them in a drawer with my lavender bags.'

He nodded, again preoccupied with his thoughts. Then he stood up. 'I'll be off then to have a look round. Come on, Jude!'

She watched dog and master walk across the yard, Jack's shoulders slumped, crushed by his obvious depression. Jude trotted beside him, watching him anxiously, sensing his mood. Her ears were back and her tail remained limp.

Five minutes later the telephone rang. It was the bank manager from Rye.

'Just pass on a message for me,' he said. 'Tell Mr Bourne I'm sorry but I've been in touch with Head Office. It's not three months, it's only two.'

'Will he know what that means?' Chloe asked.

His reply was unambiguous. 'Oh dear me, yes! He'll understand.'

Five

Wednesday arrived with a cool wind and heavy clouds. By eleven o'clock Chloe had cooked Jack's breakfast, washed up and had fed the various creatures that were now her responsibility. Now she was mashing potatoes for a fish pie and thinking about Terence Harkness. She wanted to smarten up her wardrobe before he came down again and was wondering whether to take a coffee-coloured lace collar from one dress and use it on another. This meant that the cream lace cuffs would not match and she would have to take them off. If she had a chance she could buy something in Rye but her days were very full and she didn't want to start asking for extra time off when it was clear that Jack was working round the clock without complaint.

The kitten woke up and began to play with a cotton reel and she watched her, amused by the kitten's contortions and sudden dashes across the room. She had named her Sweet Pie in memory of a cat that ruled the timber yard where Jeff had worked. The original cat had been a tortoiseshell and a terrible hunter of birds.

'But you're going to be a good cat and only catch mice,' Chloe suggested.

Sweet Pie, wrapped around the cotton reel, said nothing and Chloe grinned. Hunting was in a cat's nature and they could hardly be expected to understand the difference between mice and birds. Anything that moved was fair game.

The sound of wheels caught Chloe's attention and she saw Matty Orme clambering down from the Fairfield's pony cart. Abandoning the potatoes, she hurried to meet him. She saw at once that he looked badly shocked and that Binns was also subdued.

'What's happened?' She took hold of the old man's arm and steered him into the kitchen. He sank down on to a chair and drew several deep breaths.

'Is it Olivia?'

It was that family's nightmare that something would happen to Oliver's daughter.

Matty shook his head. 'It's Jessica. She's collapsed. You have to come, Chloe. There's no one and I don't know what to do. I've sent for Doctor Bell but he was on his rounds. Mrs Letts is all of a twitter, poor soul, and—'

Chloe tried not to show her alarm. 'Is Jessica conscious?'

'We can't tell. She's not responding to questions. She may be unconscious or she may be in a deep sleep. Or a coma!' His voice rose shakily.

'But you have managed to get her into her bed?'

'Yes. The women did it.'

Chloe stared round the kitchen, wondering if she could be spared for half an hour. Perhaps she should leave Jack a note.

Matty was still trying to recover his composure, leaning forward with his elbows on the table, his head in his hands. 'You must come, Chloe. Bertha still hasn't left her bed and there's no one else.'

'You have Alice. She's very sensible.' She was stalling for time. She found a pencil and wrote: '*Dear Mr Bourne, there is an emergency at Fairfields and I have been asked to help. I will be back as soon as I can. Please forgive hurried scribble. Chloe Tyler.*'

Matty said, 'Alice is with her now but that means Mrs Letts has to keep an eye on Olivia. For heaven's sake, hurry, Chloe!'

'I'm coming!' she cried. 'Give me a moment. I can't just walk out without a word. Jack will wonder—' She stopped, astonished. She had referred to her employer as 'Jack'.

Matty, despite his anxiety, had noticed. 'It's Jack, is it?'

'Of course not! You've got *me* hot and bothered as well. Now . . .' She snatched a shawl from a nearby chair and, glancing outside, prayed the cloudy sky did not herald rain. 'Let's go,' she said. 'I'll follow you in our trap so that I can return alone.'

* * *

84

Jessica lay in bed, her face beaded in perspiration. Alice was dabbing her face and neck with a damp flannel and looking none too confident. As soon as Chloe was ushered into the room she jumped to her feet.

'Oh Mrs Tyler! Thank the Lord you've come. Mr Orme said you would if you could. I must collect Olivia from the kitchen,' she told them. 'I know how Olivia loves to be with Mrs Letts but kitchens are dangerous places for children. Too many hot surfaces and sharp knives! Anyway, the doctor should be here before too long.'

Matty hovered in the background while Chloe took the nanny's place beside the bed. She leaned forward to study the old lady and said softly, 'Jessica! It's me. Chloe.'

At first, as Matty had told her, there was no reaction but slowly Jessica's eyes opened and she looked vaguely in Chloe's direction. Chloe stared at her in dismay. Hadn't the old lady recognized her?

Despite Matty's warning, Chloe was unprepared for the change in Jessica's appearance. Days earlier she had been fit and well but now she looked like a broken doll. Her face was chalky white and her flesh seemed to have shrunk against her bones. Her breathing was very shallow and when Chloe picked up her hand it was limp and unresponsive. Forcing a smile, she said, 'Don't be frightened, Mrs Maitland. It was just a bit of a turn. Doctor Bell will be here shortly and will soon put you to rights.'

'Chloe . . . Chloe, it's . . .' Jessica was breathing heavily.

'Don't try to talk, dear. Just rest. You're going to be fine. I daresay you've been overdoing things.' Chloe tried to sound more confident than she felt. The truth was she was herself frightened and she was greatly relieved when footsteps and voices on the stairs heralded the approach of the doctor.

At that moment Matty showed the doctor into the room and Chloe and Matty withdrew to the landing, where he clung to the banisters in obvious distress.

He said, 'You've seen her, Chloe. What did you think? She's going, isn't she?'

Chloe swallowed, fighting back her fears. 'She does look ill, I grant you.'

'Oh Jessie, old thing! Don't leave me!' Tears filled his eyes and Chloe, regretting her careless words, took hold of his arm.

'We'll go downstairs and leave the doctor to it,' she said. 'Jessica's in good hands. Now you know he will take care of her. Hold on to me. We'll go down together.'

Once installed in the drawing room, they rang for some tea and Chloe watched the colour seep back into Matty's face.

Chloe said, 'How exactly did the fall happen, Matty? You said she collapsed, but are you sure she didn't trip and fall? Maybe hit her head and knocked herself out?'

'I told you on the way over,' he protested.

'Tell me again. Please. I was in a panic and you were still badly shocked. You weren't making much sense, to be honest.'

'I didn't see what happened. I was half dozing in the drawing room and heard a muffled crash and ran into the hall. Poor old Jessie was lying on the floor. I thought she'd been speaking on the telephone or trying to make a call because the receiver was off the hook. She kept saying the same word over and over. It sounded like "Mother" but it's hardly likely. Our poor old Mother went years ago.'

'Had anything happened previously to upset her?'

He hesitated. 'We had a silly argument earlier. Nothing more than a disagreement. It's Terence. My son. I don't like to say this, with her in such a state, but the truth is, Chloe, Jessica's very jealous of him. A letter came here for him and that set her off again. She can't or won't see any good in the poor chap.'

'I thought she liked him.' Chloe was aware of disappointment. How could Jessica *not* like him? He was charming, intelligent, good company . . .

Fanny brought in the tray and Chloe poured tea for Matty and said, 'Take an extra spoonful of sugar. It will help you get over the shock.'

He obeyed and then went on. 'Jessie liked him at first but not any more. She's got it into her head that he's not to be trusted. She keeps asking me questions about him. Where does he actually live when he's not staying in London? What does

he do for a living? That sort of thing. Ask him yourself,
I told her. I don't interrogate the poor lad . . . About an
hour later this happened. I can't see that it's connected.
Can you?'

'No. Don't worry about it, Matty. You've no reason to blame
yourself.'

He sipped his tea, apparently unconvinced then he turned to
her. 'You like him, don't you? I know he . . . Well, he finds
you very attractive and that pleases me no end. I mean, you
never know. You and my son?' He winked at her. 'Stranger
things have happened, haven't they. You'd be Mrs—'

Chloe stopped him in mid-sentence. His imagination was
running along similar lines to her own but better that he did not
know that. 'I like him, Matty. Very much. We must wait and
see. As for Jessica, I suppose she feels deep down that she's lost
a son and you've found one. Perhaps there's an unconscious
resentment but I'm sure she wishes him no harm.'

Matty shrugged. 'She wants to know about his mother and
how she died. Even where she's buried! *And* what happened
between us but I can't go into details. It was a long time ago
and I can't be sure after all these years. I was half-cut most
of the time, to tell you the truth, but I can't tell her that. Can't
tell poor old Terence either.'

'I suppose he's full of questions about how you met and so
on.'

Matty frowned. 'Not as many questions as I would have
expected but it's a delicate subject for him. Probing into his
mother's past.' He sighed. 'I wish Jessica would make more
of an effort. She doesn't know how to treat him. That's the
trouble. If I refer to him as a guest she contradicts me. "I
thought he was one of the family," she says in a cool voice.
If I say that he's family she says, "We *think* he is!"'

'I see the problem,' Chloe agreed.

'I don't want him to feel unwelcome when he's here. I did
suggest he might stay overnight but Jessie put her foot down.
It's as though she doesn't want me to have a son.'

Chloe put an arm round his shoulders. 'Well, *I'm* pleased
you've got a son and I can see why you're proud of him. I'm
sure he's a very decent man.'

He said, 'Oh, he is! And if you two get together I—'

'Matty!' she laughed. 'You mustn't make plans for us. He may have a young lady tucked away somewhere.' She held her breath, hoping for Matty to reject the idea.

Matty frowned. 'He hasn't said so. Not that I've thought to ask him. Maybe I didn't want to know!' He rolled his eyes and they both laughed. 'Don't mind me, Chloe. I'm a romantic at heart! Call me an old fool—'

'I wouldn't dare!'

'We all have our dreams and mine is—' He stopped. 'No. You're right, my dear. We'll wait and see.'

Chloe refilled his tea cup, avoiding his gaze. Her own hopes had been drifting in that direction but she mustn't say so. Nothing might come of it and then there would be disappointment all round.

There was a knock on the drawing-room door and the doctor entered. Chloe and Matty sprang to their feet.

'I won't pretend I'm not worried,' the doctor told them in a low voice. 'Mrs Maitland has had some kind of collapse. Nothing major and I hope she will recover fully in time but it was enough, enough to – to disable her temporarily.'

Matty cried, 'Disabled? Oh, poor Jessie!' and Chloe took hold of his hand.

Matty asked in a hoarse voice, 'Was it a heart attack, Doctor?'

Dr Bell, arranging the contents of his bag, shook his head. 'I believe not. Maybe a slight stroke. It's too early to say. She can't speak at present but that might be the shock – and she won't be able to walk for a while without help.'

Matty sat down heavily, his face pale.

The doctor snapped his bag shut. 'She's going to need complete bed rest, I'm afraid. If you like, I'll find someone for you.'

Matty looked at Chloe. 'You'll do it, won't you, Chloe. She knows you. When you were her companion you worked miracles.'

Chloe regarded him with growing dismay. 'Matty, I'm sorry but I can't! Not that I don't want to but it's out of the question. I have a full-time job and I've only just started it. It wouldn't be fair to desert Mr Bourne now. He'd have to get a new housekeeper and . . .' She shrugged.

The doctor nodded. 'Miss Blake – I mean Mrs Tyler – is right, Mr Orme. Mrs Maitland might need care for months. You should employ a full-time nurse with proper qualifications.'

Matty was still looking beseechingly at Chloe. 'We could pay you. We could help you find another job afterwards.'

Briefly Chloe was tempted to say yes, but in her heart she knew that she was not qualified for full nursing care. 'I'm sorry, Matty.'

Dr Bell gave Matty a stern look. 'Mrs Tyler is not a trained nurse,' he repeated. 'With all the good will in the world the fact remains that she is not suitable. There is the question of accurate dosage of medicines and a trained eye to know if the patient is becoming worse. Whether she is asleep or unconscious. The workings of the digestive tract and a suitable diet . . . Only a qualified nurse can deal with all the aspects of such a patient's care. I do know someone who might be willing, however – a Mrs Williams – and with your permission I shall go now and call on her.'

Matty gave in with bad grace and listened to the doctor's instructions. Jessica was not to be given anything to drink until the nurse arrived for fear she might choke. A commode would be brought in so that she need not be carried to and from the lavatory. She was to stay in bed all day for at least a week, when she might be allowed up for an hour each day. The nurse was to decide on a suitable diet as Jessica would probably find it difficult to digest heavy food.

As they closed the door behind him, Matty gave a heartfelt sigh. 'I can't believe this has happened. I should have seen it coming. She's been doing too much and Olivia is such a lively little girl. Even her nanny gets tired, so Jessica was bound to feel it.'

Chloe took his hands in hers. 'These things happen. Jessica didn't die and she's going to make a full recovery. That's what the doctor said. Now I must get back.' She looked at him. 'Is there something else?'

'It's Terence. He was going to come down on the fifth of next month. I suppose I'll have to put him off.'

'Certainly not! Life has to go on,' Chloe insisted, unwilling to lose the chance to see Terence again. 'Mrs Letts can cope with the meals and – and I'll be here. At least I hope so.'

Matty wasn't listening. 'I can't imagine how it will be – not being able to talk properly. Poor old Jessie.'

Matty's downcast expression touched Chloe's heart. She reached up and kissed his cheek. 'You look forward to seeing your son again. Jessica won't be in a fit state to object. I doubt if she will even care. She may not even realize he's in the house. Anyway, she wouldn't want her illness to plunge the household into deep gloom – and we have to think about Olivia, too.'

'Olivia?' A fresh alarm showed in his face.

'Children are very quick to sense atmosphere,' Chloe explained. 'We don't want to depress or worry her. One day you must bring her to the farm and she can look at the animals. I'll ask Mr Bourne.'

She went to the kitchen to tell Mrs Letts what the doctor had said and asked that a spare bedroom be prepared for the nurse and that Mrs Letts should do whatever she thought best about the family meals.

'Mr Orme will be in charge for the moment,' Chloe suggested.

'Mr Orme?' Fanny and Mrs Letts exchanged worried glances but Chloe ignored them.

'In a week or two Bertha might be out of bed and able to help in some way. I'm at the farm if you need me. You can send Binns with a note if there's an emergency.'

She felt disloyal, leaving them, but she had her own responsibilities and she reminded herself that, had she still been in America, the family would have managed without her.

On the way home she thought about what Matty had said about Jessica and Terence. It must be jealousy on her part, she told herself, as he suspected, and let her mind wander back to the cause of Jessica's collapse. Matty had thought she was trying to say 'Mother'. Whatever could that mean? Had she momentarily lost her memory? Chloe knew that in some illnesses, especially those connected with the elderly, patients sometimes failed to recognize their own sons and daughters and believed themselves to be children again. Had that happened to Jessica? Was she actually worse than the doctor expected?

As Chloe arrived back at the farm she pushed the doubts out of her mind. They must all think positively. What mattered was that Jessica should recover as quickly as possible and that life should return to normal.

Sunday came all too quickly. Chloe had regretted her impulse a hundred times before the moment came when the visitors were due to arrive. Not that she was actually complaining, for the sun shone and the old house was warm and welcoming. Chloe, still in her house dress and apron, checked the two large chickens which were roasting in the oven with a dish of onion stuffing. The potatoes were browning on the shelf below and on the hob a cauliflower waited in a saucepan beside another containing neatly diced carrots. Nervously she glanced into the larder to check that the trifle had survived. At the last moment she would add the toasted almonds.

'Oh! The gravy!'

How could she have forgotten? Carefully she lifted the chickens from the roasting pan and drained most of the juices into a small saucepan. Taking an old spoon from the drawer, she filled it with sugar and held it in the flame until it caramelized, then stirred it into the juices to darken them. Satisfied, she added salt and pepper and set it aside. Her mother had always said you could judge a cook by her gravy.

'Is that good enough, Mama?' she whispered and sighed nostalgically. She had a sudden image of her mother at work in the kitchen, her thin frame bent over various pots and pans, her expression slightly harrassed as she stirred and tasted. Dorothy had been keen to learn from her mother but Chloe had listened impatiently. In her diary the young Chloe had written: *'Overcooked or undercooked – what does it matter? It will be forgotten by the next day . . .'*

Today Chloe looked at the clock and hovered uncertainly before deciding to change into her Sunday best in case the family arrived promptly. No doubt Cathy would be smartly dressed, she thought, and she didn't want to appear shabby beside her.

She took a final glance at the table in the dining room, which she had laid with the best cutlery. A jug of water and some glasses waited on the sideboard in case they were wanted. There were marigolds on the window sill.

'Everything's in order, Chloe!' she told herself. 'Stop fussing.'

She ran upstairs, praying that Jack would be around to greet Patrick and his family when they appeared. He had wandered off with Jude half an hour ago, leaving her a prey to anxieties. She pulled off her dress and put on a navy blue skirt and high-necked white blouse. She decided against lace as too showy for the occasion but she wore the pearls her grandmother had left to her.

She was pinching a little colour into her cheeks when she heard voices and rushed to the window.

'Where are you?' she asked her absent employer and went downstairs with a sinking heart.

Patrick, Cathy and Adam were already in the kitchen, making themselves at home. Cathy was wearing a dress of maroon velvet that was just a little too tight, and a long string of amber beads. The total effect was almost elegant and it made Chloe feel that the prim skirt and blouse made her look like a schoolmarm.

Patrick said, 'You're looking very smart, Mrs Tyler.'

Adam grinned at her. '*Very* nice! I might almost say "tasty"!'

Chloe muttered a 'Thank you', afraid to look at Cathy.

Cathy said, 'I hope you're going to wear an apron over that outfit. You don't want to splash it while you're serving the food.'

'I am,' Chloe told her. 'A large apron.'

Cathy stooped to pick up the kitten. 'Is she settling in?'

'Yes.'

'What do you call her?'

'Sweet Pie – after a cat we had in Montana.'

'*Sweet Pie*! Good heavens! How bizarre. Ours are called Kitty or Sooty. Very English.'

Patrick said, 'Very unoriginal, too!'

Adam said. 'Sometimes they're called "You" as in "Come out of the larder, you!"'

They all laughed and Chloe looked at him gratefully. Maybe they *would* enjoy themselves.

Patrick glanced round. 'So where is the master of the house?'

'I think Mr Bourne will be back soon. He's not far away.'

Adam said, 'I'll ferret him out.'

Cathy said, 'No I'll go.'

A little too eager, thought Chloe.

Patrick obviously thought the same. He said, 'No, you won't, Cathy. You'll stay here with me.'

Cathy bit her lip and Chloe's spirits dropped further. They hadn't been in the house five minutes but already the strains were showing.

Adam went out into the yard whistling cheerfully and Chloe swallowed and fixed a smile on her face.

'Would you like to come through into the parlour? I lit a fire because it—'

Patrick shook his head. 'On second thoughts, I'll have a look round. Jack won't mind,' and followed his son out into the sunshine.

Cathy opened her mouth to protest but apparently thought better of it. To Chloe she said, 'Typical farmer, our Patrick. Can't resist another man's farm.'

Still smiling, Chloe led the way into the parlour.

Cathy surveyed it with a jaundiced eye. 'It's always damp in this parlour. Always will be. It's not used enough. I keep telling Jack it's a waste.' She sniffed the air. 'And the fire always smokes.'

Chloe said, 'I open up the windows when it's fine.'

Cathy put a hand on the nearest upholstered chair and said, 'It seems dry enough.' Sitting down gingerly, she indicated another chair. 'Do sit down, Mrs Tyler. We have a few moments to talk before the men come back.' Her smile was an afterthought.

Chloe was tempted to refuse on the grounds that she had to see to the meal but the truth was, she was curious.

Cathy started without preamble. 'I wanted to say something about Jack – just so we understand each other. I'm probably the closest friend he has and I don't want you to think him unfriendly or odd. The way things are, he is and always will be a bachelor. Partly by nature – he's very solitary as I'm sure you've noticed. Quiet and rather shy. Not a bit like Patrick. Poor Jack works all the hours God sends because he can't afford help. When he's finished, he likes a quiet read and then bed.' She paused.

Waiting to see what I'll say, thought Chloe, and said nothing. Instead she perched on the edge of a chair and maintained an air of polite interest.

Cathy was forced to continue. 'This idea of a birthday lunch was very kind of you but I think he prefers to come to us. In future—'

'He was very keen, actually. He thought it would be fun.' That wasn't exactly true but near enough.

'Fun?' She blinked. 'That doesn't sound like Jack . . . I don't know how much you know about the past, but Jack and I were once planning to marry. I changed my mind and married Patrick.' She began to fiddle with her beads. 'Jack was wonderful. He told me he would never marry but would always be waiting for me. He thought that if anything happened to Patrick – if he dies—'

'Oh dear! He's not ill, is he?' Chloe regarded her innocently.

'Of course he's not ill. I meant if at any time in the future . . . then Jack would be free to look after me. If he'd married, that wouldn't be possible.' She gave Chloe a meaningful look. 'I only tell you in case you . . . so that you . . .'

'So that I don't get any ideas about him?' She smiled. 'Mrs Bourne, I have no hopes in that direction or any other at the moment. My husband has only been dead a few years and I am a fairly independent person. I doubt if I shall ever meet anyone else like Jeff. I think myself very lucky to have been happily married. So many marriages seem to be wretched affairs of convenience with no love in them.'

Cathy's expression changed but she said nothing.

Chloe went on. 'For a few short years we were young, hopelessly in love, wonderfully happy together. I doubt if I'll ever be that happy again.'

Cathy recovered quickly and her relief was plain. 'Exactly.

Jack would hardly measure up to your first husband but you might have been drawn to him out of misguided pity. Stranger things have happened. I wouldn't want you to face that sort of disappointment without knowing why.'

'Thank you for being so candid. I'll bear that in mind.' Chloe waited to see how Cathy would dismiss her.

'Well, I suppose you'd better get back to work.'

'Thank you. I will.'

She made her exit with conflicting emotions. A sneaking admiration, perhaps, for a woman who was so determined to protect what she considered her property. Some resentment that she, Chloe, had been so obviously 'warned off' Jack Bourne. Most of all, a certain pleasure that Cathy saw her as a threat.

'A backhanded compliment,' she muttered as she returned to the kitchen.

As she did so, the two brothers came into the kitchen, closely followed by Jude and Adam. Patrick was laughing loudly and Jack was smiling; Chloe began to feel more hopeful. Perhaps, with a little goodwill, the meal would pass cheerfully enough.

Jack gave everyone a glass of sherry which had been bought especially for the occasion and they all retired to the parlour so that Chloe could concentrate on the meal. When they were all seated at the table Cathy produced a small present tied with ribbon and presented it to Jack.

'Happy birthday, Jack,' she murmured.

'Why, thank you.'

As he began to unwrap it, Adam said, 'Not more handker-chiefs!'

Cathy glared at her son and Patrick laughed.

He said, 'He must have a cupboard full by now!'

Adam made things worse by saying, 'It's so unoriginal, Ma! Why not a tie?'

Cathy flushed under the barrage of criticism. 'Because Jack hardly ever wears a tie!'

Patrick gave his brother a sly glance. 'Only when you're visiting your bank manager, eh Jack?'

Chloe interpreted the remark immediately. Someone had seen Jack going into the bank in Rye. She said, 'A man can't have too many handkerchiefs,' and was rewarded with a brief smile from Cathy.

Desperate to deflect questions about his bank visit, Jack said, 'Mrs Tyler gave me a rather nice bookmark she had made herself.'

Chloe lowered her eyes and counted to ten. Cathy would not be pleased. There was a short silence and then Adam said, 'A bookmark for a bookworm!' and laughed. 'When I was a child, Uncle Jack was the only person who read to me.'

Cathy looked at him, hurt. '*I* read to you!'

'Did you, Ma?' He looked genuinely surprised.

Patrick said, 'Well, for the record, I never did. I was always too busy to read stories. I had a farm to run *and* a family to feed and clothe.'

Chloe said quickly, 'Well, if Mr Bourne will carve, we can make a start before the vegetables go cold.'

Jack rose dutifully and the awkward moment was averted. The meal progressed and Chloe felt that they were all making an effort. She and Jack had discussed the seating arrangement to avoid any ruffled feathers. Jack sat at the head of the table with Patrick on one side and Cathy at the other. Adam sat next to his mother and Chloe sat next to Patrick.

Chloe had brought in the trifle and was serving it when Patrick asked, 'Any more gifts, Chloe, from the phantom admirer?'

Adam grinned. 'Now don't look at me! I don't have money to waste on women!'

'Not even Marion?' Cathy challenged.

'Not expensive flowers and fancy lace gloves!'

Patrick said, 'Maybe you don't fancy her enough!'

Adam took a mouthful of trifle and said, 'Mmm! This is good. You'll have to take care, Ma, or Mrs Tyler will be voted top trifle maker!'

Patrick laughed unkindly, enjoying his wife's discomfiture.

Chloe regarded Patrick and Adam with growing exasperation. Couldn't they see that their careless barbs were not amusing and were upsetting Cathy and making matters worse? How could they be so insensitive? She said, 'I don't take any credit for the trifle. It's my mother's recipe. Not mine.' She smiled at Cathy. 'I'd be grateful to learn from an expert.'

For a moment Cathy looked confused then she said, 'I never use new-laid eggs for the custard. I prefer them a couple of weeks old.'

'I didn't realize the eggs made such a difference.'

'Oh yes!' Forgetting her annoyance, Cathy leaned forward eagerly. 'The younger the egg—'

Patrick said, 'Here we go!' and rolled his eyes.

Cathy fell silent, her expression once more sullen and unresponsive.

Patrick said, 'We don't want a cookery lesson, ladies! We were talking about the sender of the mystery gifts.' He turned to Chloe. 'So you still have no idea who is sending the gifts?'

'I'm afraid not.'

'You must have an inkling, surely.'

Cathy glanced at Jack who held up both hands in a submissive gesture. 'Don't look at me!' he said.

Patrick turned to his wife. 'You see? You needn't have worried. Jack hasn't deserted you.'

The silence was immediate. Chloe caught Jack's gaze and found herself blushing for no good reason. She thought desperately for a way to soften the impact of his accusation but her thoughts seemed to have frozen.

Cathy said slowly, 'You're a mean man, Patrick, in more ways than one.'

Adam looked nervous. 'He didn't mean anything, Ma.'

'Oh yes. He meant something, Adam.' Cathy eyed her husband venomously.

Jack said, 'Let's forget it.'

Cathy said, 'Let's not.'

Chloe's throat was dry. 'It's Jack's birthday, remember? We mustn't—'

Cathy snapped, 'You stay out of it, Mrs Tyler. You're not family – remember? You're staff.' Two spots of colour glowed in her cheeks as she stared at her husband. 'What were you trying to say, Patrick? Out with it!'

Thus challenged, he hesitated. Chloe closed her eyes. Adam

choked and spluttered as a mouthful of trifle went down the wrong way.

Patrick finally faced his wife. 'Right, I'll tell you what I meant. I'll spell it out for you. Just because someone's fallen for Mrs Tyler, you don't have to suspect Jack. And if it was Jack, so what? He's free to send flowers if he wants to. Anybody'd think you owned the man! But it wasn't Jack.'

'You sound very sure!'

'He's told you it isn't him. Aren't you listening?'

Chloe stammered, 'It doesn't matter at all. It's just a silly prank . . .'

Cathy glared. 'I've told you to keep out of this.'

Adam said, 'But we're talking about the flowers and the gloves. That's not family.'

'Oh, that's right, Adam! Take her side against mine!'

Patrick said, 'And who says it's silly? If someone is thoughtful enough to send a pretty woman a gift—'

Cathy swung round, her eyes wide. 'My God, Patrick! It's you! It's *you*! You're sending them!'

They all stared at Patrick.

'Ma! That's crazy and you know it!'

As Patrick also began to protest Chloe jumped to her feet and ran out of the room. She ran up the stairs into her room and slammed the door as hard as she could.

'And don't come after me, Jack Bourne!' she muttered. If he followed her up to the bedroom that *would* put the cat among the pigeons. Damn them all! She had worked so hard to make the day pleasant but the Bourne family were impossible. Well, let them get on with it without her. She would go downstairs and start the washing up. From now on she would not need to mingle. The meal was over. Patrick, Cathy and Adam could go home – and the sooner the better.

She stood by the window, taking deep breaths. Realizing that she was trembling, Chloe tried to will herself into a calmer state of mind and body. Was she afraid? Not exactly, but she hated friction. Was she angry, perhaps? Yes, she was. But she was vaguely aware of something that went deeper – a regret, perhaps. But what did she have to regret? If Jack Bourne had a quarrelsome family that was not her problem. He must deal with it. So was it guilt that troubled her? She didn't think she had said anything out of place, so she need not feel guilty.

She crossed to the bed and threw herself on to it face down. 'Go home, Patrick Bourne, and take your family with you!' she muttered into the pillow. All this fuss because of some stupid presents from someone who wished to be anonymous. *Could it be Patrick? Never!* He was the last man she'd suspect. But if it *were* him she could understand Cathy's reaction. But no. Patrick Bourne was definitely not a romantic man. She still suspected Adam.

'Whoever you are,' she whispered, 'don't send any more gifts. You're making my life difficult.'

Below her, the raised voices continued, so the visitors hadn't yet left. She sat up and tidied her clothes then crept downstairs into the kitchen, where she put on the big apron and set to work. Emptying the big kettle of hot water into the deep sink, she added cold from the tap. She refilled the kettle and set it back on the range. She grated some hard soap into the water and whisked it with her hand. Then she piled in plates, knives and forks and began to wash them.

A few minutes later Adam came into the kitchen. 'I'm so sorry,' he said.

She nodded without turning her head and he went out across the yard. The row in the dining room continued for another minute or so and then Cathy swept into the kitchen.

Reluctantly Chloe turned. Cathy was very pale and her red-rimmed eyes told Chloe that she had been crying. Despite her own feelings, Chloe felt a sudden surge of compassion for the woman whose son and husband had been so disloyal. She was searching for sympathetic phrases that might heal the wounds but before she could speak, Cathy took the initiative.

'I hope you're satisfied,' she told Chloe in a furious voice. 'This is what comes when you don't know your place and you interfere. If you ask me, you're the wrong person for this job and I've told Jack so. I hope he sacks you!'

Chloe, taken aback, opened her mouth to reply but at that moment Patrick appeared. He pushed past his wife and came to the sink to stand beside Chloe. With his back to Cathy he gave Chloe a large wink and put his finger to his lips. Astonished,

99

Chloe stared at him until he turned on his heel. Grabbing Cathy by the arm, he dragged her with him and together they followed Adam outside.

With relief, Chloe watched them go. Cathy's words rang in her head and her heart was thumping. Chloe waited for Jack to appear and when he didn't she picked up a tray and went in search of him. He was sitting at the dining table, his head in his hands. Silently she began to gather up the dishes and spoons. Her throat was dry and tears pressed against her eyelids. She was going to get the sack. She was going to have to tell Dorothy and the Maitlands that Jack Bourne had changed his mind. She took out the tray and came back for the remains of the celebration lunch. Water glasses, the jug, what was left of the trifle.

Still, Jack ignored her and at last she could wait no longer. 'So I'm sacked, am I?' she demanded.

He straightened up and stared at her in confusion. 'What's that?'

'Cathy says you're going to sack me. If so I'll pack and leave right now.' Thank heavens for Dorothy and Albert, she reflected. They would be pleased to have her stay until she found something else.

'Mrs Tyler, please! Sack you?' He looked bewildered. 'What are you talking about?'

'Cathy said she's advised you to sack me for – for interfering.' Her voice was shaking. 'I didn't mean to cause any trouble. I didn't expect . . . I can't help it . . .' Tears suddenly rolled down her face.

'Don't!' he cried, jumping to his feet. He searched his pockets for a handkerchief. Not finding one he picked up one of the serviettes and pressed it into her hand.

'Mrs Tyler! No one is going to sack you. You mustn't mind Cathy. She was upset. She's always been very emotional and Patrick is so cruel . . .' Clumsily he patted her shoulder. 'It was a splendid meal and I'm sorry that the company left a lot to be desired. But it's just the two of us now. Suppose we sit in the kitchen and drink a mug of tea – and forget all that nonsense.'

Chloe nodded, dabbing at her tears, furious with herself

for this show of weakness. Jack put his arm round her and she thought she should draw back but somehow she didn't. Encouraged, he tightened his hold. His other hand went round her and she thought he dropped a light kiss on to her hair. But maybe she had imagined it. It was such a long time since a man had held her close that Chloe abandoned all caution and leaned against him. Jeff had been such a passionate man. Not romantic, in the English sense, but inclined to spontaneous bursts of affection and crazy outpourings of love. He had proposed in the middle of the street with a bunch of paper roses behind his back. When she accepted, all the onlookers had applauded. Dear Jeff . . .

Jack relaxed his hold and stepped back. 'Forgive me. I had no right.'

'It doesn't matter. Truly.' She blamed herself for allowing it to happen.

Changing the subject, he said, 'You were not to blame for Cathy and Patrick. You're a splendid housekeeper and far from sacking you, I shall refuse to let you leave even if you want to!' He put a finger under her chin and tilted her face gently. 'You don't want to go, do you? I – I need you, Mrs Tyler. You surely won't desert me in my hour of need!'

Afraid to answer this, she said, 'I shall throw the gloves in the dustbin!'

He smiled at the small show of spirit. 'That would be a shame.'

She remembered Patrick's wink. 'I do hope it wasn't Patrick. I promise you I haven't given him the slightest encouragement.'

'I'm sure you haven't . . . I don't know about you, but I really could do with a cup of tea and a ginger biscuit. How would that do?'

Smiling, Chloe nodded and Jack led the way back into the kitchen.

Sunday the 28ᵗʰ of April. A very difficult birthday for poor Mr Bourne – Not to mention me. Cathy and Patrick quarrelled and I was dragged into it. Cathy thinks Patrick sent me the gifts. He gave me a large wink when he left which

*must mean something. I'm not sure now how it all hap-
pened but I was upset and Jack was so kind. Cathy tried
to persuade Jack to sack me but he didn't. He said he
needs me. We were both upset and foolishly I let him hold
me but it wasn't a good idea – we both realized that –
and it mustn't happen again. The poor man's been very
distracted lately and I took a telephone call from the bank
which sounded ominous but I can't ask about it. I think
it's money.*

*Only seven days and I shall see Terence again. It's some-
thing to look forward to. Binns came over yesterday with a
note from Matty to say Jessica is much the same but the
nurse has arrived to look after her. Apparently all Jessica
could say after her collapse was 'Mother'. I do hope her
mind's not wandering. She was trying to make a telephone
call to someone. All very odd and sad.*

*I asked Binns about Bertha and little Robert and they are
both making slow progress. Thank goodness for Terence
Harkness. He is the only ray of light in this rather gloomy
picture.*

*Sweet Pie is growing fast. She is not so frightened of Jude
as she was and has taken to sleeping in his basket, which
puzzles him.*

Six

It was Wednesday before Chloe managed to pay another visit to the Maitlands and when she did she was delighted to find Bertha there. Binns had fetched her in the trap and she was warmly ensconced on the sofa in the drawing room. There was more colour in her face and she seemed much livelier, for which Chloe was grateful.

'George's mother is looking after baby Robert,' she told Chloe. 'She felt that I needed a change of scenery. At least that's what she said.' She laughed. 'I think she actually wanted to have Robert to herself for a few hours but it suits me well enough.'

They talked for a while about the baby's progress and about George's latest commission, which was a set of wrought-iron gates for a big house in Iden. His fame was growing and Chloe was impressed. 'At least it must have set your mother's mind at ease about your future,' she told Bertha. 'And are you both still happy?'

Bertha positively beamed. 'Very happy. I can recommend married life! Oh!' She clapped a hand to her mouth. 'I'm sorry, Chloe.That was so tactless. Because we never met Jeff it's too easy to forget that you were ever married.'

'Don't apologize. I understand. Tell me now about your mother. Is she all right in her mind?'

Bertha drew her brows together. 'The doctor thinks so. She's almost recovered her speech although she is rather slow but she now seems to be obsessed with Terence Harkness. It's upsetting Matty because he would love to invite him to stay but Mama won't hear of it. She's got it into her head that he tells lies – Terence, I mean – and she doesn't trust him. It's caused a distinct coolness between her and Uncle Matty. I

103

can't help wondering if her mind is not quite as sharp as before.'

'Poor Jessica.'

'I'm not saying anything for sure and the doctor doesn't agree but sometimes what she says doesn't make sense.'

Five minutes later, when Chloe went up to see Jessica, she decided to try and find out more. Jessica's hostility towards Terence troubled Chloe and she hoped she could somehow put an end to it.

Jessica was propped up in bed and the new nurse was reading *The Times* to her. Nurse Williams was a neat little woman with iron-grey hair cut in an unbecoming bob. With her white apron she looked every inch the professional that she was and Chloe felt sure that the patient was in good hands. The nurse rose to her feet when Chloe entered.

'I'll take a break,' she told them, 'and leave you two together.'

Chloe sat down beside the bed and smiled but there was no answering smile. Instead Jessica clutched her hand and leaned forward anxiously. 'Thank goodness you're here, child. You at least have your wits about you. I can't make anyone understand that there is something not quite right about Matty's so-called son.'

This outburst seemed to exhaust her and she fell back against the pillows, breathing rapidly.

Chloe bit back a protest and prepared to hear the worst before she tried to deal with it. 'Take it slowly, Mrs Maitland,' she warned. 'There's plenty of time and it won't do you any good to tire yourself.'

'Terence said his mother was dead – and his other father, Harkness.'

Chloe nodded. She remembered it quite well.

Jessica shook her head. 'But one day he spoke of her – in the present tense! It just slipped out. I noticed it immediately and I think he realized what he had said but he went straight on. He didn't correct himself.' Jessica's eyes closed briefly and Chloe found herself wondering if Jessica's mind *was* wandering a little, as Bertha had suggested.

Jessica opened her eyes and continued but she was obviously

tiring. Her voice was weaker and Chloe had to lean closer to hear her.

'None of the others heard it, Chloe, but I know I was not mistaken. Then, on the day I collapsed, I heard from *his mother*!'

'Wait!' cried Chloe, startled. 'That's not possible.'

'There you go!' cried Jessica, waving a hand in frustration. 'You're just like the rest of them. I tell you it was his mother.' She put a hand to her heart and Chloe stroked the frail hand in an effort to calm her. 'The telephone rang and the operator put this woman through and she asked to speak to her son! I said, "There must be some mistake. You have the wrong number." But she said, "This is the number Terence gave me. He said he'd be living there with his real father."' Jessica gasped for air but waved away the offer of a glass of water. 'Imagine how I felt, Chloe. It was such a terrible shock – and I knew no one would believe me.' She leaned forward once more, her expression intense. 'I tried to question her further but she broke the connection. I turned to call Matty and that's when I felt a strange feeling at the back of my head . . . and then I was dizzy and dropped the receiver and fainted.'

Exhausted by her account, she fell back against the pillows and Chloe watched her anxiously. The story had shaken her more than she would admit. It was obvious that Jessica was very confused. Whatever the truth of the matter, the old lady was convinced that Terence Harkness's mother was still alive, which, she told herself, was impossible.

Suddenly Chloe brightened. 'We'll ask him,' she told Jessica. 'We'll ask Terence outright if his mother is still alive. He tells me he's been invited down this next Sunday and Matty has asked me to join you. He'll soon explain the muddle and then you can forget it.'

'She said she was his mother and she asked for her son. I heard her!' Jessica regarded her bleakly.

Chloe gave her a reassuring smile. Jessica could be very stubborn at times and this notion about Terence was not going to go away. 'Put it out of your mind for now,' she advised. 'The doctor says you are coming along well but all the anxiety could set you back. I promise there is nothing to worry about.'

Jessica sighed heavily. 'Fine for you to say,' she muttered with a touch of her old asperity. 'You won't have to have him under your roof. I shan't have a moment's peace until he's gone back to London for good. And don't look at me that way! I know what you're all thinking. Humour the poor old thing! Well, I may be weak physically but my mind is as clear as a bell. You'll see. You've got a nasty shock coming to you and don't say I didn't warn you.'

When at last Chloe went downstairs she made up her mind to set Jessica's mind at ease. And her own, if she was honest, for Jessica had spoken with total conviction. She truly believed something underhand was going on. Chloe knew that was nonsense. Surely it wouldn't be that difficult to disprove Jessica's theory.

She took Matty aside just before she was leaving. 'I've spoken to Jessica and she *is* confused about Terence. I suggest we do a little research. Do you know where the Harkness family lived? If so I could telephone to the local rectory and make some enquiries. The deaths and burials will be in the church records.'

'Somewhere in Leicestershire,' he told her, furrowing his brow. 'Little Modley or was it Melody . . . Something like that. A small village, he said. They were both farmworkers. She worked in the dairy and he worked the land. Good with horses, apparently, the way some men are – Got it! Lower Medley. I don't know if that's one or two "d"s.' He looked relieved. 'I hope Jessica doesn't make a scene while he's here. She can be very forthright as you know.'

'She won't see him, will she? She's confined to her room.'

'I don't want to hurt the lad's feelings.' His expression softened. 'The truth is I'd like to see more of my son. Better late than never and all that. Catch up on all that wasted time. If we can set poor old Jessie straight about him . . .'

'I'll see what I can do,' Chloe promised. 'And not a word to anyone until we have some facts.'

On her way home Chloe called in at her sister's and told her of the problem. Dorothy assured her that Albert would be able to get in contact with the rector of Lower Meddley and would let her know the outcome of one or two discreet enquiries.

The following afternoon Chloe received a note.

Dear Chloe, The Reverend Atwell was very willing to help but I don't think the outcome will please you. It seems there is no one by the name of Harkness buried in the churchyard in Lower Meddley and no mention in the church records. The only living people are a young couple in their twenties – John and Elizabeth Harkness – who have only recently moved to the village – about six weeks ago. The Reverend Atwell has never heard of a Terence Harkness or his mother and father and Lower Meddley has been his parish for nine years. Sorry. Dorothy.

The shock was enormous. It left Chloe feeling slightly sick. She read the note again, convinced there must be a mistake. Perhaps the Maitlands had misheard Terence's surname. Perhaps it was Harker or Harper. Harkwell, even. Had they ever seen his name written down?

'You're clutching at straws,' she told herself. But there must be an explanation.

Crushed and unhappy, she tried not to admit that the bad news disturbed her deeply. She told herself it was for Matty's sake that she was concerned but in fact she hated the thought that there was something less than perfect about Terence Harkness. She desperately wanted him to be genuine; to be the beloved son of Matty Orme. She recalled Matty's hopes for her and Terence – hopes that found an echo in her own heart. Since her husband's death no other man had stirred her emotions as Terence had. He was an excitement in her life; a promise of good things to come and happiness that might one day be hers.

'Terence! You can't be . . .' She swallowed hard. 'You must be *you*! Please don't do this.'

Chloe needed him to be a man she could trust and love. There! She had thought the unthinkable.

Allowing such thoughts to take shape in her mind was a big

step for her. Losing Jeff had left her desolate. She had never expected to find another man to love but now she faced up to the realization that Terence Harkness might be that man.

For the next few hours Chloe went about her work in a haze of despair. If she could only see him and talk to him. She felt certain she would learn that all was well. Jack came in with Jude just after three and looked at her in surprise.

'You all right?'

'Of course I am.' She stared at him defiantly. 'Don't I look all right?'

'No, you don't. You look upset . . . or unhappy. Are you?'

'No.'

He looked troubled. 'Something's happened. I can tell. You can talk to me, you know. I'm a good listener.'

'It's personal. Please don't bother yourself about me.' She turned quickly toward the dog. 'Here Jude! I kept this bone for you.'

They both watched the dog hurry out with the bone and settle herself in the middle of the yard. Her tail thumped once or twice and Chloe smiled.

Jack said, 'At least somebody's happy,' and went through to the little room where he kept the big desk with all his papers and bills.

Chloe heard the door close and felt immediately guilty. She had been brusque to the point of rudeness. She would tell him part of the problem. Impulsively she went after him and tapped at the door. Without waiting for an answer she went in. He was standing at the window staring out across the fields.

'I am troubled,' she told him. 'Mrs Maitland is getting very confused. We're all worried about her.'

'You said it was personal.'

She hesitated. 'The rest is complicated. But now it's your turn. I, too, am a good listener. Do you want to share your problems?'

He gave her a small, tired smile. 'I won't say they're personal but they are complicated. Financial worries. Every year the farm shows a smaller profit. The bank manager doesn't like that! He's leaning on me. Not only will he not lend me any more money, he wants me to repay what I have already

108

borrowed. He suggests I borrow from Patrick!' He sighed. 'That's it, in a nutshell. Hardly earth-shattering.'

Chloe's dismay had grown with each succeeding revelation, her own problems being overtaken by Jack's. 'That's terrible!' she said. 'I wish I could help. I could take a small cut in wages.'

'Certainly not. I pay you little enough as it is. If only I could rent, or buy, some more land . . .' He sighed. 'Old Edgeley has died – the farm that adjoins mine on the other side. His farm's going under the hammer but the land will be snapped up very quickly. I shall lose my chance.'

'You need to discover a famous oil painting tucked away in the attic! It does happen from time to time.'

His wry smile touched her heart.

'Not to me, I'm afraid.' He frowned suddenly. 'Are you expecting anyone? I hear wheels!'

Chloe shook her head and hurried to the front door, where to her surprise she saw Matty, a woman and a small boy in the Maitlands' governess cart.

With permission from Jack Bourne, she went outside to greet them. When the boy clambered down she stared at him in open-mouthed astonishment.

'Oliver's son!' The words were torn from her. There could be no doubt about it. The same dark hair, dark brown eyes and the same beautifully shaped mouth. This child had inherited all his father's looks while Olivia had some of her mother's. With an effort Chloe tore her gaze away and looked at the woman.

'Adele? Is it you?'

If anything, Oliver Maitland's erstwhile lover was even more vibrant than Chloe remembered. Her red hair had been tamed and was now swept on top of her head. She wore long silver earrings, and discreet make-up enhanced her eyes and lips. Her cheeks were rouged. Expensive clothes flattered her supple figure, silks in dull orange with black lace. She looked every inch a successful dancer and it didn't take much imagination to see her on stage at the Folies Bergère in Paris.

'Yes, Miss Blake. It is.' Adele held out a perfectly gloved hand.

Matty said, 'It's Mrs Tyler now,' but it was obvious that Adele wasn't listening.

Chloe remembered their last meeting, five years earlier. Then Adele had come from London in search of Oliver only to discover that he had had a child by one of the servants. The child was Olivia.

Chloe looked at the boy who was staring at her with bold eyes. 'And this is Oliver's son,' she said. It wasn't a question. The relationship was unmistakable.

Adele shrugged. 'I did not want a child. This you knew. This Oliver knew. I have my career, but yes. Lucien is Oliver's son. My mother has been caring for him but now she is ill. A *maladie grave*. *I* cannot keep him with me. A dancer's life is precarious. I must be free to go where the engagements take me and it is no life for a small boy. He has to go to school.'

Matty had listened to this and now interrupted Adele. 'She thought Lucien should grow up with his father. She didn't know Oliver was dead but now she thinks he should stay with the Maitland family.'

Chloe gasped. And yet, if she were Adele, the idea would probably make sense, but to hand over your only child to a family in another country! She lowered her voice. 'And Jessica?'

He shrugged. 'The poor old thing was quite hysterical at the idea. Coming so soon on top of Terence . . . And the doctor said she was to stay calm. Not much chance of that, I'm afraid.' He regarded the boy unhappily. 'He is so like his father, isn't he? She surely cannot fail to see the likeness. Two peas in a pod, I'd say. I can recall Oliver at that age. It could be Oliver – but Jessica refuses even to see him. I didn't know what to do so I brought them over to you.'

The boy said suddenly, '*Je m'appelle Lucien Dupres.*'

Adele said, 'Speak English, Lucien. You are not in France now.'

'My name is Lucien Dupres.'

Chloe smiled at him. 'And my name is Mrs Tyler. How do you do, Lucien.'

They shook hands solemnly.

Adele said, 'You are married?'

Why does she sound so surprised? Chloe wondered. Hardly flattering. She said, 'Sadly I'm a widow.'

'Then you too are alone.'

Unsure how to answer, Chloe let the comment pass. She smiled. 'You must be very proud of your son – and your mother must miss him very much.'

Adele tutted impatiently. 'Of course I am proud but I must be what you English call "sensible". The Maitlands will give him a good home. It is the best I can do for him.'

Matty and Chloe exchanged glances. Adele was assuming a great deal.

They all turned as Jack Bourne appeared from the house.

Chloe turned to him and made introductions and then explained hurriedly. 'When Oliver Maitland was killed some years ago we thought he had only one child, Olivia. Now we learn that Adele also had a child by him. This is Lucien and his mother.'

Lucien was regarding Jack with something akin to awe. 'Are you a farmer, monsieur? A real farmer?'

'I am. Would you like to come with me and see some lambs?'

Lucien gave a shriek of excitement and turned to his mother. 'Maman? May I go?'

'Yes. You may go with Mr Bourne.'

Jack held out his hand and Lucien took it trustingly. Chloe, Matty and Adele watched them set off towards the fields.

Chloe was thinking quickly. 'So what will you do now, Adele? Where will you stay?'

Matty said, 'I expect I'll have to take her into Rye. They could put up at the George for a few nights. Adele has come to England for a week. She's between engagements.' He spoke calmly but his expression said, 'Help me Chloe! What are we to do?'

Chloe remembered the spare bedrooms and an idea came to her. 'Excuse me a moment,' she murmured and left Matty and Adele staring after her.

She found Jack and the boy in a corner of the barn. A small area had been closed in with wattles and a sick lamb lay on a bed of straw. The animal's head was within reach and

Lucien, his face alive with excitement, was stroking it. Jack, crouched beside the child, was talking to him. Chloe paused a moment, watching the scene. It brought an unexpected lump to her throat. This is how her own son would have been with Jeff. Tears sprang into her eyes at the realization that that would never now happen. She would never give Jeff a child. Swallowing hard, she brushed away the tears and went forward.

'Mr Bourne, I have a suggestion to make.'

He stood up and turned enquiringly.

In a low voice she said, 'We have spare rooms and Adele and Lucien are staying for a week. Rather than let them put up in a hotel in Rye, could we offer them accommodation? We could—'

'Put them up here?'

Chloe knew at once, from the tone of his voice, that he didn't care for the idea. 'Why not? They'll be comfortable enough. I'll smarten up one of the bedrooms. We could charge them for meals and accommodation. It would be cheaper for them than the George and the money would pay a few of the farm bills. If Adele is as determined as she sounds, she'll want to visit Fairfields to press her case about Lucien and she won't have so far to travel.'

'More work for you, though, Mrs Tyler.' He looked doubtful. 'Haven't you got enough to do already?'

'I don't mind. It makes sense to me – and Lucien would love being on the farm. Adele might even leave him with me sometimes . . .' Her voice shook suddenly with longing and she was aware that Jack was eyeing her closely.

He said softly, 'You ought to have a family of your own.'

'Please . . . Don't talk that way.' She looked away, already beginning to regret her generosity. 'Maybe it wasn't such a—'

'It's a good idea. Thank you, Mrs Tyler.' He gave her an unfathomable look. 'I'll leave you to work out the details. Feed them well but cover all the costs. I can't afford to lose money on the exercise.'

'I'll see that you don't.'

Lucien was tugging at Jack's trouser leg. 'Look, *monsieur*! He is on to his legs!'

Surely enough, the lamb was struggling to his feet and Jack nodded with satisfaction. 'I thought we might lose this one,' he told her. 'Sickly right from the start. One of twins. Well, Lucien, what do you think, eh? Would you like to be a farmer when you grow up?'

'*Oui, monsieur!* But also I must be a great singer for my *grandmère* and a great scholar for Maman.'

Chloe ruffled his gleaming dark hair. Her own son would have had Jeff's fair curls . . . 'You can be all manner of things when you grow up,' she told him. 'But for now you just have to be a happy little boy. Would you like to stay here for a few days with your – Oh!'

With a flutter of soft grey wings the owl had returned to its nesting place among the rafters and three pairs of eyes watched it settle itself on the beam.

'It's an owl,' Jack told the boy. 'It lives here in the barn but it's very shy.' Remembering Chloe's interrupted question, Jack asked him if he would like to stay at the farm for a few days.

Lucien's eyes shone. 'Stay here with the lambs? Oh yes, *monsieur!*'

Jack said, 'So now we only have to persuade your mother.' He took hold of Lucien's hand. 'Shall we throw some corn to the hens? Would you like that?'

'Oui, *monsieur*. Do you have any horses?'

'One horse – and a pig.'

Chloe left them to it and walked slowly back to Matty and Adele, rapidly working out a price per day that would be fair to both parties. When she put the idea to Adele it was accepted immediately.

Matty looked years younger. He said, 'Bless you, Chloe. You're so practical. It's the perfect answer.'

Chloe, smiling, gave herself a mental pat on the back and led the way indoors. She showed Adele the rooms and let her choose, then took them into the parlour and left them with a pot of tea and some biscuits. Upstairs she ran a duster over the surfaces – she would polish the furniture later. She fetched clean linen from the airing cupboard to make up the two beds. Later she would find a few flowers for the bowl on the window sill.

It occurred to her that she was enjoying herself and she wondered whether she had hit upon a way to make money for the farm. Would anyone else want to stay on a farm in Winchelsea? There were several public houses but not all offered accommodation – and those that did might sometimes be full to capacity. If she told the local shopkeepers . . . She tugged the pillows into fresh pillowslips and plumped them up. Maybe some local people who had little space of their own might use the farm rooms to accommodate family and friends for weddings, funerals and christenings. She could talk to the rector. If she charged less than the public houses Monkswell Farm might suit those with leaner purses. With growing enthusiasm she decided they might also tempt these visitors with farm produce – eggs and home-made jams and pickles. It all depended on Jack Bourne. If he agreed she was sure she could add to the farm's income. Could he afford *not* to agree?

The following day, Saturday, Cathy sat in the kitchen and tried to make a decision. The kitchen door stood open and the two kittens that remained from the latest litter were scuffling together just outside the door to the yard. They reminded her of Sweet Pie and the wretched Mrs Tyler. Ever since the birthday lunch she had been agonizing over her life and its disappointments. In particular she grieved for the chance she had lost when she changed her mind and chose Patrick as a husband instead of Jack. She had only herself to blame but her parents had certainly influenced her choice.

'Patrick will be comfortably off and Jack will always struggle.' She could hear her father saying it. Time had proved him right, of course, but she should never have allowed that particular consideration to sway her. She should have considered his unreliability and his flirtatious character. Patrick never could resist a handsome woman.

'Damn and blast you, Patrick Bourne!' she muttered.

In retrospect she had made the wrong choice and bitterly regretted her mistake. The question was – was it too late to put matters right? And if, somehow, she *could* put matters right, would she be happier? Suppose she had married Jack –

114

would she, by now, have regretted that choice? Was it always greener on the other side of the fence?

Distracted suddenly, she focussed on a new sound coming from the far end of the yard. Cathy frowned. Was it the hive? She knew the sound of her bees and May and June were the months when a new queen appeared and set off for fresh accommodation, taking part of the hive's inhabitants with her. Forgetting her quarrel with Patrick, Cathy moved to the door and listened carefully. The familiar hum became louder and higher.

'A swarm of bees in May, is worth a load of hay!' she muttered. She had a spare hive, and a swarm at this time of the year meant the new colony would have all the summer to create honey. Pushing her worries to the back of her mind, she went outside and cautiously approached the three hives, two of which were inhabited. From one of these the bees moved in and out in a leisurely manner. From the other a stream of bees were exiting but none were entering. As Cathy watched they flew in a direct line towards a nearby oak tree. The new queen had settled on the lowest branch and thousands of bees clustered round her in an almost solid mass. They had swarmed, which meant that Cathy had to coax them into a large basket and persuade them into the third hive which was empty. If she didn't do this promptly, the swarm would fly away in search of a permanent home.

As she went back for the basket she caught sight of Patrick on his way across the field towards his brother's farmhouse. At once her pleasure at the swarm dissolved and all her previous doubts and fears resurfaced. Patrick still denied sending Mrs Tyler the gifts but she didn't believe him for a moment. She hated him for the deception and the betrayal. It was humiliating to know that both Jack and the housekeeper would be pitying her. The belief in his guilt convinced her that he had grown tired of her – if she needed conviction. It was so convenient for him – he could always insist that he had gone there to talk to Jack on farm business while all the time he was hoping to see the new housekeeper. If *she* went over there to see Jack it was very obvious. Sighing, she forced herself to concentrate on the job in hand. She retrieved the basket, found a walking stick and returned to the oak tree.

'Right, you little beauties!' she murmured. 'You're going to get into this basket!'

Moving slowly so as not to alarm them, she reached up with the walking stick and, holding the basket beneath the swarm, she struck the slender branch a sharp blow. The swarm quivered, then fell – straight into the basket. She covered them quickly and returned to the empty hive. Minutes later the queen had entered and her loyal followers were zooming in after her.

Cathy watched them for a few moments then withdrew. Back in the kitchen, she sank down on to a chair. Somehow, in that short time, she had made her decision.

'I'm leaving you, Patrick,' she whispered. 'I'm going to be with Jack. He's waited for me all these years and I'm not going to disappoint him any longer.'

She would leave a note for Patrick – or maybe she would tell him to his face. The thought of Adam troubled her but he was a grown man now and could survive the scandal. The Bourne family would be the talk of the village but she no longer cared. Patrick had lost her respect for ever and she wanted him to know it. He would probably divorce her but if he refused she would live in sin with Jack. Mrs Tyler would present no problem – she could move into Bourne Farm and be Patrick's housekeeper.

Marry her if you want to, she thought angrily. See if I care. I'll be with Jack and we'll be happy together. You won't even be lonely, Patrick. You'll have Mrs Tyler and good luck to the pair of you! Even Adam will marry eventually and leave you . . .

Jumping to her feet, she was overcome by a fierce desire to take the first step towards happiness. She stared round the kitchen as though seeing it for the first time. It was so much better than Jack's but she would encourage him to make improvements. Of course she would miss certain things – the good carpets and the good bedlinen. She would take the grandfather clock because that had been her grandmother's and she would insist on the dining-room table that had also been in her family for years. She would make Jack a wonderfully cosy home. Sad that she was too old to have a child or she could have given him a son. A half-brother for Adam. He would be surprised. She smiled.

'You're going to be sorry, Patrick!' she said aloud. 'You've gone too far and you're going to regret the way you've treated me.'

'I'll go and talk to Jack,' she said with growing desperation. But suppose Jack said, 'Stay with me,' and she never came back here. Suppose he couldn't bear the thought of her spending another night in Patrick's bed. She would need to make arrangements. Collect her things. And anyway, Patrick was over there now, so she and Jack couldn't talk privately. Hesitating, she sat down again and her eye caught the pencil marks they had made on the wall when Adam was growing up. Hard to imagine him as a little boy, pressing himself against the wall while Patrick measured him. A faint smile lit Cathy's face as she thought of him, straining his neck in an effort to be a quarter of an inch taller. He never did cheat by standing on his toes.

'You were a dear little lad!' she whispered. At least there had been some happy times.

Perhaps she should at least tell Adam what she was planning. She wouldn't ask his opinion and she wouldn't expect his approval but she would ask him to keep her secret.

Cathy stood up and clasped her hands, praying for strength. She would find Adam now and tell him. Then there would be no going back.

That same afternoon Adele returned to Fairfields and Chloe went with her. Chloe had agreed to act as a go-between between Adele and Jessica although she had very little hope of bringing about a successful conclusion. When they arrived, they saw Olivia in the garden with Alice and the latter hurried across with a request to speak alone with Chloe. Adele walked on, her head high, her every movement resenting the intrusion.

Alice's homely face was flushed and her nervousness was apparent. 'I do hope I'm not speaking out of turn, Mrs Tyler, but I know why the boy was brought here and—'

'How do you know?'

Alice had the grace to blush. 'Someone listened at a door but it wasn't me and I shan't name names.'

'I see. Go on.'

'I know you must be having to make plans for him and . . . Well, I must tell you that I'm not prepared to take on another child no matter how much they offer me. I was engaged to care for Olivia and she and I get along perfectly. In fact I adore her.'

'I can see that she loves you in return.' Chloe groaned inwardly. Here was a further complication.

'I've told Mr Orme and also Mrs Maitland and her daughter. I've nothing against the boy but we're happy as we are and I don't want to go upsetting the applecart. We know nothing about the child, do we? Suppose he's a little terror – he is French, after all.'

'He seems a nice enough child.'

'But what if he isn't? How would we get rid of him if he's a bad influence on Olivia? Mrs Letts says that last time his mother left here she just disappeared and no one could find her.'

'I can't imagine why you are so determined to think badly of him, Alice.'

Alice's good-natured face darkened. 'He's French, Mrs Tyler. My family have had some dealings with the French and none of them happy ones. I know what I'm talking about. It's not just the frogs' legs and such. They have different morals.'

Chloe wanted to argue this point but she did not know any French people.

Alice went on breathlessly. 'Do you imagine for a moment that if we took the boy for a trial period and then found him to be an unsuitable companion . . .' She threw up her hands. 'Do you really think Mrs Dupres will come across from France and take him back? Of course she won't.' She glanced over her shoulder to check on her little charge. Olivia was making a daisy chain and she looked up and smiled. At once Alice's face changed. 'Dear little pet!' she murmured. 'I'm sure you think badly of me for what I've said but I'm so afraid for

Olivia. With Mrs Maitland taking to her bed I feel I have to look out for the poor little love.'

Chloe nodded. From curiosity she asked, 'What have the French ever done to hurt your family?'

Alice rolled her eyes. 'My eldest sister was engaged to one. Paul Fontaine his name was. Wonderfully handsome in the French way. Small moustache, what my mother called "come hither" eyes! They called the banns and then he went back to France to arrange to bring over his family for the wedding and we never heard from him again. Not a word. It broke my sister's heart, poor soul. She nearly went out of her mind and she was never the same afterwards. The French! I shall never trust them again.' She was breathing rapidly. 'And look what they did to their own aristocrats. Cut off their heads with a guillotine!'

Her voice had risen and Chloe glanced apprehensively towards Adele. Hopefully she was too far ahead to hear what Alice was saying. Chloe could see that she would never change Alice's attitude. Wearily she patted her shoulder. 'Thank you for telling me how you feel, Alice.'

'So you will tell Mrs Maitland?'

'Yes I will.'

As she went into the house with Adele her hopes had fallen even further. If Alice wasn't willing to care for the boy it would make no difference whether or not Jessica *were* to be persuaded to change her mind.

She left Adele with Matty and went up to Jessica's room.

'Chloe come in, child, and close the door quietly. I have a most unpleasant headache.'

'I'm sorry. Can I fetch you anything?'

'Another head, perhaps?'

Chloe settled beside her, smiling. 'I have solved one of your problems, Mrs Maitland. Lucien and his mother are staying at Monkswell Farm for a few days. Lucien is having a wonderful time, watching the animals. He is—'

Jessica looked at her sharply. 'I can see what you are up to! My body may be weak but my mind is in good working order.' She sighed. 'I don't want to see him, Chloe. I won't see him. I don't trust that girl. Dancer indeed! She turns up

119

after five years and expects us to believe that she has borne Oliver a son. It's utter nonsense. She sees a way of ridding herself of an illegitimate child, that's all, by telling us the boy is Oliver's. If he is then why didn't she write to tell us five years ago? I'll tell you why, child. Because whoever *was* the father has now abandoned her and she cannot cope.'

Chloe said, 'He's the image of Oliver. If you would see for yourself—'

'Well, I won't and that's that. First this Terence fellow and now Lucien. Do they take me for a fool? I've told Matty his so-called son is a fraud but he won't accept the facts. And I won't he fooled either by a tuppenny ha'ppeny dancer who's no better than she should be.'

Chloe was silenced. The reference to Terence Harkness had weakened her determination. Only too clearly she saw the situation from Jessica's viewpoint. Even Chloe's own faith in Terence had been shaken by Dorothy's recent letter.

She made a final attempt. 'Why won't you take one look at him? Then if you are not convinced they can be sent away and nothing more will be said.'

It was a gamble but Chloe thought they must take it. Surely Jessica *must* see the extraordinary likeness.

Jessica hesitated. 'And if I am convinced – what then? He is Adele's son. She will start making demands. Asking for money or expecting us to bring him up . . . And who else is going to appear over the years, towing a child they claim to be Oliver's? Fairfields is not an orphanage and I am not a deep well of money into which people can dip whenever they feel inclined! The answer is "No", Chloe, and I do not want them here.'

'But we have offered them a room—'

Jessica waved an airy hand. 'You must do what you like. I don't want to hear another word on the subject.'

'But Adele is downstairs. She's hoping to speak with—'

'Is she indeed? And who invited her? I certainly didn't. I shall stay here in my room until she's gone.'

Chloe retired, defeated. She broke the news to Adele who looked perilously close to tears.

Matty patted her arm and said, 'Cheer up, old thing. It's not over yet. We'll think of something.'

120

Chloe admired his optimism. From where she stood, the outcome looked decidedly gloomy.

The following morning Chloe cooked breakfast for Jack, Adele, Lucien and herself and sat down with them to enjoy it. She had done her best not to run up expenses because she intended to keep an account of the week so that she could convince Jack of the viability of her grand idea. She had made a large pan of scrambled eggs and had fried up some potatoes left from the previous day's meal. This was followed by toast and a choice of Cathy's honey or marmalade.There was a large pot of tea and milk for Lucien.

Afterwards Adele, still subdued from Jessica's rejection, took Lucien into Hastings on the bus to spend a few hours sightseeing.

Chloe went up to their room and found the bed already made. So Adele was trying to make life easy for her. Poor woman, thought Chloe. All this way and now she was being cold-shouldered. She would be forced to go back to France, taking Lucien with her. And who would she find to care for him? It was a bleak prospect. If only she had written years ago to tell them of the boy's existence . . . but everything was clear-cut in retrospect and it was easy to see the mistakes with hindsight. Perhaps if Oliver had not been killed she would have contacted him – but no. She hadn't known that Oliver was dead and had made no attempt to tell him he was a father. Probably the hurt of Hettie's child had made her bitter. Chloe could understand that. She dipped into the tub of polish and brought a shine to the chest of drawers, the wooden bed head and the table. She picked up some petals that had fallen from the flowers on the window sill and straightened the bedside rug. She was on her way downstairs when she heard Adam call her name.

'I'm on my way!' she called, instantly distracted from Adele and her problems.

She found him in the kitchen, cutting himself a slice of bread and buttering it generously.

He said, 'You don't mind, do you?'

'Of course not.' She smiled. 'You're the nephew. I'm not

121

family – and even if I were, you'd be welcome to a slice of bread. Are you looking for Mr Bourne? He's gone into—'

'No. I've come to see you.'

His expression had changed, she thought, suddenly wary. 'Has something happened?'

'Not yet but it will. It's about my mother and Uncle Jack. She's got herself into a rather desperate state. I shouldn't be telling you this but I don't know who else to talk to and I'm worried.'

'Oh Adam . . . Is she ill?'

'Not physically but she's . . . Well, she's in a very odd mood. She's saying some very odd things.'

Chloe's heart sank. 'About me?'

He looked surprised. 'No. Should she?'

'Of course not. I wondered—'

'She says she's made up her mind to leave Pa and—'

Chloe sat down, her mind racing. 'This is not to do with the gloves and flowers, is it? I'm sure that wasn't your father! He's not the sort of man to . . .' Guiltily she recalled Patrick's wink but pressed on. 'Well, I mean he's not the romantic type. Is he?'

Adam looked uncomfortable. 'Actually it *was* him. He has finally admitted it – but it's not only that.'

He looks like a bewildered child, thought Chloe, and wondered how Cathy could inflict all this pain on him.

'Ma says she should have married Uncle Jack and it's not too late. She says she can't waste any more of her life and she's going to tell him so and move in here with Jack. There'll be the devil to pay if she does.' He looked up at Chloe. 'Honestly Mrs Tyler, I don't know what to do. I keep thinking that if I say nothing to Pa she might forget about it . . . but she might really go, especially if Uncle Jack encourages her.' He glanced nervously out of the window. 'If he comes in we'll have to say I called in to see you – to tell you about the gloves.'

Chloe regarded him soberly. 'I don't know what to say either – except that I certainly gave him no encouragement at all. You have to believe me.'

'Of course I do. Ma might not be so sure, though. When Pa

admitted it, she went mad and threw a plate at him. She said you'd put a spell on both the Bourne men!'

Mortified, Chloe could think of nothing to say.

Adam sighed. 'I told her you were seeing this chap from Fairfields – Harkness? Is that his name? I didn't know if you were but—'

Chloe hoped she wasn't blushing. 'I'm not exactly stepping out with him. I hardly know him but – but he does write to me and I'll see him tomorrow at Fairfields. I do like him.'

Adam grinned suddenly. 'I imagine he's pretty sweet on you! I'm fairly smitten myself but I have this other young lady.'

'She's more your age,' Chloe told him hastily. 'This is all rather sudden, Adam. Let me think a moment.'

The thought of Cathy marching in to take over Monkswell Farm held no appeal for her. It would almost certainly entail Chloe's dismissal. On the other hand, if it would make Jack happy it might be worth the turmoil . . . Another thought occurred. 'Of course we've got Adele and her son staying here for a few days.' She explained the circumstances and her idea for future income. 'But if your mother did come, it would be up to her and your uncle to decide about that.'

Adam groaned. 'I can't let it happen. If Ma leaves him he'll go mad. Or else he'll go to pieces. He's an awkward old devil but he does love her in his own way. What are we going to do?'

It was Chloe's turn to groan. 'You're dragging me into it and this isn't about me. Not really. It's about what happened years ago between the two brothers and your mother. Really, Adam, I have enough problems at the moment without you dropping this one into my lap!'

He crossed to the window and stared out. 'If Ma moves in here, my father might . . . he might ask you to be our housekeeper.'

'Then he'll be unlucky! I don't mean to be rude but I don't care for him at all.' Chloe had spoken hastily and immediately regretted her tone of voice. This wasn't Adam's fault but she felt aggrieved. There was no way she had brought about this terrible tangle but she saw the sag of Adam's shoulders and wanted to help. Her conscience pricked her. He was young and he had turned to her for help and she was being unsympathetic. Speaking more gently, she said, 'Would it help to speak to your father about it? Maybe you could say only that you thought your mother was depressed.'

Adam swung round. 'He wouldn't care. He's in a foul mood lately. There might be one unholy row and she might walk straight out. I keep hoping she'll give up the idea. I was wondering if you'd talk some sense into her but I don't suppose—'

'You're right. I won't. I'm the last person she wants to talk to.'

'But if you told her you're not interested in Uncle Jack she might not be in such a hurry. It's because of you she's panicking. Because of the birthday lunch and you having to sit with us. She doesn't seem to think you'll be a housekeeper for much longer.'

Abruptly Chloe's patience came to an end. Without a word she ran upstairs and returned with the gloves. She tossed them towards Adam, who caught them awkwardly. 'Give these to your mother. Say I don't want them and never did. I haven't even worn them. She might understand that I'm not a threat on either count. I don't want to steal her husband or her brother-in-law.' She realized she was breathless but rushed on. 'I don't want to cause any trouble and I've done nothing for which anyone can blame me. I simply want to do my job here as a housekeeper and to see my friend Terence Harkness.'

'I'm sorry,' Adam stammered. 'I didn't mean – I just had to talk to someone.'

'Well, now you have.' She swallowed hard. 'I'm not angry with you, Adam, believe it or not. I'm angry with a situation which casts me as the bad fairy!' She drew in a long breath.

He smiled faintly then glanced down at the gloves. 'She'll probably burn them!'

'Good riddance to them. But that's your problem now. Give them to your young lady if you like. Or throw them away. I don't care.'

He stuffed the gloves into his pocket. 'Perhaps I should talk to Uncle Jack.'

'By all means. Whatever you think best.'

'Perhaps not. He might come charging to the rescue like a prince on a white charger!'

Which made Patrick the dragon and Cathy the princess. Chloe felt slightly hysterical.

Chloe regarded him gloomily. It seemed certain that, one way or another, her own job might be in doubt. If Cathy moved in she would certainly get rid of the housekeeper. Naturally enough she would want Jack Bourne all to herself. She shrugged mentally. That would be sad but not disastrous. She would find another job. Admittedly she would miss Jack Bourne . . . But maybe she could get a job in London – and see more of Terence Harkness. Sometimes good things come from bad. And tomorrow she would see Terence again. The thought cheered her a little.

Adam had turned from the window. 'Thank you for listening. I'm sorry I worried you. I shall sit tight and see what happens. Fingers crossed. Eh?' He attempted a laugh but Chloe could see how unhappy he was.

She said, 'I honestly don't know how to advise you. They have their own lives, Adam, and whatever happens they will both still love you. None of this is your fault.'

When he had gone she glanced at the clock and saw that it was nearly ten o'clock. She must get a move on or Jack would be coming in for his lunch.

Seven

S unday morning dawned with a bright clear sky but a strong breeze, which fluttered Olivia's hair as she ran to and fro across the lawn after the ball that Bertha was throwing for her. Every now and then the little girl stopped to watch the drive.

'He's late,' she insisted. 'Mr Harkness is late!'

'He's not late,' Bertha said for the fourth time. 'He's coming around twelve and it's only eleven. Just be patient.'

She glanced towards the terrace where baby Robert slept in his pram. Bertha was regaining her strength but she now had a decision to make. Her mother was still bedridden and this time the doctor doubted if she would ever fully recover. Jessica had a strong will but her recent collapse had weakened her body and she seemd unable to raise any enthusiasm for resuming her previous existence. The full-time nurse was still in residence and Jessica appeared to depend on her more and more each day. The cost of the nurse was a heavy burden on the family finances when the cost of Olivia's nanny was also considered. Soon Olivia would need a governess and that would mean more expense. Bertha had talked to her husband on the subject. Now she had to speak to her mother.

Next time the ball came her way, Bertha picked it up and held out her hand. 'We have to go in now, Olivia. I need to speak to Grandmama.'

'May I speak to to her?'

'Not this time. You must go to Nanny and maybe she will read to you.'

'When may I push Robert in his pram? You said I could.'

'When I can be with you. Maybe this afternoon.'

Having seen the child safely into Alice's care, Bertha went upstairs to her mother's room.

Jessica was lying in bed, a book unopened on the counter-pane. She opened her eyes as Bertha entered and her face brightened. 'Bertha, my dear! Come and sit with me. I get so bored these days.'

Bertha made the usual enquiries about her health but none of the answers were encouraging.

She said, 'I have been talking to George, Mama, and we wonder if this is the time he and I should move back into Fairfields.'

Jessica's eyes widened. 'Move back? Oh, but that would be splendid!' She sat up a little straighter. 'But are you sure, dear? I know how much you love your dear little cottage.'

Bertha let that pass. 'We always knew we would come back. Eventually it will belong to Robert.'

Jessica clasped her hands. 'It would be wonderful, dear. Just like old times. But would George mind? He does so love to have you all to himself.'

Bertha shrugged. 'He's perfectly willing as long as we keep the cottage. We might find a tenant and let it out. But it would always be there if we ever wanted to return to it.'

This had been George's only stipulation. He didn't relish the idea but he had seen the force of Bertha's arguments.

Jessica said, 'You could have the three rooms at the far end of the house so that we need not impinge on your privacy. They need smartening up, of course, but that would be fun, wouldn't it. We could buy you some new furniture. You could have a little kitchen of your own but eat with us most of the time – if you wished.' She frowned as an unpleasant thought occurred. 'The doctor hasn't said anything, has he? About my health? I feel much stronger. It's this tiredness . . .'

'No, no, Mama. He's said nothing alarming though he does believe you will need your nurse for some time yet. No, it's a number of things. I thought I could take over the running of the household for you – with your advice, of course, when needed. And there's Olivia. I could give her lessons for a few years at least. That would save hiring a governess.'

'Well, Bertha . . .' Jessica positively glowed at the prospect. 'It does sound as though it would all work very well. It's been very dull here with only Matty for company. He means well but he's a daft old thing. All he wants is to be left alone with his newspaper – and his cigar, if he can hide himself away somewhere. Especially now I'm cooped up here and can't keep my eye on him. He thinks I don't know but I can smell the smoke on him.' She sighed. 'He does his best, though he has never been the same since poor Oliver was killed. But then none of us have. It changed our lives forever as death does.'

Bertha recognized the tremor in her voice and said quickly, 'And it would be wonderful for Robert to grow up with his cousin.'

Jessica nodded. 'I'm delighted, Bertha. Do go and tell your Uncle Matty. Give him something to be cheerful about.'

As Bertha rose to leave Jessica said, 'I do appreciate you, Bertha. I want you to know that. I've always loved you although I think sometimes you were jealous of Oliver. The little brother. I daresay I spoiled him but he was so like his father.'

Surprised, Bertha said, 'Thank you, Mama. Being a mother myself has helped me understand a lot of things.' She smiled. 'It does give you a different slant on life, doesn't it.' Impulsively she leaned forward and kissed her mother lightly. 'It's going to be wonderful, being together again.'

Outside the room, she closed the door quietly and smiled slowly. She *was* pleased to be coming back to Fairfields and flattered that her mother was so delighted by the idea. Perhaps after so many years of coolness, the two of them could finally be friends.

Terence Harkness arrived at half past twelve and was greeted by Matty, who carried him off to the summer house to smoke a cigar and bring his son up to date with the latest news. After about twenty minutes Terence asked about Chloe and confided his interest in her.

'She'll be here any minute,' Matty reassured him. 'A wonderful young woman. She's had a lot of tragedy, poor soul. Rather taken with her, aren't you?'

'I certainly admire her. I'm hoping she will meet me in London one day. I thought we could go to one of the galleries – if she's interested in art. Not that I know much about it but Mrs Tyler seems to be a very artistic sort of person.' He sighed. 'And how's your sister? A little better, I hope.'

Matty said carefully, 'Mrs Maitland won't be joining us. I have to tell you that she's . . . very wary of strangers. Always has been.' He glanced at his son to see if he had accepted the lie.

'Is she really? Poor soul.'

'Yes. A form of nervousness. It's not uncommon, you know. Not that she's up to it at present since her collapse. She keeps to her bed mostly. Doctor's orders.'

Terence turned to him. 'I'm glad you've told me, actually. About the nervousness, I mean. To be honest, I felt that she didn't like me. I thought that perhaps I'd offended her in some way.'

'Good Lord, no!' Matty feigned amazement at this suggestion. 'I think a cheerful young man around the place reminds her of Oliver. The son that was killed, you know.'

'Ah yes! That must have been a nightmare.'

Matty stared out of the summer house, trying to pluck up his courage. Then he said, 'You've never told me much about your life before we met. Naturally I'm interested but I don't want to pry.'

'I'm sure you won't. I'm happy to talk about my life.' His smile was open and frank.

'So . . . Were you brought up in Lower Meddley?'

'Yes. It was a good place for children to grow up in. I actually liked school!' He smiled. 'Miss Maydon was my teacher and I thought she was wonderful. I wanted to marry her, the way little boys do!'

'And Cicely didn't have any other children – by Harkness?'

'No. I don't know why. You don't think to ask these things until it's too late and they're gone.' He sighed.

'So she never mentioned me at all – I suppose she wouldn't have.'

'No. But she probably thought about you a great deal. In the circumstances, I mean. Every time she looked at me she'd remember you were my real father.'

'And her parents didn't say a word?'

'No. It was all a big secret – to me at least. Of course, they thought the world of my father – of Edgar Harkness.'

Matty closed his eyes and drew deeply on his cigar. Thank God for tobacco. For a long moment he didn't speak. At last he said, 'You must have the odd photograph of you growing up. I've missed so many years.'

'I don't think so. We didn't aspire to a camera.'

'Ah! But some schools took group photographs.'

'Private schools, maybe. Our village school never did. Sorry to disappoint you.'

For a few moments they were both silent. The summer house had always had a comforting effect on Matty and now he felt it especially. Tucked away in the little wooden house. Hidden from the harsh world outside.

He said, 'I come here often. Love the place. No one else bothers – except Olivia. She calls it her fairy house and brings her dolls in here.'

'She's a sweet child. I suppose she's related to me in a distant way. And then there's Bertha's boy. He'll inherit, I daresay.'

'Presumably – or else they'll share it all. But Olivia was born out of wedlock. Might make a difference.' He didn't like the way the conversation was heading. 'So Cicely was happy. You were all happy.'

'Yes . . . except for me. My education. I was so bright my mother wanted me to go to a university or medical school to become a doctor. She was passionate about it but it didn't happen.'

'A doctor?' Matty stared at him. 'You could have been a doctor? Good Lord!' He tried to imagine himself with a son who was a doctor. He could see Jessica's face if his son turned out to be cleverer than Oliver, who had never seriously achieved anything noteworthy. He knew it was an unkind thought but he relished the idea of anything that gave him status. Jessica had always treated him as an inferior and he had accepted his ranking. But if his son was clever enough to be a doctor . . . 'And you decided against it?'

Terence shrugged. 'Not enough money. A big disappointment. I'd always felt drawn to the medical profession. It's not too late, of course, but time's passing.' He kept his face averted. 'I wanted to make a difference . . . to help people. I could have done but . . .' He shrugged. 'It wasn't meant to be.'

A doctor. Matty could hear himself say, 'Yes, my son's just left medical school. Passed with flying colours. Always been very bright.' He asked Terence, 'Have you thought of a scholarship? If you're that bright it shouldn't be difficult.'

'I've tried that but they're few and far between. To be perfectly frank, I was wondering if there was any way you could help me out? It would be wonderful to fulfil my mother's dream even though she's gone.'

Matty regarded him sadly. 'If only I could help you but I can't. Empty pockets, old lad.' He sighed. 'Money's never stuck to me the way it does to some people.'

Some of the light faded from his son's eyes. 'It was just an idea. A faint hope . . . This house isn't yours then.'

'I wish it were. And I've no savings. As I say, I could never accumulate money. It just slips through my fingers.'

'That's a shame. I was thinking along the lines of a second mortgage which I could pay you back with interest as soon as I started in practice.'

'Out of the question,' Matty told him. 'It's all Jessica's.' Matty grinned suddenly. 'I won't get a penny, I can assure you of that. I'm sorry to disappoint you.' He laid a hand on Terence's arm.

'No need to apologize.' Terence's voice was unnaturally hearty. 'The world's full of dashed hopes. Now that I know, I'll make an effort to find something else.' His voice shook slightly. 'All this time I've been praying something would turn up . . . It'll be easier now the last faint hope has gone.'

Matty narrowed his eyes. 'Now hang on a minute, young Terence. The old grey matter's beginning to work. What you need is a rich wife!'

'A rich wife?' Terence managed a wry smile. 'They don't grow on trees – and anyway, I do very much admire Mrs Tyler.'

Matty wasn't listening. He went on. 'With your good looks that shouldn't be too difficult. Forget Chloe. She has nothing, poor girl. Now who do I know who's rich and has

131

a marriageable daughter?' He chuckled. 'By all means look for a job to tide you over but in the meantime I'll put my thinking cap on! Don't you worry, old son. We'll think of something.'

An hour later they were all seated at the dining table. Bertha opposite George, Chloe opposite Terence. Matty enjoyed his place at the head of the table while Jessica, upstairs in bed, was being coaxed to eat by her nurse. Chloe was intrigued. The relationship between Terence Harkness and Matty seemed to have blossomed since she last saw them together but she was puzzled by a slight but distinct change in Terence's attitude towards her. He was attentive, certainly, but the spark she had sensed earlier was no longer in his eyes. She told herself at first that she was imagining things but as the meal progressed she became more convinced. Terence occasionally exchanged a glance with Matty, which suggested a relaxed closeness and Matty, too, seemed less inclined to glance her way. Father and son had the air of conspirators, she decided.

Not that it was any of her business, she reminded herself, and, trying to ignore her unease, she turned away to answer a question from Bertha about Dorothy's twins.

'They are blooming,' she told her. 'And Dorothy is in her element. All those years childless and now she has two children to mother.'

Bertha smiled. 'Two for the price of one,' she joked. 'I think I must be satisfied with my one little son. The doctor feels it would be unwise to tempt fate again.'

'My son's planning to become a doctor!' Matty blurted the words out and all eyes turned towards him and then to Terence.

Bertha said, 'Gracious me. That's a long training period. Why have you left it so late?'

Terence glanced at Matty who gave an imperceptible nod. 'It's been my wish all my life but I could never afford it. Now my father is encouraging me and has promised me his help.'

Bertha stared at Matty in surprise and Chloe was piqued. She had been left in the dark about this new development and she wondered why Matty had not confided in her. Unless he wanted his son to have the pleasure of the announcement – in which case he had jumped the gun by blurting it out himself! How would it be, she wondered, to be a doctor's wife? For a few moments she imagined herself dealing with patient records, answering the door and taking messages for Doctor Terence Harkness. It had a certain charm, she thought, although no doubt the novelty would soon wear off. Not that he had said he wanted to be a family doctor. He might aspire to being a specialist of some kind or a surgeon.

Chloe listened in silence as Terence outlined his plans for the future while Matty positively glowed with pride. She wondered if Jessica knew and was curious also as to the source of his money for it seemed that Matty was somehow going to finance the enterprise although how was never specified.

George seemed very impressed. He said, 'A doctor in the family, eh? We shall know where to come with our aches and pains!' and they all joined in the laughter.

After a while Chloe found her attention wandering, wondering how Jack Bourne was coping with Adele and Lucien. She had left a large rabbit casserole in the oven and had prepared all the vegetables before she left. Jack was used to cooking for himself and had insisted it would be no trouble for him to deal with the lunch. He didn't want her to miss her visit to Fairfields, he insisted, but she had still felt a little guilty as she drove away from the farm. She had persuaded him to take in two lodgers and had then left him to cope without her.

She became aware that Terence was smiling at her and immediately banished all thoughts of Monkswell Farm and Jack Bourne.

He said, 'Are you interested in art at all, Mrs Tyler?'

Immediately warmed by his attention, she confessed her ignorance.

'Then perhaps I can tempt you to London and begin your education.'

'I'd like that. What do you have in mind?'

'A trip to one or two of the smaller galleries and then tea. We might go to the Dorchester.'

'It all sounds wonderful.'

Thrilled by the invitation, she smiled warmly at him but

before he could answer, Bertha began to tell them of their proposed move back into Fairfields. Chloe nodded and smiled but she was imagining herself alone with Terence, walking together in the galleries and exchanging intimacies over tea. Cucumber sandwiches and dainty pastries . . . There was, of course, no possibility of any privacy; no chance of spending any time together – at his lodgings, for instance. To visit a man alone and unchaperoned would be most unseemly. If only she had a place of her own, she might think of an excuse to ask him to call in but there was no prospect of that. For the foreseeable future Monkswell Farm was the roof over her head and the nearest thing she could call home.

As she drove herself home later she found herself thinking about Adele and tried to imagine her in a flat in Paris. If it was anything like the flat she had once shared with Oliver in London it would be hopelessly untidy and in need of a spring clean!

Lucien ran out to meet her and asked to help put away the horse and trap. He was a serious child, she realized, as they made their way to the barn. He asked so many questions.

'What does the horse eat, *madame*? Does he kick? Does he like being a horse, *madame*? Perhaps he would like to be a cow or a dog. What do you think?'

Chloe answered as best she could but quickly discovered that every answer provoked another question.

When the animal was safely ensconced in his stable and the trap put away in the barn, Chloe took the boy's small hand in hers. 'Shall we go back now and give the hens a little more corn?'

'They will not be hungry. Mr Bourne has fed them. And I helped him. Mr Bourne is a very good man. He likes me. He said he did. Do you believe him, *madame*?'

'Of course I believe him.'

'Maman says some men are bad. They tell lies and they do bad things. Was my father a bad man, *madame*?' He looked up at her, his expression intense.

'Your father? Certainly not, Lucien.' Chloe wondered what he knew about his father. What had Adele said to him about

134

Oliver Maitland? She searched carefully for an answer that would not confuse him.

At last she said, 'Your father was a good man who made some mistakes. We all make mistakes, Lucien.'

'Mr Bourne likes me. Did my father like me?'

'Your poor Papa died before you were born but he *would* have liked you. He would have *loved* you, Lucien.'

Suddenly he stood still. 'Did you know my father, *madame*?'

'Oh yes. He was a very good man.'

She wanted to say much more but dared not. The past for this little boy was dangerous ground. He had never seen his father and Chloe had no idea how much Adele had said.

As they walked on she took a chance. 'There are some photographs of your father at Fairfield House, Lucien. Shall we ask Uncle Matty to find them for you to look at?'

Lucien stopped again. 'Does Uncle Matty like me?'

'Yes, he does.'

His frown gave way to a smile which transformed his face. 'Then we should ask him, *madame*.'

He trotted along beside her, his small hand warm in hers and she felt again the same longing and regret that brought a lump to her throat. Her own son would be a little younger than Lucien if he had survived. She would now be living with Jeff in Montana – if Jeff had lived. So many 'ifs'. She sighed and, despite Lucien's comments about the hens, went into the barn to find some corn for them. In his excitement Lucien hurled it in all directions so that the mystified hens ran in circles to find it.

Once back in the kitchen he ran to his mother who sat in the rocking-chair beside the stove. His eyes glowed with excitement and his words tumbled out in a mixture of French and English. Adele listened, her expression wary. Once or twice she glanced at Chloe but said nothing.

Chloe waited for a protest or an accusation that she had meddled, but none came and the situation was interrupted by Jack.

He took an envelope from the dresser and handed it to Chloe with an apologetic expression.

'The postman brought this yesterday and I forgot about it. It's from America.'

Intrigued, Chloe took it from him. 'Excuse me,' she said and hurried up to her room. It had been forwarded from her old address in Montana. She opened it with unsteady fingers and read the scrawled signature. It was from a Lee M. Stocker. An attorney. Her throat tightened.

It was short and to the point.

Dear Mrs Tyler, Your father-in-law has been taken ill and has very few weeks to live. He now regrets his estrangement from his deceased son Jeffery and wishes to see you. Please contact this office and we will help you make the necessary arrangements. The costs of your travel will be met by your father-in-law. Your obedient servant . . .

Shocked, she glanced at the date and saw that the letter had been travelling for several weeks. Was Jeff's father still alive? Even if he was, she had no intention of obeying the terse command. She sat down with a rapidly beating heart. She had enough problems in England and could certainly not expect Jack Bourne to give her unlimited time off to see a man who had rejected both her and Jeff. The stark truth was that she didn't want to go back to America even if it was still possible to meet Jeff's father. Perhaps it would be enough to send a wire to acknowledge receipt of the letter and to explain why she could not return. Chloe shook her head. What would Jeff have wanted her to do? He would have understood her predicament. His father had refused to attend the wedding and had not sent a gift – not even a flower or a card. And Jeff had been adamant that he no longer wanted or needed his father's blessing on his and Chloe's union.

The minutes ticked by, filled with painful memories, but at last she came to a conclusion. A suitable compromise was how she saw it. She would find out how to send a kindly worded transatlantic message, regretting her inability to travel and to offer her condolences on his illness.

'It's more than you deserve,' she told him and went down-stairs with a heavy heart.

Later that evening Adele cornered Chloe and asked for a few moments of her time. Chloe agreed reluctantly, expecting a rebuke for the way she had talked with Lucien about his father. She was wrong, however.

'I have to talk to someone,' Adele told her earnestly. 'I cannot understand these people. These Maitlands. This mother – she loses her only son and yet she does not want the grandson. They accept the girl but not the boy. They accept the child born to the maid but not the child born to Oliver's mistress.'

Her beautiful face was suffused with the pain of incomprehension. Chloe shrugged helplessly. She, too, failed to understand Jessica's reasoning.

Adele took a quick breath and continued. 'Oliver wanted to marry me. He asked me many times but I said "No" because I want my career. He wanted a family and I did not. I am the woman he wanted for his wife, not this servant girl. Lucien is the child Oliver wanted, not Olivia. I want to tell all this to Jessica Maitland but she will not listen. Why is this?'

Chloe sighed. She felt compelled to say something in Jessica's defence.

'Sadly Mrs Maitland is not convinced that Lucien is her grandson. She *knows* that Olivia is her granddaughter because when she was born Oliver was still alive and he accepted responsibility. You should have been in touch with them right from the start – as soon as you knew you were carrying Oliver's child. Why didn't you?'

'Because I was too angry with Oliver. He had betrayed me with his mother's maid. How would you have felt?'

Chloe sighed.

Adele nodded. 'You would have felt as I did. And later I wanted to tell Oliver. To give him the child. But by that time my mother – she would not hear of it. She wanted to keep the child and I gave into her wishes. Lucien is a good boy. He loves his *grandmère* but now she is ill and she will not recover. Now she agrees he must come to England to the

137

Maitlands. She says it is his – how you say "heritage". The mother *must* understand this.'

'But she refuses to see him,' Chloe explained helplessly. 'She thinks you are . . .' She hesitated.

'She thinks I am lying!' Adele's face darkened.

'I'm afraid so.'

'She wants us to disappear. To go back to Paris and leave her in peace!' Adele's eyes flashed dangerously.

'She is like your mother – very unwell. The doctor says she must be kept quiet.'

'She has servants. A nurse. She can afford to be ill in comfort. With my mother it is not so easy. And she is truly ill.'

Chloe regarded her with regret. 'You will have to take the boy back with you. You cannot force Mrs Maitland to accept him.'

'I shall speak strongly with her! Lucien belongs here with his father's family.'

'Mrs Maitland won't see you.'

Adele's mouth tightened. 'We shall see about that.'

Not far away, Cathy was writing a letter to her husband. Sitting by the bedroom window she kept a wary eye out for Patrick's return.

> *Dear Patrick, I doubt if this letter will come as a surprise to you. After so many years together I think you know me well enough to understand that I am deeply unhappy. Our marriage was a mistake. We both know that. I can see by your eyes and by the things you say that you no longer love me, although you once did. The other day, when you admitted sending those presents to Mrs Tyler I knew that was the end of us. One of us has to take the first step and it is going to be me. I am leaving you, Patrick, for Jack – the man I should have married years ago . . .*

Cathy reread what she had written. She knew she was doing the right thing but how would Patrick react? He might go mad and come after her. Or he might be glad that she had gone. He might make advances to Mrs Tyler but she'd be a fool to have him. With her looks she could get any man. Except Jack. Dear Jack was still patiently waiting for the day when his brother would put a foot wrong – and that day had come.

I know there have been other women in your life, Patrick, but I always turned a blind eye. We have a son and I would never do anything to hurt him. But now he is almost a man and I have explained my feelings to him. Adam understands that I have to be with Jack. I shall take my things and leave your home intact so that you and Adam can carry on as you always have. I am not trying to take him from you but if he wants to follow me I know Jack will make him welcome . . .

In a way she hoped Adam would stay with his father. But was that selfish of her? The truth was that after all these years she longed for some time alone with Jack. Mrs Tyler would have to go but Patrick might employ her.

'I don't care where she goes,' she muttered, 'as long as she isn't hanging around Monkswell.'

There have been good times in our life together, Patrick, and I thank you for those. Please forgive me for what I am doing. It won't be easy for you or for me but I think we have both known for some time that this is how it would end. With regrets, Cathy

She blotted it then folded it carefully and wrote Patrick's name on the front of the envelope. She slipped the letter inside, then put it under the mattress and went downstairs. Tomorrow she would move in with Jack. The thought of his welcome brought a faint smile to her lips. Dear Jack. His waiting was over.

The following day was Monday and Matty put his plan into action. He had decided to obtain proof of his son's background and to confront his sister with it. When he found himself alone in the house he went to the telephone, picked up the receiver and waited for the operator.

'I need the number of a school,' he told her. 'The village school in Lower Meddley.'

'Is that one or two "d"s?'

'Two.'

'One moment, sir.'

He waited impatiently.

At last she came back on the line and he wrote down the number with growing excitement.

'Now . . . when's a school playtime?' He thought hard. Wasn't it somewhere in the middle of the day . . . No, halfway through the morning and halfway through the afternoon. Then there was dinner time. Briefly Matty had a hazy image of himself at boarding school, sitting at a long table with dozens of other boys, eating shepherd's pie. He always ate slowly so that he could spend less time in the playground where the bigger boys reigned supreme. Once they had tied him to the railings with his own tie. On another occasion they had stolen the bag of butter drops which had arrived in his tuck box. School had never been a happy place for the young Matty . . .

Glancing at his watch, he saw that it was five past eleven and muttered crossly. 'Just missed it. Well, never mind. She'll probably answer it.'

Not that he expected the beautiful Miss Maydon to still be at the school. With her looks she must have married and it was always considered that spinster ladies made the best teachers, untrammelled as they were with household duties. He rang the operator again and asked her to connect him to Meddley School then waited with a thumping heart.

He heard it ring and then a voice said, 'Lower Meddley School. Miss Maydon speaking.'

So she was still there. He smiled. In the background he heard the murmur of voices as the children struggled together with a class reader. Nothing changes, he thought and tried to picture a more mature Miss Maydon. A few wrinkles, no doubt, and grey hair. He wondered if she had been kind to Terence.

'I hope I haven't rung at a bad time—' he began. What luck that it was the same woman.

'I'm afraid you have but if you could be brief . . .'

Matty launched into his little speech. He pretended he was interested in tracing the young man and hinted indirectly that he was a solicitor.

'So you see,' he said, 'it would help me if you have any information. He was a very bright child and he had hopes of becoming a doctor. Terence with one "r".'

There was a short pause. 'I remember a bright child named Terence, Mr Orme,' she said. 'I never forget a bright child. They are so rare. The boy I recall was called Terence Downey. He lived with his mother and a man named Harkness. I don't think the mother was married to Harkness and they certainly didn't stay in the village for—' She broke off and Matty heard her say, 'Harold Enright! What have I told you about spitting? Stand out in the front!'

Remonstrating with one of the children. Matty smiled.

She said, 'They didn't stay in the village for long and I know nothing about aspirations to the medical fraternity.'

Matty frowned. 'I'm not sure, Miss Maydon, if this Downey boy is the person we're looking for,' he said. 'Do you have immediate access to the school records? The log book or whatever it's called.'

'I'm taking a class at the—'

'If you could just give us his date of birth and his address while he was with you? We'd be most grateful.'

'I can't deal with it now, Mr— What did you say your name was?'

'Orme.' He wished he had given a false name. He really was out of practice.

'Mr Orme, I'm in the middle of a lesson but if you care to telephone again at ten past four I will hopefully have the information you seek.'

'You're very kind. I appreciate your help. I'll telephone again.'

As he replaced the receiver he hoped the operator hadn't been listening in. He'd been rather careless. Definitely not as sharp as he used to be. But the response was not quite what he had hoped for. The facts so far did not tally. According to Terence, Harkness had married Cicely long before the boy was school age. He glared at the telephone then turned abruptly away. He would know more when he spoke to Miss Maydon again. Wandering back towards his favourite armchair, he tried to imagine her in front of the class. Probably giving young Enright what for. Spitting in class.

'Probably a hanging offence!' he muttered with a grin and changed direction in search of his cigars.

Eight

O ver breakfast the next day, Adele announced that she was not going to be insulted any longer.

'I am going to Fairfields and I shall insist on seeing Lucien's *grandmère*. I shall insist.' She glared at Chloe across the table. 'I shall drag Lucien up the stairs and we shall sit outside the bedroom door until Mrs Maitland sees us – or until the policemen take us away.'

There was a startled silence and Lucien regarded his mother anxiously.

He said, 'I do not like the policemen, Maman.'

'I am not speaking with you, Lucien. I am speaking with Mrs Tyler.'

Alarmed, Chloe glanced at Jack and back at Adele. 'You must do as you wish, Adele,' she began, 'but I must warn you—'

'No. *I* must warn *you!*' Adele tossed her head. 'I have to go back to Paris because my mother is ill. I cannot wait longer. And I do not care to stay. I do not care for England.'

Jack said mildly, 'But you want Lucien to be brought up here.'

Adele flashed him a scornful look. 'Because he has an English father. I think he is English. It is right that he should remain.' She stood up and turned to Chloe. 'Will you drive us over there or must I call a cab?'

Chloe hesitated, unwilling to be dragged into the argument. The idea of Lucien suffering hostility and rejection at Fairfields troubled her. The boy had stopped eating and his beautiful brown eyes were fixed on his mother with childish desperation. Poor child. He was too young to fully understand but no doubt he knew that his mother intended to abandon him to this strange English family.

Suddenly he said, '*Maman, je veux*—'

'Speak English!'

'I want to go home to France to Grandmère. Please, Maman, I want to go home.' His mouth trembled.

'You cannot go do that, Lucien. Your *grandmère* is sick.'

Chloe said gently, 'You have another grandmother, Lucien. She will love you when—'

Tears welled up in his eyes. 'Maman . . . ?'

Adele looked at Chloe. 'Now you have made him cry!' She stood up and held out her hand. 'Come, Lucien. We must find a cab.'

Jack sighed. 'There's no need for that. Mrs Tyler can take you in the trap – if she is willing.'

Chloe sighed. 'I may be there some time,' she hedged.

'It doesn't matter. It has to be done. For Lucien's sake, this matter has to be settled.' He smiled at Lucien, who had taken his mother's hand as directed. 'Don't cry, little one. You will have a ride with Mama and Mrs Tyler.'

Chloe, imagining the stormy scene to come, said hopefully, 'Don't you need me, Mr Bourne? What about your lunch?'

'We'll eat this evening instead,' he told her. 'I have to go into Rye to collect a new sheepdog pup. Jude is getting old and I have to train a younger animal to take her place. I reserved one earlier from a litter at Neasden Farm where Jude came from.' He smiled at Lucien. 'When you come back we'll have a puppy for you to play with. How will that be?'

Lucien's face lit up with delight and Jack ruffled his dark hair.

When Adele had taken him upstairs to put on his jacket, Chloe and Jack regarded one another with resignation.

Jack said, 'She won't give up!'

'Neither will Jessica! Lord knows what will happen but as you say, something has to be settled one way or the other.'

'He's such a sweeet child. I shall miss him. He loves the farm. So many questions!' He smiled. 'I wonder what sort of life he would have with his mother – always on the move, I suppose. A gipsy existence.'

'But he loves her. Of course he does. She's his mother.'

'But he's grown up with his grandmother.'

Chloe shrugged. She felt helpless and confused. A small part of her admired Adele's determination. A larger part wondered what *would* be best for the boy. 'I'd better harness the trap,' she said without enthusiasm. 'They'll be down any minute and, to tell you the truth, I'm dreading this. The sooner we go, the sooner we'll get it over with.'

Jack watched Chloe go with the familiar sense of loss. He had finally admitted to himself that he looked forward to their time together and it wasn't because of the meals she produced, although she was a good cook. Plain food, carefully prepared. He sighed.

'Watch yourself, Jack!' he muttered.

Don't let yourself fall for her. She's the housekeeper. She's taken a job to tide her over financially until the day she marries again. And that won't be too far away. Terence Harkness is already in the running and if Adam hasn't thought about her, he should have done. Mrs Tyler would make any man a good wife. Pity Adam was so young. Mrs Tyler would settle him down . . . although Marion Lester was a very decent young woman and financially she would make a better match for him. Patrick was keen on the idea of getting in with the Lester family.

Jude crept forward and laid his head on Jack's knee. Patting her absentmindedly, Jack thought about the new pup but couldn't summon any real enthusiasm. If the bank was going to foreclose on him, a second sheep dog would hardly be necessary. He thought about Lucien and the feel of the small hand in his own and wished he had not waited so long for Cathy.

Patrick was never going to leave her. He had made the promise in the heat of love and disappointment. 'If he ever leaves you in the lurch, I'll be waiting.' And he meant it. He had waited eighteen years but Cathy had never complained about the marriage and, for better or worse, Patrick had never deserted her. He had never been called upon to honour his words and now it was never going to happen. And he was glad because Mrs Chloe Tyler had come into his life and suddenly there was hope.

He thought of Adam, who should have been *his* son – and of little Lucien. Was there a slim chance, now, that Jack might one day have a family of his own? He was getting older and the farm was failing. What did he have to offer any woman except perhaps Cathy and that was out of the question. He had waited for Patrick to grow tired of her but that hadn't happened. True, he had dallied once or twice but the women meant absolutely nothing. Cathy was Patrick's only true love. Cathy had never known of his infidelities or she would have come to him – of that he was quite certain. He had never told her of Patrick's indiscretions nor had he done anything to encourage her to leave her husband. Patrick was his brother and Jack would never hurt him.

If he was honest, his feelings toward Cathy had finally cooled. The passion had given way to a loyal friendship.

Jude whined softly, gazing up at her master with a puzzled look. Jack smiled and stood up.

'I can take a hint!' he told her. It was time to make a move or he would be late getting to Rye. He would start walking and someone would offer him a ride. He was reaching for his cap when Jude suddenly swung round and raced out of the door, barking a welcome.

'Cathy!' He smiled. Talk of the devil, he thought affectionately as he went outside. What would it be this time? he wondered. A jar of chutney or a fruit cake? One look at her face stopped him in his tracks and his smile vanished.

'Jack!' She rushed up to him. 'I have to see you. To talk to you.' To his surprise, instead of the usual chaste peck on the cheek, she threw out her arms and clung to him.

Wonderingly, he put his arms round her. She was murmuring his name over and over.

'Cathy? What's the matter?' His first thought was that there had been an accident. They were common enough on farms. 'Who is it? Tell me what's happened.'

Instead she burst into tears and he led her slowly indoors, with Jude fretting behind them.

'Oh Jack! My dearest Jack! I've done it! I've finally left him.' She looked at him tearfully. 'I should have done it sooner, I know. You must forgive me. I've been such a coward. But

I've done it now. I've left him a letter.' He handed her a towel from behind the the door and she mopped her eyes.

Jack stared at her fearfully. Had he understood her properly? She hadn't left Patrick, surely – or had she?

'You'd better sit down,' he told her and sat down himself. A black cloud of dismay was fogging his brain. 'What exactly have you done?'

She drew a long breath. 'I've left him. I told him I want you. It should have been you all along.'

'Oh my God! You've *told* him? What did he say?' He could picture his brother's face, white and shocked.

'I haven't actually told him but it's all in the letter. Jack, please say you forgive me. I'm so sorry for all those wasted years. It was cruel of me not to realize. I've . . . I've been such a coward and . . . and then there was Adam and he . . .'

'You mean he hasn't read the letter yet?' Jack clutched at the small straw.

'What?' She stared at him.

'Has Patrick read this letter?' He was aware that his voice was rising as panic took hold.

'Not yet. He's out shooting rabbits with Adam. But as soon as they get back he'll see it. I've propped it on the mantelpiece. I've told him the truth – that it's you I love. He'll get over it, Jack.' She wiped away a few last tears. 'Tell me you're pleased, darling. Say you love me. I know you do.'

Her entreaties added to his distress. He saw disaster descending upon the family and struggled to avert it. 'But we can't do that to him,' he stammered. 'You can't leave him, Cathy.'

'I can, Jack, and I have. I keep telling you. It was my fault. I abandoned you for Patrick and that was wrong of me. It's never too late, Jack.' She regarded him with quivering lips. 'I can make you happy, dearest Jack. We'll be happy together. Just the two of us. Mrs Tyler can go with a good reference. She might even go to Patrick. He fancies her, you know. She's not the first, either. There was the woman from the bakery and Maudie at the pub . . . I pretended not to know. I was so humiliated. I hate him, Jack. I know he's your brother but—'

'You don't hate him.' Jack regarded her with something akin to desperation.

'I tell you I *do*!'

'He loves you. You can't do this to him. We can't hurt him.'

'But you love me, Jack. You've waited all these years and now I'm here. Asking you. Begging you to forgive me. To give me a second chance.'

There was a long silence.

'Jack . . . You do still love me, don't you?'

He couldn't answer. He didn't want to hurt her but he didn't think he did still love her. He said, 'I thought it was all over . . . years ago. I mean, that special kind of love. Over the years . . .'

'Jack!' She clutched his hand. 'It's still the same love, Jack. I promise you it is. It will be wonderful. You'll never regret it.'

Jude, watching from his basket, growled softly. They both turned to him.

Jack said, 'She knows we're upset.'

'Poor Jude. It's all right, girl.'

Jude leaped from his basket and hurried to her. Cathy busied herself, making a fuss of him and Jack watched her bent head sadly. This was his chance and he couldn't take it because he didn't feel enough for her.

Slowly she raised her head and looked at him. 'Don't say you don't love me, Jack. I couldn't bear it.'

'Of course I love you. I always will. But this isn't . . . I don't feel happy about this, Cathy. You should have talked to me first. I need time to think.'

All the colour fled from her face. 'Time to think? But you've always loved me. We've always known this would happen one day. You promised me . . . Oh Jack, darling, don't look at me that way. I'm still the same Cathy.'

He stood up, withdrawing his hand. How on earth could he tell this sweet woman that she no longer moved him?

Cathy stood up. 'Just tell me that you don't love me and I'll go away.'

He looked into her eyes. 'I love you in a different way. Please try to understand. I promised that if Patrick left you I'd be here for you. I never said I would take you from him.'

'What's the difference?'

'There's a lot of difference.'

There was desperation in her face. 'Will you take me in, then? Let me live here with you? I'll housekeep for you – until you feel better about it all.'

'I'm sorry.' He closed his eyes. Hearing her move towards the door, he opened them again. 'Cathy . . . Come back. I have to explain. Please listen to me.'

Her expression changed. 'It's her, isn't it? It's Chloe Tyler. She's taken my place.'

'Certainly not!'

'You're lying – to me and to yourself. You're in love with your housekeeper and you don't even know it! My God, Jack. I never would have thought it of you.'

'It's nothing to do with Mrs Tyler!'

'Are you blind? She's bewitched you, Jack. And you've let her do it. After all you said . . . After all your promises. I come to you – I give up everything for you – and you're going to throw it all—'

Jack stepped forward and caught hold of her arms. 'Cathy, don't! Don't say things you'll regret. I haven't fallen in love with anyone else. I've fallen out—' He stopped himself in mid sentence but he had gone too far.

She wrenched herself free. 'You've fallen out of love with me! That's what you were going to say.' Her voice was shrill as shock and grief held her. She stared at him wildly then fell back against the door jamb as the anger left her.

They regarded each other warily. Jack tried to think of a way to end it gently but all the time he was aware of time passing and he kept imagining his brother reading the letter. Once Patrick saw that, it would all be over.

Suddenly she said, 'Let's go upstairs, Jack! Let's go to bed together and see if you still feel that you've stopped loving me.'

He shook his head. 'Go and get the letter. Tear it up. Patrick's looked after you all these years. You can't—'

She cried, 'Jack! Do you hear me? I want you. I want us to go upstairs . . . If you turn me down it will be the end of me, Jack. I want one chance to show you how happy we could be.'

149

But Jack pushed her gently from the doorway into the yard, stepped out after her and closed the door behind them.

Cathy was looking at him in disbelief. 'You mean it, Jack? This is the end of everything between us?'

'We can still be friends, Cathy. For God's sake!'

She turned and stumbled, then ran heavily across the yard in the direction of Bourne Farm.

'Cathy!' She looked broken, vulnerable. Jack cursed beneath his breath. He had been too abrupt. He had handled it badly. He should have given her some hope . . . but then that would have been cruel. Her accusations rang in his ears as he watched her hurry through the trees, across the field and out of sight. Leaning back against the door, Jack tried to imagine her reaching Bourne Farm, entering the kitchen and tearing up the letter. Unless, instead, she found Patrick reading it.

What would he do? There would be an almighty quarrel but what then? They had quarrelled before and made up. But this was different. Suppose Patrick lost his temper and struck her?

'Go after her, you fool!' he muttered but didn't move. If Patrick *had* found the letter, Jack's presence would make matters worse. Patrick would almost certainly hit him and they would fight. 'Damn!' If only he could be certain she had destroyed the letter – although she hadn't said she would do so.

He made his way into the parlour and poured himself a whisky. '*Why*, Cathy?' he wondered. Why had she made this sudden decision after all this time? Was it the gloves and the flowers? If so, no one could blame Chloe Tyler. He felt ashamed that she had been dragged into this mess. It was an impossible situation and there was no way, that he could see, that it could end happily. Leaning back on the sofa, he closed his eyes.

'I'm not in love with Mrs Tyler!' he muttered angrily. 'Never was and never will be.' Cathy was wrong about that. He thought about Cathy's offer to go to bed with him. Perhaps he should have accepted. Perhaps if they had become lovers just once, Cathy would have felt she had punished Patrick enough. She may have felt that her infidelity with Jack would serve her husband right. It might have satisfied her in more ways than one. The truth was that even if he still desired Cathy, he could never have betrayed Patrick. Brotherly love? Or misguided loyalty. Perhaps that was a failing on his part.

'Hell!' The truth was he had no idea what to do next.

He poured himself another drink and downed it in one gulp. Then he remembered Lucien and his promise about the new pup. He leapt to his feet, whistled to Jude and set off towards the road and a lift into town.

As soon as Chloe arrived at Fairfield House with Adele and Lucien, Matty told them that Jessica was sleeping. He was in a state of some agitation and before long he drew Chloe to one side and whispered that they must talk. They stood inside the French windows, looking out across the garden.

'Not about Jessica. It's about Terence,' he told her.

Chloe noticed that he cast anxious glances towards his son, who was in the middle of the lawn with Adele, Olivia and the nanny.

Chloe saw them all laugh and smiled. 'Your son has natural charm,' she told Matty. 'Nanny and Adele are quite taken with him – and look at Olivia. She's made him a daisy chain!'

They both watched as Olivia presented it to Terence and gave a small curtsey. When Terence gave an exaggerated curtsey in return there was more laughter. Matty, however, only sighed.

'I don't know how to say this but there's been a bit of a hitch and I daren't tell Jessie. She's very frail at the moment and I think it would worry her.'

'Oh dear! It's not Bertha, is it?'

'No, no! I've just told you!' He took a deep breath. 'It's Terence. I got in touch with the village school in Meddley where he went as a child. Where he told me he spent many happy years with Miss Maydon as his teacher. The same Miss Maydon is there today but—'

'But older and wiser, no doubt!'

Matty ignored the interruption. 'It seems that her version is a little different. She says Terence was only there for a few months and that his name was Downey, not Harkness and that

151

it was rather shocking that Harkness lived with the mother out of wedlock!'

'Oh dear!' Chloe tried to hide her dismay. She desperately wanted Terence to be genuine for her own selfish ends as well as for Matty. 'Is she sure of this?' she asked. 'It was years ago.'

'It's all in the records, Chloe. She had attendance records, the school's log book, the punishment book . . . Not that Terence was a naughty boy. He wasn't and he was very bright, as he claims, so he could have been a doctor, couldn't he?'

'Certainly.' Chloe tried to imagine him in a white coat, making his rounds in a hospital ward. With his warm personality and good looks, Terence would be a firm favourite with patients and nursing staff. But . . . was his charm natural or was it a screen for something less attractive? They now needed to be sure.

'But he was often absent, apparently. Poor lad,' Matty went on. He shook his head.

Chloe nodded. 'So where else did they live?'

'She didn't know that – but she also said the father had a bad reputation. Seems he was in and out of trouble with the law and she thinks that might be why they moved around so much. But the worst bit is this, Chloe – that his date of birth doesn't tally with what he told us.'

Chloe groaned. 'Which means . . . Oh Matty! Does it mean what I think it means?'

He nodded. 'He was born almost two years after I left the area. I know that for sure because although I'd said I was going to join the Navy I went up to London instead and got a job in Hatton Garden in a jeweller's shop. I remember that exactly because my landlady was very taken with me. She liked what she called "my posh voice" and she made such a fuss over my birthday. She made me a birthday cake and put thirty-eight candles on it for a laugh!' He frowned unhappily. 'I'm sixty-four now, so that birthday cake was twenty-six years ago.'

Chloe stared at him, stricken. Words deserted her.

Matty turned to her, his disappointment obvious in his mournful expression and the sagging shoulders. 'So the boy can't be mine. It's all a pack of lies.'

Chloe felt almost as bad as Matty, who looked as though the sun had gone in forever. She had been so strongly attracted to Terence and now she, too, was going to have to face unpalatable facts. 'I'm so sorry,' she told him. 'What are you going to do?'

He shrugged. 'He's not what he seems, Chloe,' Matty sighed. 'I'll have to tackle him, won't I, although I haven't got the heart for it? Then I'll have to stop seeing him . . .'

'Oh Matty! How awful! Maybe you could write to him. Save you both some embarrassment.'

He shrugged. 'And I'll have to confess to Jessie that I've been well and truly hoodwinked. I was casting around for a rich young wife for him – oh!'

'Matty! How could you?' Chloe couldn't hide her shock.

'I know, my dear,' he said. 'I'm a very self-centred man. Not at all nice. He had asked for a loan, you see, and I have no money. Jokingly I suggested a—'

'I don't want to hear about it!'

It came out a little harder than Chloe had intended and Matty's expression was now a mix of grief and guilt.

He said, 'In view of this I wonder if that's what he really meant to do with the money. Be a doctor, I mean. If he's just a young con-man he might have just scarpered with it. Spent it all on the gee-gees or drunk himself to death.'

Chloe had already forgiven him. She said, 'I don't think he's that type, Matty. He can't be all bad. No one is.'

Matty shrugged plump shoulders. 'I'd be awfully grateful if you'd break it to poor old Jessie. I can't face her.'

Chloe nodded. That wouldn't be too difficult because it merely confirmed what Jessica had suspected.

From upstairs the bell rang and they heard the nurse's footsteps as she hurried into Jessica's room.

'She's awake,' said Chloe unnecessarily. 'I'll go up in a minute and tell her. I also have to say that Adele's insisting on seeing her.'

'It never rains but it pours!' Matty regarded her with deep gloom.

Chloe stood up. 'So what *is* the truth about Terence? Is he

Cicely Downey's son? And if so, do you think she put him up to this deception?'

'Oh no! His mother's dead.'

'But is she? Maybe she isn't. Maybe he's Harkness's son and Cicely saw a chance to improve her son's fortunes . . . Would she do that, do you think? The Cicely you knew?'

Matty shook his head. 'I trusted him. He was so – so convincing. Open. So jolly *decent*. And I swear I saw a likeness, just now and then. I keep wishing I didn't know the truth.'

Chloe put a comforting arm around his shoulders. 'I know how you feel. I was getting rather too fond of him myself.'

'Oh Chloe! You must put that out of your mind now. Goodness only knows what else we'll discover.'

At that moment the nurse came down the stairs and Chloe asked her if she could speak with Jessica.

'I don't see why not. She's had a good sleep.'

Chloe glanced at Matty, who gave her the thumbs up sign. With a heavy heart she made her way upstairs.

Quickly explaining that Adele and Lucien were downstairs, Chloe made a heartfelt request that Jessica should see them but for no more than five minutes.

Jessica refused point blank. While Chloe argued, there were sounds of a scuffle and raised voices. A rush of footsteps sounded on the landing and the door was thrown open.

Adele, red-faced, rushed into the room shouted, 'Take a look at your grandson, you spiteful old woman! I am tired of your—'

There was a cry from Lucien and an angry slap from the nurse. As Jessica and Chloe stared, Adele was snatched from view.

Jessica clutched her bedjacket to her. 'What on earth is going on?' she demanded. 'That wasn't Adele, I trust.'

They heard the flow of furious French and the sound of a boy sobbing. The nurse shouted, 'And I say you *won't* go in. I'm in charge here and I say Mrs Maitland is—'

Adele cried, 'Let me go! Take your hands—'

The nurse, red-faced and breathless, appeared in the doorway and stood with arms widestretched to bar Adele's entry into

154

the room. From outside the door, Lucien began to cry in earnest and Matty was heard in the background trying to quieten them.

Chloe turned to Jessica, 'Let them come in, for heaven's sake! This is becoming ridiculous.'

Jessica cried, 'No! I won't see them. How dare they try to force a way – oh!'

Her eyes widened as the nurse, pushed violently by Adele, came flying backwards into the room. Arms flailing, she caught her heel in the rug, lost her balance and crashed to the floor. Jessica screamed as Chloe rushed to help the nurse and Adele ran into the room, pushing Lucien before her.

'This is Oliver's son!' she shouted. 'You *will* see him! You cannot deny your—' She stopped abruptly and stared at the woman in the bed. Chloe turned.

Jessica was clutching her chest and her eyes were dark with shock. 'Help me!' she croaked. 'Help me! Chloe!'

By now the nurse was on her feet and she ran to her patient with a cry of alarm. Jessica was contorted with pain and the colour had fled from her face leaving the skin paper-white. Her lips had taken on a blue tinge and it was obvious that she was in severe distress.

The nurse cried, 'Oh God! It's her heart! Get out, all of you! And send for the doctor at once.'

Chloe dragged Adele from the room and Lucien followed them out.

Chloe glared at Adele. 'This is your fault!' she told her. 'Don't you dare go back into that room. Either of you.' She raced downstairs and out into the back garden, where Binns was raking out weeds from the vegetable garden and peacefully minding his own business. Minutes later he was on his way to the barn to collect the trap while Chloe went in search of the horse, which was grazing in the paddock. As soon as Binns was on his way to the doctor she returned to the house, where she found Adele in the hallway with her arm round her son. Lucien was clinging to his mother, his face pressed against her, his small shoulders shaking with sobs.

Matty appeared from the drawing room and Chloe told him

what had happened but warned him against going up to Jessica until the doctor had seen her.

He hesitated. 'I'll ask the nurse if I may go in.'

As he made his way upstairs Adele turned to Chloe. 'I am sorry. It was wrong of me but . . .' She paused and gave her son a shake. 'Stop these tears, Lucien. Be a man.'

'He's only a child,' Chloe protested. 'He was frightened and I'm not surprised!' Seeing no real remorse in Adele's eyes, she snapped, 'You had no right to push that nurse. Who do you think you are?'

'I'm the mother of Oliver's child. I have a right—'

'You have no right to behave so badly.'

'I have made the apology.'

Lucien peeped nervously from the shelter of his mother's skirts and Chloe choked back further reproaches. He had suffered enough, poor child, she thought and smiled at him.

Matty came back downstairs. 'She's very poorly,' he whispered. 'I couldn't speak to her. Nurse is furious. No one has ever treated her like that. She says it was an assault.' He looked at Adele and for once his geniality had deserted him. 'She says that if Jessie dies she will tell the police it was your fault!'

Adele drew back, shocked into silence. 'Mine?'

Chloe stammered, 'If Jessica *dies*? She's not going to die, surely!'

Matty regarded her soberly. 'It seems possible . . .' He swallowed. 'Where the devil is that wretched doctor?' He looked at Lucien and suddenly managed a faint smile. 'Now then, little man. Shall we go and find Olivia? Would you like to play with her on the see-saw? Or we could play bat and ball.' He held out his hand and Lucien glanced at his mother.

'Go then,' she said. 'Play with your stepsister.'

When they had gone Chloe said, 'We had better wait in the drawing room,' and led the way. She then rang for Mrs Letts, told her what had happened and asked for a tray of tea. Angry as she was with Adele and shocked by her behaviour, she was nevertheless partly in sympathy with the woman's cause. Jessica should see the boy. If she did, she would see the likeness and would love him. She sat down on the sofa but Adele remained standing, her mouth a tight line, her face pale.

156

For a while she said nothing but then she sat down abruptly opposite Chloe.

'You think I have killed her.' The statement was made in a hostile way but Chloe detected fear behind the façade.

'Let's hope not,' she said.

'I do not kill anyone in my whole life! She was ill already. You said so yourself.'

'She certainly wasn't at all strong. That's why we were supposed to keep her calm.'

Adele's fingers fumbled nervously with the folds of her skirt. 'She will not die. The police will not come.'

'I hope you're right.' Chloe began to feel sorry for her. 'I don't think she'll die,' she said and crossed her fingers.

'I shall pray for her.' Adele glanced up. 'Oh! Lucien is a Roman Catholic,' she said. 'You must always remember that.'

'I don't think he will be staying here.'

Adele gave her an enigmatic look but said nothing.

Mrs Letts brought in a pot of tea and a plate of raspberry buns and Adele ate hungrily. She had had a cooked breakfast not so long ago, Chloe reflected in amazement as Adele ate three buns in quick succession.

Then Adele said, 'Lucien has a bath once a week. Every Saturday morning.'

'I've told you, Adele – he won't be staying. Especially after what has just happened.'

Before Adele could reply, a rattle of wheels announced Binns' return with the doctor.

Matty came in and reported that Alice was reading to the two children.

Chloe, Adele and Matty waited in silence for the doctor's verdict and when he came back downstairs they rose to their feet as one. His expression was grim and he avoided looking anyone straight in the eye by fumbling in his doctor's bag. When he had closed it he straightened up.

Matty asked, 'How is she?'

'It's not looking good,' he announced, dabbing his face with a handkerchief. 'I'm afraid it was a severe attack and it has left her very weak indeed. Mrs Maitland is too ill to be moved, so she must be nursed in situ. She must be closely watched around the clock.' He glanced at Adele. 'The nurse tells me she had a very bad shock which brought on the attack.'

Adele swallowed hard. 'Why look at me? I did nothing wrong. Yes, I shouted at her. To make her listen. That is all. I am not to blame.'

Chloe's sympathy for her vanished at this outburst. 'How can you say that? You forced your way in to her room. You struggled with the nurse and pushed her over! You were very angry and you frightened Mrs Maitland. It was appalling behaviour.'

Adele's small chin jutted. 'You all want to blame me but it was not my fault.' Her voice began to falter and there were tears in her eyes. 'She should have agreed to see me. She should have—'

Matty raised a hand and she fell silent. He asked, 'Is the poor old thing going to survive this, Doctor? I'd like you to speak freely. What are her chances?'

The doctor pursed his lips, considering his answer. 'Speak freely, you say? Then I would have to say "No". I rather doubt it. It is a major setback and she has so little stamina. But . . . stranger things have happened. Love and tender care can work miracles – if the will is there.'

Matty sat down heavily and covered his face with his hands. Chloe, badly shaken by the verdict, patted his shoulder.

Adele faced them all, white faced. 'So . . . you will tell the police I killed her?'

Matty said, 'We'll simply give them the facts. You didn't mean to harm her so . . .' He pulled a handkerchief from his pocket and dabbed his eyes. 'Poor old Jessie! Oh Lord. Don't let her die!'

Adele glanced at the doctor who shrugged. 'I shall give the facts as I see them, Miss Dupres, but I don't think you should worry on that score.'

'You *think* I shouldn't worry.' Her lips moved soundlessly and she crossed herself.

The doctor turned to Chloe. 'And how is Bertha's son, Robert?'

'He's doing well, thank you. Slow but sure, I believe.'

The doctor turned to Matty. 'Don't let Mrs Maitland know how ill she is. She needs to believe she will recover.'

Minutes later he had gone and they were left to come to terms with the bad news, each in their own respective way.

Chloe settled Adele and her son in the trap and they set off for home in an uneasy silence. The horse was inclined to be lazy and took advantage of Chloe's distraction to trot along at a leisurely pace. Lucien watched his mother anxiously while Adele stared straight ahead with a show of bravado that did not convince Chloe. She felt that she ought to say something conciliatory but she was very angry with Adele and couldn't trust herself to speak calmly. Whatever Adele might choose to believe she had directly brought about Jessica's heart attack – an attack which might well prove fatal. Too ill to be moved to the hospital. That sounded ominous. As did the round-the-clock nursing she was going to need. Presumably the nurse would need some relief from her duties, which meant they would need to bring in a night nurse. It was too much to expect Bertha to cope with so much when she had scarcely recovered from the birth of her child.

Chloe tried to imagine Fairfields without Jessica and felt a chill of despair at the thought. Was there some kind of curse on the place? First Oliver was killed and now this bizarre dispute between Adele and Jessica might result in another death. Suddenly she realized that Lucien was crying softly. Perhaps he understood that his mother was out of favour.

She heard herself say, 'You weren't entirely to blame, Adele.'

Adele refused to be comforted. 'That is what you say now. What will you say if she dies? You will tell the police. That nurse! Hah!' She glanced at Lucien. 'Stop that noise at once. Be a man, Lucien. Find your handkerchief. What would your *grandmère* say if she could see you?'

Chloe said 'He's upset. You shouldn't punish him.'

'I don't punish him. I teach him. My mother is right. His tears flow too easily.'

Chloe said nothing but she was heartily glad when they

159

reached the farm. Jack opened the door to them and a new puppy danced around his heels.

'Oh look!' cried Lucien, his tears forgotten.

He jumped down into Jack's outstretched arms and for a moment Chloe was surprised by a frisson of envy. There were so many times when she missed the reassuring bear hugs that had been Jeff's way of showing his affection for her. She now found herself wondering how it would be to be greeted that way by Jack Bourne.

Briefly she explained what had happened, omitting the ugly scene which had brought on the attack.

'I would like to alert Bertha,' she told him as Adele alighted and hurried into the house.

'Of course you must,' he agreed. 'And on the way back would you call in at Bourne Farm and ask if I can borrow the spare trough? Ours has sprung a leak. And see . . .' He hesitated. 'And make sure everything is all right there.'

Chloe blinked. 'All right? In what way? Is someone ill?'

'No. Not exactly. That is, Cathy is in a bit of a state. Or was. She came over earlier and . . . Well, I'd just like to know she's recovered.'

Looking down into his face, Chloe could see real concern. 'Wouldn't you prefer to go?' she asked. 'Now that you have the trap.'

'No. I can't.' He looked away then back again. 'It might make matters worse if I go. I can't explain . . . But Patrick will lift the trough into the trap for you. Just make sure everything is . . . as usual. If you would, please.'

'Of course I will.' She hoped she was hiding her curiosity. She glanced down at Lucien, who was playing with the puppy while Jude looked on with a bored expression. She said, 'It has been rather disastrous at Fairfield House but I'll tell you about it later.'

Nine

Chloe found Bertha in the garden with Robert in his pram nearby. She was arranging newly ironed clothes on a wooden airer to take advantage of the sunshine. Her smile of welcome faded as she saw Chloe's expression and she listened in horrified silence to Chloe's account.

'Poor Mama! Oh, I could strangle that wretched Adele! What a little madam she's turned out to be! I'll go across as soon as George returns, then I can leave Robert here with him. Oh Chloe! You don't think she really *will* die, do you?'

'I think she might, Bertha. I'm so sorry.'

'We'll have to see that she doesn't,' Bertha replied. 'Thank heavens for the nurse – but as you say we shall need to hire a night nurse. What a good thing we are moving back into Fairfields. We were planning to go in a week or two but we can move in tomorrow and sort everything out later. We have a tenant for the cottage and—' She stopped and took a deep breath. 'Poor Mama! She must be so frightened.' She finished arranging the clothes and carried the empty basket back into the house while Chloe pushed the pram.

Robert was asleep and Chloe thought regretfully that now he and Olivia would probably grow up unaware of Lucien's existence. Not that she could expect Bertha to mind very much. At present her son was the heir to Fairfields. Oliver's son, if legitimized, would have had prior claim. Certainly Jessica might have left him a share of what remained of the estate. Bertha had never spoken of this but Chloe felt sure she must be aware of the ramifications. She would also realize that since Oliver was dead it could not be proved that he was the boy's father.

Half an hour later Chloe reached Bourne Farm and pulled

161

up at the front door. It was suspiciously quiet and she sighed with relief. There was no one at home. To make sure she went round to the back but there was no sign of life. The back door was open but that meant very little. Perhaps Cathy was dealing with the bees. Chloe decided not to investigate that. She had a deep mistrust of bees and had heard horror stories of people dying from bee stings.

She stepped into the kitchen, uneasily aware that if Cathy appeared she would probably accuse her of spying!

'Cathy? Adam?' She didn't want to meet Patrick.

A sound from above made her look up.

'Who's down there?'

It was Adam's voice. She called, 'It's me. Mrs Tyler.'

After a pause he said. 'You'd better come on up!'

She frowned. There was something odd about his voice.

She made her way up the curving stairs and was instantly aware of the difference in quality between Patrick's farmhouse and Jack's. There was a polished wood staircase and well-framed pictures hung on the walls.

Adam appeared suddenly in the doorway of one of the rooms at the far end of the landing. He was holding a sheet of paper in his hand. He said, 'She's gone. Ma's gone.'

'Gone where?'

'I don't know. It's because of my father.' He sounded dazed and Chloe followed him into the large bedroom. There was a large bed with brass rails top and bottom. A lovingly made patchwork quilt in jewel colours almost glowed in the beam of sun that lay across it. There were flowers on the table by the window and a faint smell of lavender polish.

'Look!' He opened the door of a mahogany wardrobe and Chloe saw that it was full. 'I came to see if she'd taken any clothes with her but I don't think she has. I saw her at breakfast and she seemed a bit quiet. Nothing was said.'

Chloe swallowed nervously. Was this what Jack had meant? Had he known or suspected that Cathy would do something desperate? If so, why on earth hadn't he warned her? On reflection, he may have been reluctant to break Cathy's trust. She may have made him promise that he would say nothing.

Adam thrust the note into her hand and sat down on the bed.

'You opened your father's letter?'

'It wasn't stuck down. And there's a note for me.'

'So has he seen it?'

'I don't think so. Knowing him, he'd have ripped it to pieces. Read it.'

'I don't think I should.'

'Read it, for God's sake!' He covered his face with his hands for a long moment then looked up. 'If I could find her it's not too late. She could come back. Pa needn't even see the letter.'

Reluctantly Chloe read the short letter.

Dear Adam, Please forgive me. I love you,
Your loving Ma.

A cold shiver ran through Chloe's body. 'She's left home.'

He nodded. 'It's about Uncle Jack – but she says in my father's letter she wishes she'd never seen either of them. I know she said she was going to leave him but I didn't quite believe it. Is she with Uncle Jack?'

His eyes were full of anguish and Chloe longed to comfort him but was there time?

'No. I've just come from there. Your uncle sent me over to see that everything was all right here. He said your mother had called in and was very upset.'

His confusion deepened. 'Maybe Ma and Uncle Jack had a row – although he's never said a cross word to her before . . . Oh Hell! . . . Sorry. I can't think where she'd go. Unless to her parents. I could telephone them but that will mean telling them what's happened and if we get her back the fewer people who know . . .'

Chloe read the note again. A coldness had settled in the pit of her stomach. There was no mention in either letter of where she was going nor any suggestion that she would get in touch eventually. Not even a few words to reassure her son. If Cathy simply vanished would the family have to inform the police? Chloe could imagine how Patrick would react to that idea.

Speak of the devil, she thought, as footsteps sounded outside and they heard Patrick enter the kitchen.

'Adam? You there?' He sounded cheerful, thought Chloe. He hasn't seen the letter.

Adam snatched the note from her and stuffed it into his pocket. 'I'm up here.'

Chloe rolled her eyes. How would it look to Patrick, to find the two of them in the bedroom. She and Adam stared at each other in panic but it was too late to hide. Too late even to concoct an innocent explanation for why they were together in Patrick's bedroom. Patrick was coming upstairs. He came into the room and his mouth fell open in shock.

Chloe said, 'It isn't the way it looks, Mr Bourne.' Even to her own ears it sounded like a feeble excuse.

'You two?' A dull flush rose in Patrick's face and anger flared in his eyes. He glanced toward the bed and Chloe felt a flash of resentment. How dare he imagine that she and his son had been caught in a compromising situation? She opened her mouth to protest but caution won and she remained silent. Maybe the less said the better.

'You and her?' He glared at Adam.

Adam said, 'Pa, it's not . . . that is, it's nothing between us. I swear it.'

Patrick remained firmly in the doorway, blocking any possible escape. He looked at his son. 'If I find out there is I'll knock your bloody head off!'

Chloe knew suddenly that this encounter could end in serious trouble.

Patrick turned to her. 'Say something, you stupid woman!'

'She's not doing anything wrong!' cried Adam. 'Leave Mrs Tyler out of this!'

Chloe stepped forward. 'Adam's telling the truth. I came over with a message from your brother and Adam was up here. That's all. Your brother wants to borrow—'

'My brother! Oh, he's your alibi, is he? You must think I'm daft. I've seen you look at him. Don't think I don't know what's going on over there!'

'Pa! You're wrong. Uncle Jack did send her but . . .'

Chloe looked at him unwilling to influence him. Personally, she thought they would have to show Patrick the letter but that was for Adam to decide. She was not going to meddle. Hopefully she need not become involved. She wondered whether Jack had known that Cathy was threatening to leave home.

Patrick was breathing rapidly and Chloe was aware of a moment's compassion. He reminded her of a large, dull animal that was being baited.

He looked at his son. 'If you've laid a finger on Mrs Tyler I'll—'

'Oh, don't talk such nonsense!' Chloe gave him a withering look. 'And I haven't tried to seduce your son, so please stop these wild accusations. They make you look foolish.'

'Not as foolish as you two look,' he shouted, 'hiding in the bedroom with guilt written all over you!' To Adam he said, 'We'll see what your mother has to say about this. Don't think you've heard the last of it. Maybe she'll get the truth out of you.' He turned to Chloe. 'She was right about you. She's said all along you're—'

Adam's fist flashed out but Patrick moved fast and it struck a glancing blow. Patrick lunged forward with a roar but Chloe rushed between them.

'Show him the letter, Adam!' she cried. 'This has to stop. He has to know.'

Patrick, about to return Adam's blow, drew back abruptly. 'I have to know what?'

Silently Adam passed him the letter and they watched him read it. As the full meaning registered, all the anger vanished and Patrick staggered to the bed and collapsed on to it, ashen faced and trembling. Adam explained that he had been checking the wardrobe for Cathy's clothes.

After what seemed an interminable interval, Patrick raised his eyes to meet Chloe. 'D'you know where she's gone? Is that why you came?'

Chloe told him again that Jack had asked her to bring a message about the trough.

Patrick nodded. 'Adam'll hoist it into the trap for you.'

'Thank you.'

Adam said, 'Blow the trough, Pa. What's happened to make Ma go off like this?'

'Don't ask me. You know how moody she can be.'

165

'I know you two don't get on on too well but she's never gone off like this without a word. Suppose she doesn't come back? What then?'

'She'll come back. Your mother knows which side her bread's buttered . . . I've given that woman everything,' he muttered. 'She only had to ask. What more can I do?' He rubbed at his hair until it stood up in spikes.

Adam turned to the window. 'You didn't make her happy. Money isn't everything.'

'Oh, and you'd know all about that, would you?' He glared at his son's back.

Chloe, exhausted by the tension, decided it was time to go. 'Well, if someone will help with the trough I'll be getting back. I have to get tea for all of us.'

'All of you?'

'We have friends of the Maitlands staying with us. Which reminds me, Mrs Maitland has had a heart attack and is very ill.'

'I'm sorry,' Adam told her. 'I know you're very fond of the old lady.'

Patrick pushed himself upright and led the way in silence to a small shed and he and Adam swung a small but newish trough into the rear of the pony trap.

Chloe said quietly, 'Shall I tell your brother what's happened?'

Patrick hesitated. 'And if I say no? You'll tell him anyway, won't you?'

'Yes. I think he should know. He might be able to help.'

'How's that then? What can he do?'

'You might want to go out and look for her – if it get's late.'

'What? Go traipsing round in the dark looking for her? She knows where she lives. She can find her own way home when she's good and ready.'

'Mr Bourne . . . your wife may have had an accident. She may be regretting leaving but not be able—'

Patrick's eyes narrowed. 'It's not your damned business, is it, Mrs Tyler? It's family business and you aren't family. So stop poking your nose in where—'

Adam said, 'Shut up, Pa. You're making things worse. Mrs Tyler's right. If Ma's not back by morning I'm going to the police and you can't stop me.'

'She'll be back and I'll be waiting for her.'

'You'll be drinking, you mean. Getting drunk, so that if she does come back you'll be in no—'

'That's enough lip from you. I don't need a lecture from my son. She was always too soft on you but she couldn't see it.'

Chloe had had enough. To Adam she said, 'Pop over and let us know if there's any news – or if there's anything we can do.'

'Thanks.'

He walked with her for a few yards until he was out of his father's hearing. His handsome face was etched with worry. 'You can see what he's like,' he said. 'He'll start drinking now. If Ma does come back there'll be a Godalmighty row!'

'Maybe.' She climbed up into the driving seat and picked up the reins. The horse shook his head and snorted. 'Look, Adam, it's hard for you but they'll have to sort things out for themselves. It's not your responsibility.'

'But how can I sleep, wondering where she is? She may have had a breakdown. Or been run over or lost her memory. I want to go out and look for her but I don't know where to start.'

'And I don't know what to say?' Chloe sighed. 'Try not to worry. Your father's right. She'll probably come back. Maybe she's decided to teach him a lesson. Give him a fright.'

He seized on the idea. 'And that's why she hasn't taken any clothes.'

'Of course!' Chloe reached down and he gripped her hand fiercely.

He said, 'She'll come back.'

Chloe smiled. 'You know where we are if you want us.' She hesitated. 'Would it help if your uncle came across?'

He shook his head. 'Probably not.'

As Chloe urged the horse into a trot she knew that in spite of their confident words, they both had terrible doubts.

Later that evening Matty knocked on the door of Jessica's room. The nurse opened it. She looked, as always, entirely

167

professional. Her uniform was immaculate, the hair tucked neatly beneath the flowing white kerchief that covered her head. She smiled, putting a warning finger to her lips.

'I need to talk to Mrs Maitland,' Matty whispered.

'I really don't advise it, Mr Orme. She needs to be kept very quiet.'

'Is she awake?'

'Not quite awake. She is aware but the medicine keeps her in a drowsy state. Difficult to know sometimes just how much she understands.'

Still Matty lingered. 'How would it be if you popped down to the kitchen for a quarter of an hour for a bit of a chat and a cup of tea while I sit with her.'

'We-ell . . . that is rather tempting.' She glanced back towards her patient. 'As long as you promise to call me at once if there's any need.'

'I promise.'

'I must be back at my post when Nurse Allan arrives.'

Matty nodded, understanding her caution. The two nurses were in undeclared competition with each other as to which of them performed her duties best. The rivalry was obvious from the moment they first met. Nurse Allan came in at nine p.m. and left at seven in the morning after she had eaten breakfast in the kitchen. During the meal she uttered a small criticism of 'the day nurse'. As soon as she had left the house her rival made her way into the kitchen to grumble about the state of the bedroom and the higgledy-piggledy appearance of the patient.

Now, Matty walked softly across the floor to take his seat beside the bed. On the table he saw a glass of lemon barley water, various medicines and pills and a bible. Perhaps he should ask the vicar to call in and see her. At Icklesham church Albert was including Jessica in their prayers and so far it was working, thought Matty, because she hadn't died but surely a personal visit could do no harm. He had never been a regular churchgoer but now he was reconsidering his position on God and all things holy. Perhaps he would go along one evening and add his prayers to those of the congregation. Not that the idea appealed to him. All that incense and he never could remember the responses. He'd been a choirboy once in the far distant past but had been thrown out for fighting in the graveyard.

He looked at Jessica as she lay against the white pillows with her mouth slightly open. Her eyes were shut and her skin looked paper-thin.

Matty tried to remember her as a child. He had been so jealous when she was born and he had been forced to share his mother's affections with a new baby as well as a new husband. Later the baby sister had adored her big brother and he had blossomed in the warmth of her adoration. It was only much later that the scales fell from Jessica's eyes and she saw him for what he was.

'It's Matty here, old thing,' he told her with a smile. 'Your big brother! Just you and me. I've got rid of Nursie.'

By the time she was a grown woman she had become aware of his faults. Unambitious, lazy, sparing with the truth when it suited him, irresponsible. The list was endless.

'But you never disliked me, Jessie.'

She'd tried to rally him and he hadn't wanted to be rallied. She'd told him that somewhere inside the waster there was a great man wanting to get out – but he had never been convinced. He didn't want to be a great man. He wanted to do as little as possible.

'I've got it wrong again, old thing,' he told her, keeping his voice low. 'Made a fool of myself over young Terence and now I know he's nothing. Not to me, anyway. You were right as usual. He's lied to me, that's the crux of the matter. Lied to all of us but mostly me. Because I wanted to believe him . . .' He shrugged, then leaned forward, peering into Jessica's face. Had she heard any of this he wondered. *Was* she asleep? She wasn't snoring but then snoring wasn't ladylike, so it was unlikely she ever did such a thing.

Not that lies were so terrible, he reflected. He'd told a few himself along the way and he could understand the temptation for Terence. 'But I never claimed to be anyone's son, Jessie. I never caused heartbreak . . . Well. Maybe once or twice . . . But he was born too late to have been my son and worse still, he lied for money. Yes, I know it all now. I had a telephone call just after lunch. Guess who?' he sighed heavily. 'Cicely

Downey! The boy's mother. Not dead as we were led to believe but very much alive and demanding to speak to her son.'

Cicely had been most insistent. 'I know he's there. He gave me this number and said he'd be living there for a few months. If he's not there then I want to speak to Matthew Orme.'

'He's in London as far as I know.'

He hadn't wanted her to know who he was.

'Is that you, Matty?'

Matty had remained silent, his mind racing.

'It *is* you, Matty! I never forget a voice.'

He tried to imagine Cicely Downey, recently returned from the grave and frowned at the picture this created.

'I know it's you, Matty. I want to speak to my son . . . to our son.'

'He's not here.' With a tremendous effort Matty had found his courage and went on quickly. 'He said you were dead. He said he was my son but he isn't. Can't be. Not possible. I've checked up on him.'

'Checked up? On your own son?'

'He's not mine, Cicely. The dates don't tally. Not by a mile.'

Long silence. Then she said, 'Worth a try, wasn't it?' And hung up on him.

Suddenly Jessica opened her eyes. She looked at him and smiled. 'No fool like an old fool!' she whispered.

He blinked foolishly. 'I thought you were dozing.'

'I know you did . . . I'm sorry, Matty. About the boy.' Her voice was very faint and he had to lean forward to catch the words. 'Was it money, Matty? That he was after?'

'He said he wanted to be a doctor. I wanted to help him. To make up for . . . Well . . . You know what I mean.' He patted her hand. 'I didn't want to tell you. Mustn't upset you, you see. Doc's orders and Nursie said—'

'I already knew. That first time I collapsed. It was her. On the telephone. I knew then that he was lying . . . didn't know how to tell you.'

'I don't know what to do now.' He brushed his eyes hastily. Mustn't cry. That would never do. 'He was a nice lad. At least I thought—'

'Let him go, Matty dear.' She closed her eyes wearily but eventually opened them again. 'Write to him in London . . . If he telephones . . . tell him the truth. That you know.'

'I will. Yes . . . I'll say it was a good try.' He swallowed and stood up. He felt better now. So the old dear had known all along. Amazing woman, Jessie.

He said humbly, 'You're not going to die old thing, are you?'

She gave a low throaty chuckle. 'No, Matty . . . not going to die.'

He leaned down and kissed her and as he tiptoed from the room his lips moved silently as he thanked God. Now he needn't go to church.

Chloe awoke next morning from a strange dream. She had been trying to run away from something but unseen hands were pulling her back. She gave a little cry of fear and opened her eyes. In the gloom of the pre-dawn she saw Lucien standing by the bed, tugging the counterpane.

'Lucien!' She smiled as she struggled into a sitting position. 'What is it, dear?'

'*Où est Maman?*' His eyes pleaded with her.

Chloe frowned. She had almost no understanding of French. 'Speak English, please, Lucien.'

'Maman. Where is Maman?'

'Where is your Mama? I expect she's gone downstairs. Wait. I'll light a candle.' By its flickering light, Chloe glanced at the clock, assuming that she had overslept but it was only quarter past five. She slid out of bed and took his hand. He had dressed himself after a fashion and his shoes were on the wrong feet. 'Mama will still be in bed, fast asleep. You must go back to bed.'

In the guest room she had a surprise. It seemed that Adele *was* already up and about and her bed had been made. Perhaps she was ill – or had gone downstairs to . . . to do what?

'I want Maman,' Lucien wailed and his face crumpled.

'We'll find her. Come along.' They went downstairs to find the kitchen empty. She wondered about Jack. Was he still upstairs or had he and Adele gone somewhere together? To the doctor? Her anxiety was mounting. Remembering the drama of the previous day, Chloe wondered if it was anything to do with Cathy. But how could it be? She could see no possible connection.

She crouched beside Lucien and put her arms around him. 'Don't cry, little one. We'll find—'

Jack's voice interrupted her. 'What's going on? I thought we had burglars!'

He stood frowning at the bottom of the stairs. He had pulled on a shirt and trousers but was barefooted. Chloe explained quickly that Adele was missing.

He frowned. 'Do you think she's gone back to Fairfields for a last try?'

'I don't know what to think.' She was uncomfortably aware that she was still in her nightdress and Jack was staring at her.

'Maman . . .' Lucien was crying in earnest now and Jack and Chloe regarded him with dismay.

Jack said, 'Let's have an early breakfast – when you've had time to dress.'

'At half past five?'

He shrugged. 'Can you suggest something better? Adele might have gone for a walk and will turn up later.'

Chloe nodded. He was right. What else was there to do? Lucien would never go back to sleep now that he knew his mother was missing.

Jack went to the back door and let Jude and the puppy in and at once the boy's face was wreathed in smiles as he bent to play with them.

Jack said, 'That reminds me. I heard Jude barking earlier and thought it must be a fox. Probably it was Adele leaving the house.'

Upstairs, as she washed hurriedly and dressed, Chloe thought long and hard. What on earth was happening? First Cathy made an exit and now Adele had wandered off. She shook her head despairingly as she buttoned her blouse and laced her shoes. Back in the kitchen she cooked enough for four but there was still no sign of Adele and the three of them ate their food in a subdued mood.

Suddenly, however, Jude rushed barking towards the back door and Chloe glanced out of the window to see a figure on a bicycle. Chloe followed Lucien outside and found him admiring both the vehicle and its rider – a boy of about thirteen with his cap on sideways. He handed her a folded sheet of paper. 'For Mrs Maitland,' he announced. 'Is that you, missus? She said you'd give me a sixpence.'

'Sixpence? What cheek!' cried Chloe. 'And Mrs Maitland doesn't live here. She lives at Fairfield House in Icklesham.'

'This is where she sent me. She said Monkswell Farm as clear as day and I'm not going anywhere else. So where's me sixpence?'

'I won't give you sixpence.'

He glared at her. 'Then you can't have the letter!'

'It's not my letter, I tell you. It's—' She stopped. She would have to accept the letter and pass it on to Bertha. She already had a nasty suspicion that she knew the identity of the sender. 'You must make do with threepence.'

The boy took it so willingly that Chloe wondered if he had actually inflated the promised reward – or even invented it.

Lucien had picked up the puppy and now held it out shyly to show the boy.

He said, 'Yeah. Nice little dog,' and rode off whistling.

Chloe looked at the paper. Guiltily she read it twice then hurried inside to show Jack.

Dear Mrs Maitland, I have gone back to Paris. Lucien is your grandson and a good boy. You must care for him as I cannot. If you die I am sorry but I did not kill you. The police will not find me. Lucien must be an English gentleman but I beg you do not let him forget me. Tell him many times that I love him. Yours gratefully, Adele Dupres

He said, 'It's unbelievable! The nerve!' He glanced out at Lucien, who was rolling with the puppy. 'How could she leave him like this? Her only child. Hasn't she even said goodbye to him?'

Chloe sat down, close to tears. 'How do we tell him?' She

tried to imagine a kind way to explain that he might never see his mother again.

Jack sat opposite her. 'I think we should pretend for the moment that she has gone to London and will be coming back. Let him get used to being without her. Then . . . We'll have to think of something. Meanwhile he can stay with us if the Maitlands won't have him.'

'Maybe Adele will miss him so much she will change her mind and come back for him.'

Jack raised his eyebrows. 'You really think so?'

'No. Not really. Maybe Bertha and George would take him in for a short time. But then again, here on the farm he has plenty to amuse him.'

He smiled suddenly. 'Poor Chloe. Are you beginning to wish you'd stayed in America?'

'It has crossed my mind,' she laughed but then abruptly was sober again. 'I wonder whether Cathy is back.'

'I expect so. If she is I hope Patrick is properly grateful. He doesn't deserve her. I'm going up there this morning. I can't pretend I don't know what's happening. If I'm not welcome there I'll be back.'

Chloe jumped to her feet. 'I'll wash up the breakfast things and then, if I may, I'd like to take this letter to Fairfields. I'll take Lucien with me. I'll show the letter to Matty and he can talk it over with Bertha. I think Bertha and George will be moving in to Fairfields today or tomorrow, which will make life easier for all of them.'

Jack set off in the direction of his brother's farm with a heavy heart and with no idea what sort of reception he would receive. If Cathy were there, he would leave them to it. Better not to confuse the issue. If she had not returned Patrick might be willing to talk. He would be in a blue funk at the prospect of contacting the police. The local men drank with him on occasions in the Star and he would not want them to know he had a runaway wife.

'Serve you right, you old bugger!' he muttered as he climbed the first stile but he knew that Cathy's desperation was due in part to his own refusal to take her away from Patrick. He couldn't repress the feeling that he was responsible and the deep sense of guilt weighed heavily on him.

The sheep hurried towards him from the far corner of the field, their black faces inscrutable, then veered away as they caught sight of Jude. Jack ignored them, his mind full of nameless horrors. Suppose Cathy had gone forever. They might never see her again; might never know what became of her . . . If only he hadn't been so blunt with her, but at the time it had seemed the right thing to do. He thought now that he had handled the matter badly and had forced Cathy to take this action – whatever it was.

With some relief, he saw a figure in the distance and recognized his nephew. It was Adam. Jack waved his arm in greeting. At least he would get some news. His relief was shortlived, however, for, as Adam drew closer, Jack could see his expression and knew that he was going to hear bad news.

'She hasn't come home,' Adam told him breathlessly. 'Pa went on a bender and is completely hungover. Can't get a word out of him so I don't know what to do. I was coming over to you.'

'You look terrible.'

Adam's eyes were darkly shadowed and his hair was dishevelled.

'So do you,' he said. 'I doubt we got much sleep last night. I didn't go to bed but sat downstairs waiting. I kept thinking I heard footsteps and went rushing out but – nothing.'

Adam went on. 'We'll have to go to the police – but Pa will be livid when he comes round and finds out.'

'Damnation!' Jack ran fingers through his hair. The day had started badly but it was getting worse and he knew there was more to come. His brother would wake in a foul mood and it would be impossible to talk to him. 'Have you thought about Cathy's parents? She might be there.'

'Wouldn't they have let us know?'

'You could get over there and find out. I'll rouse up Patrick and get some hot tea into him. Then we'll decide what to do next.' He was trying not to let Adam see how agitated he was. He had been so hopeful that Cathy would have turned up by

175

this time and his thoughts lurched from one possible scenario to another.

Adam said, 'I think she must have wandered off and then got amnesia, so she doesn't remember her name or where she lives. That does happen sometimes. The police may have found her – or she might be in the hospital.'

Or on a train going anywhere but Bourne Farm, thought Jack, but he nodded. No point in alarming Adam further. The lad had enough to cope with.

They set off again in opposite directions and Jack reached his brother's farm and let himself into the kitchen.

'Patrick! It's me – Jack!'

There was no answer but he hadn't really expected one. He found his brother sprawled across the bed and shook him roughly.

'Wake up! There's a lot to be done. Wake *up*!' He shook him repeatedly until Patrick opened bleary eyes and mumbled something unintelligible, then left him while he went downstairs and made some strong tea. Patrick stumbled down the stairs, missed his footing and fell headlong. A few oaths followed, which told Jack he wasn't seriously hurt, so he let him pick himself up. He appeared in the kitchen with one hand to his head and the other to his back.

'Christ, Jack!' he muttered thickly. 'I feel like death! What the hell are you doing here?'

Briefly, Jack reminded him of the previous day's events and was pleased to see his brother's face fall.

Scowling, Patrick muttered, 'Silly cow!' He sank on to a chair with a loud groan and rested his elbows on the table. With his head in his hands he muttered, 'She'll be back.'

'I don't think so.'

Patrick raised his head. 'What do you know about it? She's my wife, remember.' He rolled his eyes. 'O-oh! My back! I might have broken my ruddy neck on those stairs!'

Jack put a mug of tea down in front of him and sat close. 'Listen, Patrick. Cathy's been out all night. It doesn't look good. I think we should make a quick call to the local hospital and see if Cathy's been admitted. She may have had an accident and just maybe we can keep the police out of this.'

Patrick clasped his mug of tea with trembling hands. He sipped in silence for a moment or two and then nodded. 'You do it, Jack. I'm not up to it.'

'She's your wife. Remember? The hospital will expect the husband to—'

'Say you're me.'

'No . . . If you want her back you'll have to—'

'But do I? Maybe I don't. Not after what she's put me through.'

'She wouldn't have gone if you'd made her happy! Those other women – you really think she didn't know? The whole damned village knew. You can bet someone told her.'

Patrick's face flamed and he struggled to his feet. 'Don't you come here preaching to me, Jackie boy! You get out of here!' He pointed to the door. 'D'you hear me? Get out before I throw you . . . Oh Jesus!' Clutching his head, he sat down again and began to cry.

Jack watched him, feeling no compassion. The situation was too familiar. He remembered a day at school when he was nine and Patrick was nearly eleven and had been caught behind the school shed with one of the younger girls and the headmistress had caned him. Ten strokes on each hand. The two brothers had trailed home followed by the jeers of the other children. Jack had never forgotten the feeling of shame that he had felt. The big brother in disgrace and weeping publicly.

Ignoring Patrick's threat, he went to the telephone and asked the operator for the local hospital. When she put him through he chose his words carefully.

'Do you have any patients who came in yesterday or overnight.'

'I'll check for you but I don't think so . . . No. No one at all. Is anything—?'

Jack hung up. 'The answer's no. Thank God for that. She's not hurt.'

'So what now?'

'Adam's gone over to her parents.'

'That poor kid! What sort of mother would put her son through this sort of caper?'

Jack bit back a caustic reply. 'A mother who was feeling desperate?' he suggested.

'That's right. Take her side against mine. You probably put her up to this. You and your housekeeper. She was jealous. You knew that, did you? Thought her faithful old Jack had deserted her! So if she's upset it's your fault as well as mine.'

Stung by the accusation, Jack stood up. 'I'm going home. You don't want my help – fine! You sort out your own mess, Patrick.'

'I will! I don't need your help . . . But what can I do?'

'I'd go to the police and ask their advice.'

'Oh! I've done something to my back!' He groaned. 'I can't turn properly. It's ruddy agony!'

Jack hesitated. Patrick needed him but Jack knew his brother would only talk to the police as a last resort. Best to let *him* decide when that point had been reached.

'I'm off home then,' he announced. 'I'll be mending hurdles if you need me.'

Chloe wrote in her diary:

Wednesday May 8 – What a day this has been and thank heavens it's over at last. I am so tired with worry yet I doubt if I shall sleep tonight. This morning Adele left – and without Lucien. The poor mite is so bewildered but is trying so hard to be brave. He wants his Maman but the truth is he may never see her again. Lord knows what will become of him. I have spoken to Bertha but she refuses even to consider bringing him up at Fairfields. At least he is reasonably happy here. He is afraid to sleep alone in that big room, so for the time being we have used two screens and brought his bed into a corner of my room so that he knows I am nearby. Jack is wonderful with him. Of course, when Adele departed she left no payment for their bed and board, so my clever scheme to help Jack has come to nothing but so far he hasn't reproached me.

Cathy is still missing and Jack and Patrick are almost at each other's throats. Adam is worried to death and to make matters worse he forgot he was meeting Marion Lester the night Cathy went and she is none too pleased at being 'stood up', as she put it.

Worst of all from my own point of view – poor Matty has discovered that Terence was simply an opportunist and that his mother, Cicely, had encouraged him to 'try his luck'. I can hardly believe it. Terence was so convincing. I would have vouched for him any day – until now! Thank goodness our friendship hadn't blossomed into something deeper. He would have broken my heart.

Jessica is no better and no worse. I keep hoping the doctor is wrong and that she will recover. Nothing has gone right for the Maitlands since Oliver died. Except Olivia, of course. She's a sweet child.

Roll on tomorrow. Things must get better – mustn't they?

Ten

They did not get better. The first thing that greeted them when they gathered for breakfast at Monkswell Farm on Thursday morning was Adam with the news that Cathy was not at her parents and Patrick had sobered up enough to alert the police.

'They've sent a man to search the grounds,' he told them.

Chloe took one look at his terrified eyes and pulled another chair up to the table. 'You can eat with us,' she told him. She filled a dish with porridge and passed the milk jug and sugar bowl. 'Has your father eaten?'

'He's had two whiskies, that's all.'

Chloe caught Jack's glance but neither commented.

Adam said, 'Ma's got a friend who lives in Hackney. They used to send each other Christmas cards but we can't find the address. Pa thinks she might have gone there. They asked him so many questions – the police, I mean. Pa thinks maybe they think there's something suspicious. That maybe they think he's . . . he's had a hand . . .'

'That's nonsense!' cried Chloe. 'We saw him read the letter, remember? That wasn't acting, Adam. Your father was genuinely shocked.'

Adam glanced at Jack who nodded. 'Don't give it another thought. I know your father. Patrick would never – *could* never – do something like that. He's a bit of a roughneck at times, but he knows when to stop. Don't even think it, Adam. Your father is as worried as any of us.'

He hesitated a moment and then looked from Chloe to Adam. 'I think I have to tell you something before I have to tell the police. Cathy came to me the morning she disappeared and wanted to leave Patrick and . . . She was planning – or hoping

180

– to move in here with me.' As Adam opened his mouth, Jack held up his hand. 'Not yet, Adam. Hear me out. I didn't think it the right thing to do and told her so and she was very upset.' He pursed his lips. 'She then jumped to the conclusion that I had become . . . involved with Mrs Tyler' – Chloe gasped and turned her head away – 'but I tried to assure her that was untrue.'

Adam said, 'Ma thought that right from the start and maybe Pa thought so too and wanted to upset things. So he sent the flowers. I don't know. I don't seem to know anything anymore. Why does everything have to change?' Tears shone in his eyes but he blinked them away.

Chloe said, 'Please, Adam. There was nothing for your mother to be jealous about – nothing between me and your uncle. If you must know I was . . . I was rather taken with Terence Harkness and I thought it was mutual. He was very charming and attentive . . .' Her voice faltered.

Adam frowned. 'Mr Orme's long lost son? The one everyone was talking about?'

Chloe took a deep breath. 'We *thought* he was the son but we now know he was an imposter. He was totally convincing. I feel such a fool.'

Adam stared at her. 'He's *not* his son?' For a moment, surprise made him forget his own troubles. 'Poor you.'

Chloe shrugged. 'I'm simply trying to prove to you that your uncle and I—'

Jack said quickly, 'The police might be able to trace this friend in Hackney by name alone. Can't you remember any of it?'

Adam screwed up his eyes in concentration. 'Her name was Nancy and I think the surname began with a "P" or a "B" – or even a "T". Bit of a long shot though, even for the police.'

Lucien said timidly, 'May I have some bread, please?' and they all turned to look at him.

'Oh you poor lamb!' said Chloe. 'We've forgotten all about you!' She gave him a bright smile and reached for the breadknife. She fetched plum jam from the cupboard but, seeing Cathy's handwriting on the label, returned it to the shelf. 'I'll make some scrambled eggs for all of us,' she promised but at that moment a police constable cycled into the yard.

Here we go, thought Chloe with a chill of apprehension. It seemed that with the appearance of the law, the potential for disaster had grown immeasurably.

Twenty minutes later she left Jack giving his statement to PC Moss and watched Adam set off in the direction of his home. It had been agreed that in view of the trouble, Lucien should once again be left with the family at Fairfields. Chloe knew that Dorothy would willingly have cared for him but Lucien didn't know her and it seemed unfair to put further strain on the boy. He could play with Olivia and hopefully that would take his mind off his mother.

Outside the large barn Chloe told Lucien to wait while she wheeled out the trap.

'Then we'll give the horse some breakfast and then we'll have a ride. Would you like to play with Olivia again?'

Lucien nodded. 'May I take the puppy? Olivia will like the puppy.'

'No, dear. He might get lost – and anyway I think he is going out with Jude and Mr Bourne, who are teaching the puppy how to be a sheepdog.'

She pulled open the heavy door and stepped inside. After the sunshine, her eyes were unaccustomed to the gloom and, almost blindly, she stepped towards the trap. She tripped and almost fell and was surprised to see a pair of steps lying on its side.

'Now that's careless, Jack!' she muttered. Tutting, she bent down, retrieved it and set it upright. As she did so something brushed her hair and instinctively she ducked and turned, expecting to see the owl fly out. Nothing. Vaguely puzzled, she moved on, hands outstretched for the painted wooden shafts. Suddenly, from the corner of her eye, she saw something that made her freeze in her tracks.

'Please, *please*, no!' she whispered as her heart began to race. She forced herself to look upwards. With a gasp of fear she closed her eyes in a desperate bid to delay the moment of truth but she knew that it was only a matter of time. Slowly, fearfully, she opened her eyes. She saw a pair of dusty buttoned boots and above the boots she saw a petticoat and skirt. With a sharp intake of breath Chloe stepped back. Cathy's lifeless body moved slightly on the rope which had been thrown and tied over the beam. Her head hung at an awkward angle and her long hair had fallen forward, mercifully hiding most of her face. Her hands dangled at her sides, the fingers limp and uncurled.

Chloe cried, 'Cathy! *Cathy!*' and a deep sound that was part moan, part sob burst from her as a long shudder filled her body. Her legs almost gave way beneath her but somehow she stumbled back, still staring at the figure hanging above her in the gloom. To one side of the rope the owl still perched. It appeared unperturbed but the large eyes were watchful.

Chloe's next thought was for the boy waiting outside. 'Lucien!' she whispered. He mustn't see this terrible sight. She backed away towards the door. She then thought of Adam and thanked heaven that he was on his way home. Once outside the barn, she pushed the door shut and stared round her. For a moment her mind seemed frozen with shock, unable to function properly but then she saw Lucien staring up at her.

'Lucien!' She took his hand. 'Quick now! We must go back . . .' She led him away from the barn, her thoughts chaotic. The police would have to be informed. Yes, that was it. She had to tell the policeman what she had seen. As they crossed the yard her one thought was to share the terrible news with someone who would take responsibility. The knowledge of Cathy's terrible death was a nightmare from which she would never wake.

Reaching the door, she stepped into the kitchen and received another shock. Adam had obviously turned back for some reason and was standing beside the policeman. Jack and the policeman were still sitting at the table but it was Jack, facing the door, who saw Chloe first. She opened her mouth to speak. No words came out but her horrified expression alerted him. He stood up slowly.

'Mrs Tyler! What's happened?'

Adam and the constable swung round to look at her and she

tried again for the unwelcome words that would shatter both Adam and Jack.

'It's . . .' She couldn't utter Cathy's name. Not in front of her son. 'In the barn . . . Oh God! I'm so sorry!'

Adam still stared at her unaware but Jack cried, 'Not Cathy?'

The constable jumped to his feet, dropping his pencil in the process. 'Mrs Bourne? In the . . . You don't mean . . . ?'

With a hoarse cry Jack leaped to his feet and ran from the room in the direction of the barn and now the policeman was preparing to follow.

Adam, dazed, hesitated and Chloe clutched his arm. 'Don't go, Adam. Please. I don't want you to see her . . .' She tightened the grip on his arm but he tried to free himself. Chloe thought frantically. How could she prevent him from seeing his mother. She must give them time to get her down.

'Wait!' she urged him. 'I – I must tell you something, Adam,' she gabbled. Anything to delay him. 'It was her choice. You have to remember that. Her decision. Nobody is to blame—'

He looked at her, trembling, as his brain allowed the truth to sink in. 'You mean she's dead? Ma is dead? No! *No!*'

He swayed then sat down heavily.

'Adam, I'm sorry but she is,' Chloe told him. At the sight of his haunted expression, Chloe too began to shake and then her own fragile composure gave way and she burst into tears.

Adam watched her for a moment, uncomprehending, then he stood up and put his arms around her. 'Don't!' he murmured. 'Don't cry. You said it yourself. It's nobody's fault. Oh Ma! Poor, *poor* Ma!'

For what seemed an age they clung together in the kitchen and then Lucien's small arms were around Chloe's legs and he had buried his head in her skirts.

'Oh Lucien!' She reached down to stroke his dark curls in a daze of misery but somewhere at the back of her mind, Chloe's mind was working and she was thankful for the small delay. With any luck, by the time Adam went into the barn, his mother would have been taken down and laid out on the straw.

184

That would be a hard enough sight for him but the alternative would have been unbearable.

At last Adam said, 'Are you all right? I have to go to her.' She nodded. 'I'll stay here with Lucien.'

After they had gone she saw that the boy was crying softly. 'I want Maman,' he sobbed and she lifted him on to her lap and held him close while she murmured comforting phrases and wished she knew some French.

When PC Moss came in to use the telephone Chloe decided she would take Lucien for a walk down the lane with Jude and the puppy. That way he would miss most of the turmoil that was bound to follow the discovery of Cathy's body.

Lucien cheered up as he threw sticks for the dogs who obligingly raced after them. While he was thus happily engaged, Chloe's thoughts returned to Cathy and her last hours. When had she come to the barn? It must have been during the night . . . unless she had come earlier and had been hiding, trying to gather the courage for her suicide. Was her choice of a place to die a deliberate reproach to Jack? If so, his feelings of loss would be compounded by a sense of guilt. She thought of him spending the rest of his life alone and pitied him with all her heart . . . And Adam – so young to be burdened with the awful knowledge that his mother preferred death to life. It was inevitable that, in the years to come, he would constantly wonder whether he could have done anything to prevent her death.

A fresh thought struck her. They would have to bury Cathy in a separate part of the graveyard, for in the eyes of the Church she had committed a mortal sin by taking her own life.

'Look, Mrs Tyler! A squirrel!' Lucien pointed to a nearby tree where the dogs were now barking frantically and trying unsuccessfully to reach a small brown squirrel which was poised for flight on one of the lower boughs but which seemed determined to enrage the dogs before it went with tantalizing flicks and curls of its bushy tail.

'A squirrel! So it is!' Chloe agreed cheerfully. 'I think he's laughing at the dogs. Cheeky little thing.'

They watched it for a minute or two before it finally leaped away through the tree, leaving the dogs running in disconsolate circles, their ears flattened with disappointment.

Suddenly Lucien slipped a trusting hand into Chloe's and she glanced down at him. His face was bright with excitement and Chloe was reminded how quickly a child's emotions could turn from joy to sorrow and back again. She tried to imagine Adam at Lucien's age, running in these fields, walking the lanes with his hand in Cathy's. His childhood must have been mainly happy and she hoped he would eventually remember the good times.

Not that childhood is ever truly carefree, she reflected. There are always small griefs and woes to be borne – a preparation for life as an adult. Adam would be an adult from now on, she thought sadly. Any last vestiges of childhood had now been snatched from him by his mother's unhappy end. Was she somewhere, even in death, regretting her actions? Was there remorse after death – and was that Hell?

With an effort she shook off the dark thoughts and returned to the task of cheering up her small charge.

'I think that squirrel liked you,' she told him.

'He did,' Lucien agreed eagerly. 'Is he an English squirrel? Does he know any French? I could talk to him, couldn't I, on the way back? I could tell him my name.'

'You could. That's a very good idea.'

'Will he tell us his name?'

'I don't think so. He can only talk squirrel language. But we could think of a name for him.'

They wandered on hand in hand, inventing names for the squirrel. In her heart Chloe was deeply grateful for the excuse to walk away from the scenes that she could now imagine were taking place at Monkswell Farm. No doubt Patrick had been sent for and an undertaker. Maybe even a police photographer. But at least they knew the worst. Their darkest fears had been realized and must now be faced. The lives of the Bourne men had been changed forever and it would be a long, painful road back to anything approaching normality.

Chloe thought about Jack, who already had problems with his farm. He had lived for so long without the love of a wife and now the slim chance that that might change had been taken from him. How would Jack face the lonely years ahead? And Patrick? He seemed tougher altogether than Jack. Chloe couldn't imagine him living alone. Perhaps after a decent interval he might marry again.

They turned and walked back. Now Lucien was absorbed in his search for the squirrel. They had decided to call it Peeper because it peeped out of the branches at them.

'*Voilà!*' cried Lucien and he pointed to a squirrel that was sitting on the ground, holding a nut in its paws.

'There he is!' Chloe agreed. 'Good morning, Peeper!' Fortunately the squirrels were indistinguishable, so they would meet Lucien's squirrel frequently!

'Good morning, Peeper!' Lucien echoed, his little face alight with pleasure.

Chloe cupped a hand to her ear. 'Did you hear that little squeak, Lucien?'

'Yes, I did!' He copied Chloe, one hand to his ear.

'I think he is saying, "Good morning, Lucien," in squirrel language. Does it sound like that to you?'

'Yes, yes! *Mais certainement!* Certainly he is! Oh!' In his excitement he pressed the fingers of both hands to his mouth then glanced up at Chloe to share the moment with her. In that moment, as his dark eyes met hers, Chloe knew with a rush of longing that she could love Oliver's abandoned son.

An hour later, Chloe and Lucien were on their way in the trap to Fairfields but first Chloe called in at the vicarage to tell Dorothy what had been happening.

Dorothy, busy with some of the babies' washing, shook her head appalled.

'What a wicked thing to do – may God forgive her! Whatever will Albert say?' For a moment the small woollen clothes lay forgotten in the soapy water. 'You must leave that farm at once,' she told Chloe. 'I *knew* that job was a mistake, Chloe,' she insisted. 'Sharing a house with a single man! I told you but you wouldn't listen to me. You never do! You were never meant to be a housekeeper – especially to a farmer who can scarcely scrape a living.'

Chloe stared. 'How did you—?' she began.

'Oh, I know more than you think.' Dorothy returned to the

task in hand, squeezing the tiny garments and setting them to one side for rinsing.

She looked at her sister with the expression that reminded Chloe of their mother. 'Everyone knows everyone in this place and I hear things. Monskwell Farm is in trouble financially and now this has happened. One way and another you are getting yourself talked about, Chloe. Mama would have been horrified.'

Beside them at the table Lucien glanced up. 'We saw a squirrel. His name is Peeper.' He returned his attention to the book Dorothy had found for him.

'That's nice, dear.' Dorothy shook her head. 'Poor little mite. How could his mother—'

'Shh!' Chloe put a warning finger to her lips. 'So tell me how Bertie and Clara are getting on?'

'You're trying to change the subject.'

'Maybe I am.' Chloe helped herself to another biscuit and began, albeit reluctantly, to tell her sister about Terence Harkness.

Dorothy's face fell as she listened. 'But he was such a nice man!' she exclaimed. 'I really liked the sound of him. "He'd be just right for Chloe," I told Albert. And he agreed.'

'We all make mistakes,' Chloe murmured.

'But how could he do such a thing? That's fraud, isn't it? Trying to get money under false pretences. Are they going to prosecute him?'

'I doubt it.'

'Poor Chloe! I know you liked him a lot. And he appeared to be fond of you. He owes you some kind of explanation, surely?'

Chloe shrugged. 'I don't think I want to know *why* he did it. It wouldn't change anything. I admit I did like him.' She sighed. 'The truth is, Dorothy, I *more* than liked him! I was beginning to fall in love with him . . . But thank goodness we found out in time. I might have married him.'

Dorothy tutted. 'You *must* come back here, Chloe. I'll talk to Albert but I know he will think as I do. We both missed you and it would be wonderful to have you with us again. The truth is, Chloe, you're too trusting to be out in the world on your own.'

Chloe smiled. 'Remember I went to America on my own, Dorothy. I'm really not that helpless. As for Terence, it seemed dreadful at the time – especially for Matty – but now, with Cathy going like this, it rather pales into insignificance.'

Dorothy dropped the clothes into clear rinsing water and concentrated for a moment on the washing. Chloe sat silent, exhausted by events and emotions.

Then Dorothy turned to her, wide-eyed. 'You are sure it was an accident, aren't you, Chloe? I mean, the police *are* sure it was suicide.'

Chloe stared at her sister. 'What do you mean?'

'Well, awful things do happen. It might *look* like suicide . . .'

'Dorothy!' Chloe was astonished. 'You of all people! Of course it was suicide. She left that note!'

'Oh yes. So she did.' She had the grace to look a little ashamed. 'I only wondered. You have to be sure about these things.'

'We are sure. The police are quite satisfied – but there'll have to be a post-mortem, of course.'

'And she'll have to be buried in unconsecrated ground! Oh, how dreadful for the family!'

'It's all dreadful,' said Chloe wearily. 'Just when I thought nothing more could go wrong . . .'

'I'll ask Albert to include them all in next Sunday's prayers.'

'Thank you, Dorothy.' She stood up reluctantly. It was time to move on to Fairfields and to break the bad news all over again.

When Adam returned to Bourne Farm and stepped into the kitchen, the first thing he saw was his mother's apron hanging on its hook beside the dresser. Desolation washed through him. He would never, never see her again. She would never wear that apron, never bustle about the kitchen with pans of stew or trays of cakes. Adam unhooked the apron and, closing his eyes, pressed the cloth to his face. Breathing in, he hoped to discover any lingering trace of his mother but it smelled of soap and he hung it up again. They would never sit in church again as a family – it was him and his father from now on. It was a bitter prospect.

He looked up as his father entered from the yard, his face pale and lined with worry. Seeing Adam, he gave him a quick nod then slumped into a chair.

'Bloody police!' he muttered. 'I'm sick of their questions. Of course we didn't know she was going to do herself in. How the hell could we know something like that?' He sighed and rubbed bloodshot eyes. 'This is all your uncle's fault. Leading her on all these years. Promising to be there for her if she needed him. That's why she's done this. It's all Jack's fault and he knows it.'

He got up and opened one or two cupboard doors, then wandered into the larder. He came out with a lump of ham on a plate.

'I'm starving. Do you want a sandwich?'

Adam shook his head. 'I'm not hungry. Sick to my stomach. And don't go blaming Uncle Jack when you're the one who's to blame! You're the one that had flings. You're the one—'

'Oh! You don't think your ma had her little flings? You know she was always up at Jack's place. Jars of jam and home-made pies. And he encouraged her. He's no knight in shining armour.' He had found some bread and was now cutting a slice. 'If you ask me, it was six of one and half a dozen of the other.'

'I'm not asking you. I just don't know how you could have driven her to this. To hang herself. You're her husband, for God's sake!'

'And you'd have done better, would you? You're the smart one, is that it? Just you wait until you're wed and see how it feels.'

'Are you saying Ma wasn't a good wife?' Eyes flashing, he dared his father to agree.

'I'm only saying that women aren't the easiest of creatures. Not to live with. You'll learn when your time comes.'

'I hope not.'

'You'll see!' He cut a lump of ham, folded it into the bread and took a large bite.

'You're disgusting,' said Adam. 'Your wife's killed herself and all you can do is stuff your face with—'

Patrick reached out and grabbed his shirt. 'Watch your

190

tongue, you young . . . You just watch it. This is my house and—'

'It was hers too. It was *our* home! And now it's nothing. Without Ma—'

Patrick leaned across the table and punched his son in the shoulder. Adam jumped to his feet, picked up the plate of ham and hurled it against the far wall where the plate smashed.

Taken aback, Patrick stared at the ruined food. 'If your ma could see—'

'That's the whole point, Pa,' Adam shouted. 'She can't see what I've done. She will never be able to see what any of us do. Never again . . . never . . .' His voice broke. He sat down again, laid his head on the table and sobbed.

For a moment Patrick watched him uneasily, then he looked from the bread to the ham which lay among the broken shards of china. 'You can bloody well clear that up!' he said without much conviction.

He made another trip to the larder, came back with a piece of cheese, which he began to eat in the stricken silence.

Adam eventually looked up. He wiped his sleeve across his eyes and said dully, 'I can't stay here. Not without Ma.'

'Can't . . . What does that mean?' Patrick was startled. 'Where else can you go? This is your home. This is – will be – your farm.'

'It's not home without her. It's just four walls. I shan't stay.'

'And I say you *will*!' Patrick glared at his son, leaning closer, threatening him without words. 'Your mother always wanted you to have the farm. She was always looking forward to—'

'She's not here, though, is she? She can't look forward to anything. Maybe I'll go and work for Uncle Jack.'

'You think he'd do that to me?' Patrick blustered. 'Take my son away? He wouldn't dare try it.'

'You couldn't stop me.'

Baffled, Patrick regarded him helplessly. Suddenly he said, 'Sod off then. Go where you like. I don't give a damn.'

Adam smiled grimly. 'Oh yes? You know you won't manage without me.'

Patrick hesitated fractionally. 'Jack does all right.'

The hesitation told Adam that his father was worried and the knowledge gave him confidence. His father had always been a bit of a bully, his excesses always kept in line by Cathy's moderating influence. Now his mother was gone but Adam sensed that the pendulum was swinging his way. His father needed him. Bereft and shaken, Adam felt much older and a little wiser.

He said, 'But Uncle Jack's got a much smaller farm.'

'I'll hire some help.' Patrick spoke with bravado but they both knew that Patrick wasn't exactly popular. He might find it easy to hire staff but he wouldn't find them easy to keep.

There was a knock on the door and they both turned guiltily. Marion Lester, Adam's girlfriend, stood in the doorway. Her eyes were red-rimmed and her face was pale. Her smooth fair hair was tied back with a black ribbon.

She looked nervously from one to the other. 'I came to say how sorry I am. We just can't believe it. Oh Adam!' Her lips trembled.

Patrick rallied quickly and gave her a faint smile. 'Come in, lass. We were only talking. The way you do.'

He smiled at her but she moved towards Adam and he gave her a self-conscious hug.

'My parents send their love,' she told him. 'We're all so shocked.'

Patrick said, 'News travels fast in these parts.' He tossed the remains of his bread and cheese to the dog, who snapped it up greedily.

Marion's grey eyes searched Adam's face. 'Mama didn't want me to come. She—'

Patrick said, 'Afraid of the scandal, I suppose! Hardly the sort of thing—'

She gave him a sharp look. 'Not at all. She thought you wouldn't want to see anybody at a time like this but I had to come – to see if there was anything I can do. To help.'

Adam said, 'The police were down there all morning. Questions and more questions. Poor Ma. If only we'd known . . . If only we could have stopped her . . . Found her in time . . .'

Patrick tightened his mouth. 'No point in going over and

over it,' he said harshly. 'It's happened and we have to make the best of things.'

Marion glared at him. 'People need to talk at a time like this! It's only natural.' To Adam she said, 'Shall we walk for a bit?'

He nodded. To his father he said, 'I'll be back later.'

'Please yourself!'

Outside, Marion slipped her arm around Adam's waist and as they crossed the yard Adam knew his father was watching. They climbed the gate and moved off across the field.

'How did you hear about it?' Adam asked.

'The farrier heard it from his cousin who's married to a policeman.'

'What did your folks say?'

'You really want to know?'

He nodded. He didn't want to hear it but there was going to be a lot of gossip and he'd have to get used to it.

'They said I was to keep away. Not get mixed up in it all. You can imagine, can't you. Papa said he'd never liked your father but he was a good farmer and knows cattle. Mama said your mother was a goodhearted woman.'

'Damned with faint praise!' Adam felt a surge of resentment.

'You did ask. Grandmama said—'

Adam smiled faintly. 'Oh no! Not pearls of wisdom from your canny grandmother!'

Ignoring this, Marion went on. 'Grandmama said that the Bournes' stars were in the descendent—'

'She's right there!' He shook his head.

'She said I should "put a clear distance between us", meaning you and me. I said I wouldn't. I thought – I *hoped* – you'd need me.' She gave him a sideways glance. 'I wanted to be near you. I thought I might be able to help in some way. Comfort you.'

'It's a bit late for words. Nothing can bring her back.'

She stoppped and gave him a quick hug. 'It doesn't matter what my parents say, I shall still see you, Adam. I couldn't bear it if I thought we'd never see each other again.'

Adam tried not to show his surprise. He had never taken the

relationship that seriously but Marion appeared to be very fond of him. He was touched by her earnestness and by the fact that she had defied her parents. The truth was that he had never taken any woman seriously. Nor had he ever contemplated marriage, having been deterred from an early age by his parents' uneasy relationship. Cautiously he returned the hug and they walked on, hand in hand.

'Why on earth did she do it, Adam? She was such a sweet lady. I couldn't believe it when I heard.'

He drew a long breath. 'Ma was desperate. She told me she was unhappy. I suppose she couldn't bear it any more.'

She looked up into his face. 'They're saying she always loved your uncle – so why did she marry your father?'

'Heaven only knows. Perhaps she should have married Jack.'

'But then you wouldn't be you, would you? I mean you'd be their son but you'd be different. Maybe I wouldn't love you so much.'

He stopped abruptly. 'I didn't know you loved me. You've never said you loved me.'

'You never asked me, Adam.' They walked on and she said, 'I'm not going to ask you if you love me. I don't suppose you know yet. I don't suppose you can even think about me and you at a time like this. I don't mind. I understand.'

They walked over the grass, through the sheep, who turned their heads enquiringly, down the slope to the small copse and into the shelter of the trees.

Once there, Adam took her in his arms. 'You're right, Marion. I can't think straight at the moment. But I think I might love you. Is that enough for now?'

By way of answer, she held him tight and kissed him and a little of her warmth found its way into his frozen soul.

Eleven

The next two days passed in a daze of uncertainty, grief and regret. For Chloe, drawn into the general gloom, the days were lightened only by Lucien, who seemed to blossom in the attention he received from Jack and Chloe. The little boy found pleasure in so many things that Chloe was cheered by his obvious happiness. Occasionally, when something reminded him of his absent mother, there were tears but Chloe did what she could to comfort him. His future looked bleak for there was no news from his mother nor was there any sign that the Maitlands would soften their attitude towards him. Only Matty was in favour of accepting him into the family. Jessica would not talk about it at all and no one pressed her because the state of her health was still extremely worrying. Bertha shied away from the subject whenever it was raised.

Sunday morning, in a show of solidarity, Jack, Patrick and Adam attended church in Winchelsea leaving Chloe to look after Lucien and to prepare Sunday lunch for all of them. Despite his confused feelings, Jack had taken pity on his brother and nephew. Neither could cook and without Cathy he guessed they were existing on bread and cheese and had decided they should have at least one decent meal. At quarter to twelve Chloe was making mint sauce when she heard a knock on the front door.

'Who on earth is that?' she muttered and hastily wiped her hands and tidied her hair. Most local callers came to the kitchen door so this person was presumably a stranger.

A large woman stood on the step, smiling somewhat nervously at her. 'Mrs Bourne?'

'No. I'm Mrs Tyler, Mr Bourne's housekeeper.'

'I'm Miss Edwards from Doctor Barnado's. May I come in for a moment?'

Chloe was aware of a frisson of unease. 'Doctor Barnado, the philanthropist? The orphanage man?' Had this woman come to the right house? 'Was Mr Bourne expecting you?'

'Not exactly. I was given this address by Mrs Brier in Icklesham.'

Chloe was confused. Why on earth should Bertha send a complete stranger to Monkswell Farm?

The woman said, 'We understand that you have an abandoned child living with you. I'm hopeful—'

Chloe blinked. 'An abandoned child? Here?' Even as she spoke, it dawned on her that Lucien was exactly that and the realization shocked her.

Miss Edwards looked nervous. 'We're hoping that we can help in some way.'

Chloe opened the door reluctantly. 'You'd better come in.'

Silently she led the way into the parlour. Why on earth had Bertha decided to meddle, she wondered resentfully? And she hated the phrase 'abandoned child' even though it might be seen as apt by some people. It made poor Lucien sound like a baby left on a doorstep.

Chloe led Miss Edwards into the parlour, where they were suddenly joined by Lucien, who was chasing the puppy with shrill screams of laughter.

Chloe said, 'This is Lucien Dupres. Does he look abandoned?' There was a distinct edge to her voice.

'Well no, he doesn't. He's a most attractive child.'

Miss Edwards sat down and Chloe sat down nearby.

She said, 'I'm in the middle of preparing Sunday lunch, so if you don't mind I'd like you to make this brief.' She gave her visitor a challenging look.

The woman flushed at Chloe's tone but straightened her back and folded her hands in her lap. 'It has come to my notice,' she began, '– that a child has been abandoned by his mother who has returned to France and that she has sent a letter requesting that he be brought up by the Maitland family, who are unwilling to accept him. Am I right so far?'

Chloe wanted to deny it but the information was correct.

Instead she turned to Lucien. 'Go and play in the yard, dear, will you. Puppies need plenty of fresh air.'

Obligingly Lucien scooped up the puppy and staggered out of the room.

Miss Edwards then continued but her well-modulated voice was already beginning to grate on Chloe's nerves. She sounded, Chloe thought, like an adult speaking to a fractious child.

'I am on the board of a small orphanage in Kent. We have thirty-one children at present but we could take another nine. As a member of the Board I am—'

'Excuse me, but do you normally do business on a Sunday?'

The woman flushed. 'Not normally but . . . but I am here unofficially. If you allow me to continue . . .'

Chloe nodded and she continued.

'I can recommend children for entry. The children are well cared for and all are found work when they leave us. If the Maitlands were to apply through the proper channels—'

'Miss Edwards, this is all rather premature.' Chloe fought down rising anger. If this was Bertha's idea of a solution to Lucien's problem . . . 'I am still hopeful that Lucien's mother will change her mind. A few days without Lucien may bring her to her senses. If that happens Lucien will be going home. Back to Paris. Placing him in an orphanage at this early stage—'

'You are in contact with his mother?' The feigned surprise was exaggerated and Miss Edwards' expression was almost triumphant. 'I was led to believe that she, Miss Dupres, had left no forwarding address and that she had vaguely mentioned Paris. Paris is a big place, Mrs Tyler.'

Chloe stiffened. 'I don't need a geography lesson, Miss Edwards.'

'I wasn't offering one but as a nation we are not very adventurous and not everyone has been to that city. *I*, in fact, have had that pleasure and I can assure you—'

'Not everyone's been to America, Miss Edwards, but *I* have had *that* pleasure. America is also a big place!'

For a moment they eyed each other with undisguised antagonism until Chloe realized how foolishly she was behaving.

197

She was allowing this wretched woman to bring out the worst in her. 'I'm sorry,' she muttered. 'Do go on.'

Miss Edwards gave a small nod. 'The reason I am here is not only to inform you that the child would be welcome at our orphanage should it prove necessary but also to ask you to consider an alternative which you might prefer. I happen to know personally of a very decent couple – friends of mine – who would be willing to give the boy a good home. To adopt him, in fact. If an adoption were to—'

Chloe felt a distinct tightening in her throat at this prospect. 'It's out of the question!' she cried.

Miss Edwards barely paused. '—were to go ahead after a suitable probationary period, it could be dealt with privately to everyone's satisfaction. I could help with the preparation of the application forms and—'

'I've told you this won't happen. You're wasting your time.'

Miss Edwards remained very cool but her smile was thin. 'If I explain this to Mr Bourne—'

'The decision doesn't lie with Mr Bourne,' Chloe told her. 'It's nothing to do with him. It doesn't really lie with anybody – not even the Maitlands. Lucien happened to be staying here as a paying guest when his mother returned unexpectedly to France. Mr Bourne and I are caring for Lucien and are in no hurry to see him placed in a children's home – no matter how good it may be. You would have to have his mother's agreement before he could be adopted . . . And since Paris is such a big place how would you find her?'

Miss Edwards' mouth tightened. 'I'm beginning to think you are being deliberately awkward, Mrs Tyler.' The colour in her face had now faded with her hopes. 'You seem determined to misunderstand my motives and you are doing the young boy a great disservice.'

Chloe was near to tears but she battled on. 'No one has decided to give Lucien up for private adoption and I shall speak with Mrs Briers on the matter. She was not within her rights to assume—'

'From what I have been told I think she *was* within her rights.'

Chloe frowned. Her heart was thumping with the suddeness of this potential disaster. The idea of Lucien in an orphanage was intolerable. How could Bertha have suggested such a thing? How dare she? Fear and anger sharpened Chloe's voice. 'How exactly did you come to learn about Lucien? Did Mrs Briers write to the orphanage?'

'Not at all. Officially we know nothing about the boy. The matter came to my knowledge through mutual friends – Elspeth and Ian Palmer. The Palmer's maid is a friend of Mrs Letts, the Maitland's cook. Elspeth Palmer was told about the boy and the rather bizarre goings-on. She has a niece who has been married for ten years and has not been able to have a child of her own. The niece and her husband are desperate to adopt a child and although they would have preferred a younger child—'

Chloe was staring at her. 'But you said it was Mrs Briers' idea!'

'No.' Miss Edwards drew in an exasperated breath. 'I said that Mrs Briers gave me this address. I have been to Fairfield House this morning but Mrs Briers chose not to discuss the matter of the boy with me except to say that there was no plan for the boy to be taken into *her* family. I asked where the boy was and after some prompting she eventually gave me this address.'

Chloe sighed with relief and with it came the realization that she had done Bertha an injustice. She, Chloe, had jumped to the wrong conclusion and she felt very ashamed of herself.

She stood up. 'I can only say that at present Lucien is in good hands and that at some stage all those concerned will come to a decision about his future. But this I can tell you – he will never need a place in an orphanage nor will he be available for adoption by strangers.'

Miss Edwards rose to her feet. 'You cannot possibly be certain of that, Mrs Tyler.' She fumbled in her handbag and handed Chloe a small white card. 'This is the name and address of the matron at our orphanage. You are welcome at any time to visit and see for yourself how well we care for the children. We frequently take in children for a few weeks or months while the families decide what to do. Young Lucien could be given a temporary placement. Then if the Maitlands are still adamant that they do not want him, he could be privately adopted by the Palmers' niece and her husband.'

Chloe had also risen. 'Miss Edwards, I appreciate your concern but I doubt we shall take up your offer. We could look for the boy's mother. I think a private detective might help us and if we change our mind at any time we shall undoubtedly look into that.'

Chloe forced a smile and led the way to the front door. Closing it firmly behind Miss Edwards, she leaned back against it. 'Not while I have breath in my body!' she whispered.

The menfolk returned from church looking morose and saying little. Chloe guessed that they had had a mixed reception from their fellow churchgoers.

She was saving the news about Miss Edwards' plan until she and Jack were alone. The idea of allowing Lucien to be put into an orphanage appalled her. She had a ghastly vision of him among more than forty children, in the care of nurses. No matter how kind they were they could never replace the love and attention of caring parents. The idea of a young couple adopting the boy was also distasteful to her although she knew in her heart that they might be delightful people who would adore him. The truth was that Chloe didn't want anybody to bring him up except his mother.

Or herself! The idea was growing within her that *she* would adopt Lucien – but there were difficulties to that plan. Firstly she was a widow with no money except her wages and secondly she had no husband and no home. Given the choice, the authorities might deem Mrs Palmer's niece and her husband to be a better prospect for Lucien's future. On the other hand, if Jack would guarantee her a job that would mean she had a permanent roof over her head and life on the farm might be considered a healthy environment for a boy to grow up in.

The meal was a sober affair. The memory of the last meal they had shared at that table was in everyone's mind. Cathy had been alive and well then and it seemed her absence was like a heavy cloud. Just a few days had passed but in those few days the lives of all of them had been scarred. Chloe glanced at Patrick. He looked sullen and his expression was one of hopeless defeat but his appetite had survived. Adam tried to eat, but grief had robbed him of his pleasure in the meal. His mind was on other things and he hardly spoke. Jack was trying to be cheerful for Lucien's sake but his voice was different in a way Chloe could not define and his eyes were haunted.

Lucien was saying little, his natural cheerfulness dimmed by the sombre atmosphere around him. Dutifully he ate his greens, keeping a watchful eye on Jack and giving him a shy smile whenever their eyes met.

Finally Adam glanced at Chloe. 'They said a prayer in church – for Ma's soul.'

'That was nice of them.'

Patrick snorted. 'Fat good that'll do anyone, least of all Cathy!'

Jack looked at him. 'Why did you go if you don't believe in it?'

'It was expected, in the circumstances.' He helped himself to more potatoes without being invited and drained the last of the gravy over them. Adam, mortified, pretended not to notice this breach of good manners and Chloe thought what a good job Cathy had made of bringing up her son.

Patrick said suddenly, 'So how come Miss Lester was in our church? She should have been with her parents in Rye.'

Adam stared at his empty plate. 'She wanted to be with me. Marion knows what happened to Ma and she thought I'd—'

Patrick's head had jerked upwards and his eyes blazed. 'Nothing *happened* to your mother, Adam. Get that straight, for God's sake. *She did it to herself!* It wasn't an accident.'

Jack said, 'Drop it, please, Patrick. We're trying to enjoy our meal.'

'Not much chance of that. Not much chance ever again.'

Chloe smiled at Adam and said quickly, 'Marion sounds like a really nice girl. I'd like to meet her some time.'

'Oh she is. She *is*. Very nice.'

He was suddenly beaming and Chloe felt a debt of gratitude towards the absent Marion who had managed to bring some joy into Adam's life at such a sad time.

Adam went on. 'Her parents told her to stay away from me because of . . .' His voice shook. 'Because of what Ma had

201

done. Marion told them she wouldn't. She's going to go on meeting me.'

Patrick drew his brows together. 'Told her to stay away? Bloody cheek!'

Jack said sharply, 'Watch your language!' To Adam he said, 'Rather brave of her in the circumstances.'

Chloe said, 'Maybe you could bring her to tea one day – if your uncle—'

But she had gone too far. She knew it the moment the words had left her lips.

Patrick reared his head and laughed. 'Oh! *You're* the one issuing invitations now? So that's how the land lies, is it Jack?'

Chloe cursed inwardly but Jack came to her rescue. Ignoring Patrick, he said, 'Good idea, Mrs Tyler. We could ask her to Sunday lunch.'

Adam gave Chloe an imploring look and she returned it with a reassuring smile. How awful, she thought, to grow up with such a father.

She cleared the plates and served stewed apples and custard and the conversation dwindled again.

As soon as Patrick and Adam had left, Chloe stacked the crockery in a sinkful of hot water and told Jack about the morning's unexpected visitor. She wanted to tell him her own wishes on the subject but somehow the right moment never arrived. The idea of expecting him to guarantee her a job when his financial position was so desperate seemed unfair and she shrank from putting him in an invidious position.

He listened thoughtfully and she thought how generous he was to find time for her problems when his own life was full of present sorrow and fears for the future.

At last he said, 'We needn't be too hasty, Chloe. Nothing can happen until we find Ma'mselle Dupres and I suspect that will take some time. Perhaps you could talk with the Maitlands, tell them what's happened and ask them to employ a private detective. In the meantime Lucien is happy here and I'm willing for him to stay as long as it's necessary. He's a dear little chap.' He broke into a smile. 'It's nice to see somebody happy.' He stood up. 'Oh, by the way, I apologize for Patrick.

He's a clumsy devil. Never has had any social graces. Never wanted any, actually. I don't know what they'll do without Cathy. He'll have to get himself a cook or a housekeeper.'

Chloe, tying on her apron in preparation for the washing-up, looked at him.

'You called me Chloe!' she accused.

He gave an awkward laugh. 'It just slipped out. I hoped you hadn't noticed.'

'I almost missed it.' She realized her heart was racing. 'Does that mean that I can stop calling you Mr Bourne?'

'Would you like to?'

'Yes, Jack. I would. Very much.'

They stared at each other across the room, surprised by this turn of events.

Chloe heard herself say, 'It's much friendlier and I do hope . . . that is, I'd like you to see me as a friend. Someone you can talk to about anything.'

'Thank you.' He regarded her uncertainly.

'A shoulder to cry on if needed.' She laughed nervously, telling herself she had gone far enough but found she could not hold back the rush of words. 'Someone to give you an occasional hug,' she said and tried frantically to blink back the unexpected tears.

Jack took a few paces towards her and she could see the surprise in his eyes.

He said hoarsely, 'It does get lonely sometimes.'

Chloe thought of all the years he had waited for Cathy. She held out her arms and after a slight hesitation he stepped forward and they clung together in disbelief.

Abruptly Chloe released herself from the embrace. 'Now I must wash up,' she told him briskly and saw the relief in his face. She had been disgracefully forward, she told herself, and Dorothy must never know.

Jack grinned at her. 'That was short and sweet!'

'I'm sure we'll improve with practice!' she said and reached for the first plate.

Monday dawned fair with a brisk breeze which blew in the postman with a letter for Chloe from London.

203

Dear Mrs Tyler, This is to inform you that your father-in-law has died peacefully in his sleep. The will has been read and the bulk of his fortune as well as the cattle ranch and stock has gone to his nephew Charles Warby. He has, however, left you a small legacy as his son's wife, which converts into sterling as the sum of four hundred and fifty guineas. You will need to sign the legal document appertaining to these monies by appearing in person at the London branch of our offices in Wigmore Street.

I trust this news will be welcome and your father-in-law hoped that past frictions will not prevent you from claiming this gift. Your obedient servant, Arnold D. Holler

Chloe wanted to pinch herself as she reread the letter. Four hundred and fifty guineas! She could buy herself a house and have money left over. It was unbelievable. She thought fleetingly about Jeff and his disappointment when his father refused to see them.

'But would you mind, dearest Jeff, if I accept this now?' she asked his ghost. The gesture was, after all, a small admission of regret on the father's part. Maybe even a request for forgiveness.

Chloe's immediate thought was for her own position with regard to Lucien. Would the money make it easier for her to bring him up? Another thought edged its way into the confusion. Perhaps she could lend some of the money to Jack to help him through his current difficulties.

Impulsively she kissed the letter. For the first time in her life she was not struggling. She had money of her own. It was a heady feeling.

'Dorothy! Just wait until I tell you!'

The euphoria lasted for an hour or so but then it was replaced by a certain caution. Money changed things. It changed people and not always for the best. Would Jack regard her in a different light because of the windfall? Almost certainly, she decided. It might change things between them, she reflected anxiously. Now that they were closer she didn't want to risk spoiling the relationship. They had not embraced again but

Chloe admitted to herself that she was hopeful. Did she want anything lasting to come from this shift in the relationship? One moment she thought she did and the next she was fearful of the commitment. Loving someone meant that you were vulnerable to the pain of loss. She had learned that much from Jeff's death.

'Would you approve, Jeff?' she murmured. 'Would you mind if I loved someone else? It would never be the same. No one can ever take your place but . . .' She thought of Jack's words – *It does get lonely sometimes.*

She put the idea from her and thought again about the windfall. Perhaps she should keep the news to herself for the time being until she knew what she would do with the money and exactly how it would change her life. She felt somehow thankful that it wasn't a larger amount. She would have to open a bank account and pay in the cheque as soon as she received it.

She took Lucien out for a walk after lunch and they found his favourite squirrel. Or one very like it.

'Peeper!' cried Lucien and threw down the scraps of bread he had brought with him. The squirrel sprang to and fro in search of the boy's offerings, the little body curved itself and the elegant tail arched.

'Freedom!' Chloe whispered as the revelation dawned. She was free to go anywhere in the world. Back to America if she wished. She could turn her back on the Bourne family and all its difficulties. And they were many. Patrick was not a man she could ever warm to. The mixture of arrogance and insensitivity was unbearable. Jack might be forever haunted by the loss of Cathy and the part he had unwittingly played in her death. The scandal would linger and fingers would be pointed at the Bournes for years to come. Even Adam would not be immune. The funeral was fixed for Thursday the sixteenth and tongues would wag. People would attend out of curiosity and the unmarked grave would be a talking point for weeks to come.

At Fairfields Jessica was not expected to live long, Matty was a disappointed man and Bertha was becoming proprietorial now that she had a son who would inherit whatever was left of

205

the estate. Everything was changing – but should she, Chloe, object to that? Wasn't there something to be said for accepting change and making a success of whatever fate had provided?

'May we take Peeper home with us?'

Lucien was looking up at her with earnest eyes and Chloe immediately recognized that here was the reason that she could not disappear from the scene. Lucien . . . and Jack. With a jolt of excitement she faced the truth. She wanted to build her future around the man and the boy.

'Peeper wouldn't like it,' she told Lucien. 'He only likes to be free to play all over the fields and to climb every tree.'

'He could go in the puppy's box.'

'I don't think so, little one,' she smiled. 'The puppy would bark at Peeper and frighten him and then he would run away. We should leave him here. We can always see him when we come for a walk.'

As they walked back Lucien asked, 'When's Maman coming back?'

Normally Chloe answered this with 'Soon' but now she took a calculated risk. 'I'm not sure, Lucien. I expect she'll write to us and tell us.'

'Why doesn't she write?'

'She's too busy, Lucien. She has to dance every night on the stage. She is such a clever dancer and all the people love to watch. And then they clap their hands.'

'Like this?' He clapped his hands enthusiastically.

'Just like that! Your Mama is so clever. But she will write one day . . . You don't mind waiting, do you? You like it here with me and with Uncle Jack?'

He nodded. 'But I have to go to school. Maman said that I must go to school in England so that I can be an English gentleman like my papa.'

'We'll think about that then, Lucien . . . Oh look at the big birds in that field! They have white rings round their necks, so they must be collar doves.'

Schooling. Of course. He could go to the village school or Bertha might agree to include him in the lessons she was going to give to Olivia. Or she might not.

Chloe sighed deeply. Everything was possible, she told herself firmly. The trick was never to give up believing.

The sixteenth of May was cloudy with occasional squally rain. By the time the mourners reached the church for Cathy's funeral, many were wet and thoroughly depressed. The vicar had been adamant on the question of the service. No trappings at all to lighten the gloom. Not even a hymn. Chloe had left Lucien with Dorothy with the promise that they would make some gingerbread men. Chloe sat in the second row behind Jack. Adam was next to his uncle and Marion Lester sat with him, her hand in his. Chloe had only spoken a few words to Marion but already she had formed a favourable opinion of the girl. Three of Patrick's farm workers had come to the church, there were a few neighbours but to Chloe the rest were strangers. There was no sign of Patrick.

'Probably getting drunk somewhere,' Jack whispered.

'Oh no!'

He shrugged. The church was about a quarter full when the vicar, his expression grim, stepped out in front of the altar and began the service. Jack leaped to his feet and walked up to him and there was a short exchange of views. As Jack returned redfaced to his pew the vicar said, 'We will wait a further ten minutes as the husband of the deceased has not yet arrived.'

Chloe stared at the coffin. Plain wood with only a small posy of freesias. Jack had protested to Patrick that at least they should buy her a decent coffin.

'It's nothing to do with you!' Patrick had replied dourly. 'You've meddled enough in my affairs, Jack. She did what she did to spite me and I'm not wasting good money on her! After all I've done for that woman . . .'

Chloe suspected that in his heart Patrick knew that he would never again have the respect of his fellow men. A wife who chose death reflected badly on her husband and he would never forgive her for that. The fact that he showed no remorse but wallowed in defiant self-pity would also not endear him to those who knew the family.

Ten minutes passed. People whispered among themselves and heads turned frequently to the church door in a vain hope that Patrick would appear. Jack looked at Chloe and rolled his eyes. He pulled out his watch. 'Nearly quarter past,' he whispered. 'He's not coming! Can you believe that?'

The vicar made a second appearance before the altar and without more ado said, 'All kneel. Let us pray.'

There was a rustle of skirts and a scrape of boots as the small congregation knelt. Chloe listened in astonishment as the vicar rattled through the prayer in an expressionless voice, apparently determined to impress on his listeners the fact that this service was not to his liking.

No forgiveness there, thought Chloe. In his eyes Cathy had committed the worst sin of all – she had taken her own life. She wondered if in those final agonizing moments, Cathy had regretted her decision. When it was past the point of no return had she had the smallest regret?

The vicar closed his prayer book with a snap. 'Mister Jack Bourne will now read the lesson which is taken from the Gospel of—'

There was a scuffle from the rear of the church and Chloe swung round. A dishevelled figure was leaning over the last pew, gasping for air. As they watched, he slowly sank to the floor, groaning. Chloe froze. This was not her family, she reminded herself. Don't meddle, she told herself.

Jack muttered, 'God Almighty!' and rose slowly to his feet. Adam had also risen but Marion was trying to pull him back on to his seat.

The vicar cried, 'What on earth . . . ?'

Patrick, bleary eyed and with his clothes askew, had hauled himself to his feet and now began to weave his way down the aisle between the pews.

''Scuse me . . . Sorry . . .' he muttered as he lost his balance and fell against a middle-aged lady.

'I'll give you "Sorry"!' she cried. 'Look at you! You're a disgrace, Patrick Bourne! A disgrace!'

Adam caught Chloe's gaze. 'Her husband used to work for us.'

Someone else muttered, 'Drunk at his wife's funeral!' and thus encouraged, another woman leaned out from her seat and hit Patrick a glancing blow across the shoulders with her black umbrella. 'That's for Cath!' she cried. 'She was a good woman.'

Jack hurried up the aisle. Chloe looked at Adam, who was hesitating.

'Let your uncle deal with it,' she whispered and Marion gave her a grateful glance. Hesitating, Adam sat down only to come face to face with a white-faced vicar who was almost speechless with rage.

'You tell your father . . . this is God's house and . . . That man is drunk. *Drunk!* In the house of God! . . .'

'I'm sorry,' Adam stammered. 'I apologize for him. My uncle will—'

The vicar was not prepared to be mollified. 'I won't have the house of the Lord treated with such disrespect!' he hissed loudly. 'If you don't get him out of here I shall cancel the service.'

Marion glared at him. 'But he's the husband,' she protested. 'You have to let him stay.'

He gave her a scathing look. 'I have to do no such thing, young lady.'

Adam looked desperately at Chloe, who reluctantly joined the argument. 'I shall personally write to your bishop,' she told the vicar, 'if you *do* cancel this funeral.'

That stopped him in his tracks. Shaken, he stared at her, searching for words but Chloe rushed on. 'Some men are weak. They can't deal with grief and anger without resorting to drink. We should feel sorry for them. You, as a minister, should certainly try to understand.'

He found his voice at last and was beginning to tell Chloe that she was the rudest woman he had ever met when there was a crash and all heads turned once more to the aisle. Jack and Patrick were on the ground and a third man was trying to help Jack up again. The vicar faltered in mid-sentence and he closed his eyes.

Chloe said quietly, 'I meant what I said about the bishop.'

She wondered if Cathy, in her ghostly state, could see what was happening and, if so, what she would make of it. It was to be hoped she could see the funny side of it. Chloe herself was close to hysterics, somewhere between laughter and tears. She was willing to bet that Winchelsea had never witnessed such goings-on before. It would be the talk of the town for years to come.

At last Patrick was on his feet again, being supported by his brother. They made their way slowly down the aisle and sat down in the front pew. The murmurings of outrage died down and the church was silent. All eyes were on the vicar, who was breathing heavily. Chloe held her breath. Whatever would they do if he cancelled the funeral service? She would definitely write her letter but that would not solve the immediate problem. Cathy's coffin waited before them on its trestle and it could not remain there indefinitely.

Slowly the vicar walked back towards the altar, his back stiff with disapproval. Chloe wondered if they could carry the coffin outside without the vicar's blessing and hold an impromptu service of their own. The Lord's Prayer and a few kinds words from Jack and Adam. Better not risk allowing Patrick to speak.

She waited as the vicar turned to his congregation. He was making a big performance of opening his prayer book, she thought, but he was finally ready.

'All kneel. Let us pray.'

She fell to her knees thankfully. They had at least avoided the worst that could have happened. Restricted on both sides, Patrick was unable to do much. His version of the Lord's Prayer was a jumbled affair given in a slurred voice – but at least he did kneel and he did say the prayer. Jack read the lesson and the entire service lasted about five minutes, which included a few words from Adam.

'My mother was a sweet woman,' he began shakily. 'I expect she had her faults like the rest of us but if she did, I never noticed them. She was a wonderful mother. Her family was everything . . . She did her best for us and I wish we had appreciated her more when she was alive . . . No one will ever take her place in my heart.'

He sat down and Marion slipped her arm through his and whispered something to him. Chloe saw him smile faintly and he leaned towards her so that their heads touched briefly.

When Cathy's coffin had been lowered into the newly dug

grave, the vicar gave Jack a brief nod and set off in the direction of the vicarage without a word to anyone. After the remaining mourners had drifted away, Jack, Patrick, Adam and Marion remained. They stared helplessly at the gravedigger, who was already busy shovelling the earth back into place. Each spadeful of soil fell with a soft thud on to the coffin-top and seemed to Chloe to be taking Cathy further and further from them. Patrick began to cry, loud raucous sobs.

Jack patted his shoulder. He looked at Adam. 'Why don't you take your father home and put him to bed. Then come down to us for a bite to eat. Marion, too.'

The young woman's face lit up. 'Thank you. I'd like that. I'll help Adam with his father.'

Chloe watched them go then turned to Jack. 'I admire that girl. She's got what Jeff used to call "true grit"!'

'Let's hope she sticks by him. The family's in for a rough ride.'

They began to walk back to the farm in a thoughtful silence. Suddenly Chloe started to laugh and once she had started she could not stop. Spluttering an apology, she leaned against Jack, her shoulders shaking, her eyes streaming.

After a moment Jack found the laughter infectious and soon he too was laughing.

'I'm so sorry, Jack!' Chloe cried, as she mopped the tears and hiccuped to a stop. 'I truly don't mean any disrespect. It was that woman . . . Oh Jack!'

'The one with the umbrella! I know! Poor old Patrick!'

They both began again and then they were clinging together until the hysteria began to lessen and they faced each other sheepishly.

Jack said, 'Cathy wouldn't mind. She'd understand. We've been through a lot. You in particular. You were the one that found her.' He looked at her soberly. 'I haven't thanked you yet. You've been such a rock. Jeff Tyler was a very lucky man. I envy him, you know. Every minute of every day.' He swallowed hard. 'I lied to the police and to Patrick. I implied that you were nothing to me. It isn't true, Chloe.'

Chloe waited breathlessly. She felt some words were needed but none came to mind.

Jack said, 'Just lately I've had this dream. Fantasy. Call it what you will . . . You and me and Lucien . . . but I don't suppose it's ever going to happen. I've no right to ask you to be anything more than a housekeeper, for I'm poor as a church mouse and always will be . . . And for God's sake, Chloe! Who'd want to marry into the Bourne family?'

Chloe felt lightheaded as the words struck home. Jack wanted to marry her. At least she thought he did.

She asked, 'Jack, is that a proposal?'

He shook his head. 'I daren't ask you in case you refuse. Not that I wouldn't understand and I'd still want you to be—'

'Take a chance, Jack. Ask me.'

He stared at her. 'Will you? Marry me, I mean?'

'Yes, I will.'

For a moment shock robbed him of speech but then he whispered, 'Chloe! *Chloe!* My dearest girl!'

As he drew her closer, Chloe felt a moment's panic. It had happened so quickly. Had she done the right thing? What on earth would Dorothy say? But then Jack kissed her and she knew that she no longer cared what anybody else thought about them. She had said, 'Yes'. The deed was done – and the few tears that now filled her eyes were tears of happiness.

Epilogue

C hloe sat in the headmaster's room at the Priory School in Rye. Lucien, now nine years old, stood beside her. He had grown into a handsome child and Chloe, glancing at him, felt the familiar rush of love and pride.

The headmaster, Clarence Sutton, was studying the papers on his desk with interest and now looked to Chloe for clarification.

'I see, Mrs Tyler, that your son is adopted and yet you have another child – a little girl and, if you will pardon my candour, you have a second child on the way.'

Chloe smiled. 'My daughter is Emma Jane. At the moment she is with my sister and Emma's cousins. Dorothy is taking them all to a birthday party. We adopted Lucien several years ago when his mother decided she could no longer care for him due to her profession. Adele Dupres is a well-known dancer who travels frequently around Europe. Lucien was staying with us at the time and we became very fond of him. His mother finally agreed that we should adopt him.'

Clarence Sutton looked at Lucien. 'So your real mother is a famous dancer. You must be very proud of her.'

Lucien's face lit up. 'Yes, sir. I am, sir. We're going to Paris in August to see her dance. Mama Adele – that's what I call her – is going to send us tickets. Emma can't come to France with us because she is only four but Mama and I will go.' He grinned at Chloe. 'Poor Papa has to stay home to look after the sheep.' He turned back to the headmaster. 'Papa is my father now but I did have a real father but he died.'

'How very sad. But your Papa has a farm. That must be very nice. Will you be a farmer when you grow up?'

'Yes, I will. It's a large farm in Winchelsea.'

The headmaster glanced at Chloe.

She nodded. 'The farm is a joint venture, Mr Sutton. I am a partner in the business.'

Mr Sutton hid his surprise and returned his attention to the form Jack had completed plus several other sheets. 'I see Lucien's arithmetic is above average and his English grammar is . . . Let me see. Ah yes. Fifty-five out of a hundred. Very fair results . . . And you speak a little French, Lucien?'

'So that I can speak with Mama Adele's friends,' he explained.

Chloe said, 'When Lucien first came to us he spoke mostly French because he was raised in Paris. A close family friend, Mrs Bertha Brier, has acted as his governess for the last five years but now we feel he should take his place in the mainstream of education.'

'I think I agree with you, Mrs Bourne. I also think he will do very well here. Lucien, do you like lessons?'

'Some of them, sir. I don't much like geography but I can draw maps.'

'Do you think you will enjoy being with so many children? School is not at all like home. It's a different world altogether.'

'I'm used to other children,' he insisted. 'I have two cousins, Bertie and Clara as well as Olivia Maitland and Robert.'

Chloe said, 'Lucien's a fairly confident child. I think he'll cope very well.'

Clarence Sutton rose to his feet. 'I'm sure he will, Mrs Bourne.'

They shook hands and the headmaster gave Lucien a friendly pat on the shoulder. 'See you next term, young Bourne.'

'Yes, sir.'

They walked in silence through the little town to where they had left the trap. Climbing in, they set off along the road towards the Bridge Inn and on up the hill to Winchelsea.

They were half way home before Lucien made any comment on the interview. Chloe had waited patiently for his comment.

'Why did he call me young Bourne? Why not Lucien? Is it because it's a French name?'

'No, dear. It's a tradition at some schools. The boys are called by their surnames. There'll be Smith and Wilson and Grey . . . and Bourne!'

That apparently satisfied him. He said, 'Papa will be pleased that I can go to that school. Will Robert go to that school when he's old enough?'

'I expect so.'

'And Bertie?'

'I don't know about Bertie. Maybe not. We'll have to wait and see.'

Chloe was almost certain that the fees at the Priory would be too much for the vicar's slender purse. Clara and Bertie would probably stay at the village school. She sighed. Since Chloe's legacy, there had been a slight restraint between the two sisters. Dorothy, struggling on her husband's meagre salary, had tried hard to rid herself of resentment. Fortunately their shared background and the mutual interest in their children had created a bond that had proved strong enough.

Lucien looked at Chloe. 'When will I have a pocket watch, Mama?'

'When you are eighteen, Lucien.'

'What is the time now?'

'I don't know exactly but I heard the clock strike three when we were leaving Rye.'

'Will we be late for Uncle Matty's birthday?'

'Only a little – but they won't start the birthday tea without us.' She smiled at him. 'They are only playing baby games. You wouldn't like that, would you?'

'Pass the parcel?'

'Probably.'

He wrinkled his nose. 'Have we got Uncle Matty's present?'

'It's under the seat.'

Matty was a survivor, Chloe reflected. He was very fit for his age although his zest for life had waned since Jessica's death. She had survived the heart attack by only a few months and Matty missed her more than he would admit. They all missed her but Bertha had stepped very naturally into her mother's shoes. She was now very much in command at Fairfield House, where she was fiercely protective of her son's position in the family. Olivia was treated with the utmost kindness but she had never been adopted by the Briers. When Matty suggested that *he* might adopt her the idea was firmly quashed, a compromise had been reached and her name had been legally changed to Maitland.

Twenty minutes later they reached Fairfield House and Lucien's patience was rewarded. He waved to the children who were playing on the lawn and they abandoned their game to run to the newcomers.

'Auntie Chloe! Lucien!' Olivia reached the trap just as Chloe descended. Lucien clambered down after her.

Olivia's hair flew in a tangle of coloured ribbons as she hurled herself into Chloe's arms. Over the last few years she had become a little more relaxed. Less demure and more her age, thought Chloe, hugging her. When they had exchanged hugs and kisses Olivia took hold of Lucien's hand with a bright smile. She was ten years old and within a few years would be a beautiful young woman.

'Come and see the cake Mrs Letts has made for Uncle Matty's birthday!' she urged him. 'There wasn't room for all the candles so she has written the number in blue icing!' She dragged him away and Chloe watched them go with the usual sigh of regret. Oliver's children, she reflected. If only he were able to see them. How proud he would be.

Fanny, holding the door open, greeted Chloe with a smile and then Bertha came to welcome them and five-year-old Robert came with her, shyly hiding behind his mother's skirts. He was a slight child with his father's neat features and pale smooth hair. Underweight at birth, he had never been robust and Bertha was constantly anxious about his health because several members of her husband's family had died young.

'Hello, Robert. My, you're growing into a big lad!' Chloe bent to kiss him, holding the frail child in her arms for a moment or two. She straightened up and smiled at Bertha. 'He's looking very well,' she told her and saw Bertha's expression lighten with pleasure.

Robert said, 'It's Uncle Matty's birthday. I made him a birthday card with a ribbon and a lace doily and coloured crayons.'

216

'How very clever! I'd like to see it.' Taking his hand, she followed Bertha into the hall, where Mrs Letts hurried to exchange a few words. When she had returned to the kitchen Bertha said, 'We're losing her shortly. Mrs Letts, I mean. She's given in her notice. It's the rheumatism. Sometimes it's worse, sometimes not so bad. She's going to live with her sister in Worthing. I've advertised for someone and I'll be interviewing next week.'

They found Matty in the drawing room, watching from the window as Alice and Dorothy supervised the children in a treasure hunt which had been laid out across the garden. Chloe saw Dorothy's twins following the coloured threads together. They were not identical twins but *were* almost inseparable. She smiled and looked for her own daughter and saw sturdy little Emma tumble over on the grass and scramble to her feet again without a word of complaint. A girl after my own heart, Chloe thought with a smile. A tough little girl who takes after her father. A girl with a mind of her own and a winning smile that quickly charmed all who met her.

Chloe stepped forward to greet Matty and Lucien proudly presented him with his present. They watched as he unwrapped it with loud exclamations of delight.

'A brass inkwell! Why that's exactly what I wanted! How did you know, Lucien?'

Lucien said, 'I didn't know but Papa thought it was a good idea.'

'He's right. You must tell him I'm delighted with it.'

'Papa's sorry he couldn't come,' Lucien explained. 'He's helping Uncle Patrick with one of his cows.'

Matty held up the inkwell and admired it from all angles. 'With an inkwell like this I can write a letter to *The Times*!'

He and Chloe exchanged smiles and Chloe thought how important Matty was to the Maitland family. The one member of the Maitlands who had remained unchanged by the passage of the years.

He said, 'A penny for them, Chloe!'

'I was thinking of this family – and what it has meant to me.'

'You've meant a lot to us, Chloe. I hope you realize that.'

217

She smiled. 'We've been through some bad times, Matty, but we've survived . . . It's good to see the next generation out there at play.'

Matty took her hand. 'You may have married into the Bourne family, Chloe, but you're an honorary Maitland,' he told her. 'You know that, don't you?'

'I do – and I deem it an honour,' she replied with a laugh that was full of genuine affection. 'Long may we all flourish!' She held up an imaginary glass.

Matty did the same. 'I'll second that!' he said.